THE WITCH OF WATERGATE

THE WITCH OF WATERGATE

A Novel by

Warren Adler

DONALD I. FINE, INC.
New York

Copyright © 1992 by Warren Adler

All rights reserved, including the right of reproduction
in whole or in part in any form.
Published in the United States of America by Donald I. Fine, Inc.
and in Canada by General Publishing Company Limited.

Library of Congress Cataloging-in-Publication Data
Adler, Warren.
The witch of Watergate / by Warren Adler.
p.   cm.
ISBN 1-55611-296-3
I. Title.
PS3551.D64W58   1992
813'.54—dc20   91-58668
CIP

Manufactured in the United States of America

10 9 8 7 6 5 4 3 2 1

Designed by Irving Perkins Associates

1

THE PUNGENT AROMA of the awakening spring earth and the manure of the hundred-odd horse entries of the Middleburg Hunt Races wafted over the soft greening field. Spaces allocated to patrons of the races were filled with elaborately decorated tables, some with candelabra, crystal and silver tureens, colorful flower arrangements, linen tablecloths and exotic food concoctions.

Some were tented and served by waiters in black tie and the air was often punctuated by the sounds of champagne bottles popping. Others were merely sumptuous tailgate parties complete with full bar and more rustic food placed elegantly on checkered tablecloths.

As always, Fiona FitzGerald noted, there was less interest in the races and more in the imbibing and socializing. Chappy Chapin's bash was a case in point. There he was, ex-Ambassador to Switzerland, now a bachelor man-about-town, holding forth alongside his yellow and black antique Rolls complete with a horn that trilled "Pop Goes the Weasel" on command. As a long-standing patron of the races he had a choice up-front location.

Chappy, although he did not ride, looked the part of the gentleman horseman. His tall frame was ramrod straight and his clipped moustache on a pink complexion gave him an outdoorsy look that belied his sedentary life. His relaxed hosting of this little group of ten bespoke a practiced social elegance. He wore a plaid deerstalker cap and matching cape, which, on him, looked perfectly normal.

Chappy always had a good group to the hunt races, and he was usually a patron of most of them in the Washington area. His menu was invariable, made with his own hands in his lovely house in Georgetown: spicy fried chicken, delicious syrupy baked beans and bacon, his own secret formula, and lush chocolate brownies. And, of course, pitchers of Bloody Marys, champagne and whatever else alcoholic his guests might desire.

"What race is this?" Harvey Halloran asked, turning casually toward the field, where a number of horses were steeplechasing around the track. Few of Chappy's guests paid any attention to the races, except to place an occasional bet with the various gentlemen bookies that collected slips near the official tent. Halloran was a lobbyist for the oil and gas industry. The other guests included a Congressman and his wife, a State Department Assistant Secretary and his girlfriend, the Peruvian Ambassador and his wife and a stockbroker and his male live-in lover. To Fiona, they were familiar Washington types, par for the course.

An invitation to one of Chappy's tailgating racing parties was a hot ticket and Fiona was often invited as Chappy's date when he didn't have a steady on his arm and she wasn't toiling in the Eggplant's homicide vineyard.

Today she was here out of her own sheer therapeutic necessity. Things downtown were depressing. Drug gang wars and the accelerating introduction of automatic weapons had considerably raised the homicide body count, putting unbearable pressure on the entire department. A hurricane of death was sweeping through Washington and homicide was in its vortex.

The Mayor and his appointed Police Commissioner were being harassed by the media, especially the Washington *Post*, which had dubbed Washington the "murder capital of the U.S.A.," and the Chief of Homicide, Captain Luther Greene, called the "Eggplant" by his underlings, was taking flak from all sides. Eggplant was, of course, a term of affectionate derision, its origins murky, but its tradition tenacious.

Because of the pressure, Capt. Greene had become even more irritable and subject to tantrums as he pushed the squad to find the perpetrators. He also worried incessantly about the dangers that this new and bloodier environment posed to the squad.

So far no one on the squad had been hurt, although cops in other departments had been killed. Ironically, the Eggplant had become an object of pity and, although it would seem less than macho to mention it, Fiona knew that his troops were deeply worried about him.

The fact was that everyone in Homicide was edgy and nervous and naturally disgruntled by the longer hours and often futile searches for trigger-happy, ruthless drug gang members, many of whom were juveniles. It simply meant that everyone had more on their plates than they could possibly handle.

Thus, Chappy's invitation on one of her rare days off came as a godsend and she was enjoying it immensely. Theirs was a kind of old-shoe, nonsexual, but very intimate relationship. He was a widower, a friend of her late father the Senator, and had a reputation as a womanizer.

Fiona, as Chappy's date, played the hostess role at this outing, helping him load up and clean up, as well as making sure the guests were properly fed and watered. Most of the other race patrons and their guests were also less interested in the races than in socializing and groups of people strolled by in a roundelay of cheery hellos and double-cheeker kisses.

There was a cachet, of course, in getting Washington's version of a celebrity to be a patron's guest and, scanning the crowd, Fiona saw any number of Senators, Cabinet Members, high-profile journalists, Congressmen, Ambassadors and important Administration types. It was, as everyone who attended knew, a place to show off, aside from horsemanship, the colors of power and prestige.

"The weather is glorious," the wife of the Congressman said.

"Nothing like a delicious Washington spring," Fiona commented. It was true. The air was pristine and refreshing, the odor rich with awakening fecundity, the sky a seamless royal blue.

A roar went up from the crowd as the horses passed close to the rail and headed over the flat to the finish line.

"Who won?" the Peruvian Ambassador asked.

"Who cares?" Chappy said, laughing as he poured champagne into proffered flute glasses.

"Don't you love all this decadence?" Halloran, the lobbyist, said.

"Makes you want to throw off your clothes and ride naked over the field in glorious abandonment," the stockbroker's lover said.

"Interesting image." Chappy said with a laugh, raising his eyebrows.

There was an air of good feeling here, helped along by both the alcohol and the weather. It was, therefore, surprising to Fiona to see Chappy's face suddenly become gloomy. He was staring toward one of the more elaborate spaces about thirty feet away, guests crowding around a long table groaning with food and covered with a lace tablecloth on which, at either end, stood two silver candelabra.

"I can never look at that cunt without my stomach doing flip-flops," Chappy said.

She recognized the object of his anger. Polly Dearborn, who did those long bitchy pieces in the *Post* that laid bare enough deep and dark secrets to impale whoever it was she chose to assassinate. In a city where image often surpassed substance, Polly Dearborn could eviscerate the vulnerable or, at the least, make the invulnerable appear impotent.

Everyone knew that the *Post* editors and management treated her with kid gloves and it was rumored that she had enough on the editor and owner to neutralize any efforts, short of libel, to stop her stiletto stories. But the fact was that her work was enormously popular, a real circulation booster. Washington newspaper readers loved to see blood as long as it wasn't their own.

"It was a long time ago, Chappy," Fiona said.

"Not to me."

Chappy had allowed Polly Dearborn to interview him and she had effectively ruined his diplomatic career, suggesting that he made profitable investments in Switzerland while he was Ambassador, based on information that was accessible to him only because of his position. The accusation was oblique and subtle enough to escape a libel action. But it was coupled with the revelations of his so-called womanizing, told in such a humorous way, with just enough sarcasm to subject him to ridicule, that he was never able to recover the image that he had carefully projected as a man of integrity and sterling character. He was never again offered a diplomatic post. Or, for that matter, any other government job.

Polly Dearborn was tall, mid-fortyish, with a slender neck that was far too long and gave her face a horsey look. Her hair was cut short, bobbed close to the head. She was dressed in a tweed suit with a single discreet strand of pearls around her neck. Her shoes were low-heeled and sensible. All in all she was properly attired for the occasion, exuding a kind of arrogant, country aristocratic look, quite appropriate to her role as a fawned-over, but ever-feared darling of the Washington elite.

She was surrounded by "powerful" figures, some of whom were recognizable to Fiona. Chester Downey, the Secretary of Defense for one, and the Senate whip, Allen Farr. She had her arm under Downey's and they were laughing uproariously over something said between them.

"Watch them all play kissy assy," Chappy said. "As if that would make a difference if she ever chose to drag any of them over the coals. Listen carefully and you can hear the ice cubes in her blood rattle."

"She does pile up the body count," Fiona sighed. "Amazing she has the guts to appear in public."

"And without bodyguards."

Of course, Fiona read every word of Polly Dearborn's bitchy stories. She, too, was not above vicarious thrills, although she was deeply sympathetic to Chappy, whose attempt to have the record corrected had met with little success.

Actually, there was a core of truth in the accusation. Chappy had made some clever investments in Switzerland, but, he assured everyone, they were not made on any basis other than his instincts and good business sense. She believed Chappy. Besides, he was already rich when he took the Ambassador's job.

"I'd like to personally add one more to the massacre," Chappy muttered. "Her."

"That would create a business relationship between us," Fiona joked.

"In my mind it's a serial crime with a single victim. You'd be surprised how creative my imagination has been in stringing out the pain, killing her over and over again. And in my heart there is never remorse."

"Shop talk again. And I've come here to get away from it all," Fiona bantered. "Frankly, I'd like to keep our relationship on the pleasure side."

"So would I," Chappy said, the gloom beginning to fade. He turned away from contemplating Polly Dearborn and moved toward Fiona, kissing her lightly on the lips.

"How long must I be kept at bay?" he whispered.

"I'll say this for your tenacity, Chappy. It's world-class." It was the way in which she fended him off, little jokes and sarcasms.

Over the years, it had become a game between them, a verbal joust. He never crossed the bounds of propriety. Nor did she ever let down her guard. Not that such a possibility was distasteful. He was not unattractive and he was certainly well preserved and, by all accounts, quite virile.

What she feared most was a change in their relationship. After a period of sexual intimacy, he always severed relationships irrevocably with his girlfriends, as if he feared commitment more than anything. They had discussed this together often, analyzing it quite seriously, even touching on the idea that he was either still committed to his dead wife or guilt-ridden about his continuing to live on after

11

she was gone. These discussions, however, did not stop him from his verbal pursuit.

But their little exchange did not completely shift his attention from Polly Dearborn. Before coming back to his guests, he glanced at her once again. He seemed to mumble a curse word under his breath.

"Sticks and stones," Fiona said, grabbing him forcefully under the arm, pulling him toward the group huddled around the back of the Rolls.

"That would be a delight," Chappy muttered, managing a smile and letting her lead him to his guests.

2

A WEEK LATER Fiona called Chappy from the office. Polly Dearborn's latest story was spread out on the top of her battered squad-room desk. Some of it had absorbed coffee stains and smears from the sticky bun she had brought in with her from the basement carry-out.

"You must be prescient," she said.

It was morning and his voice was still hoarse with sleep.

"I am?" He seemed confused, not yet oriented.

"I woke you."

"Busy night," he mumbled.

"Are you alone?"

"Just a minute, I'll check," he said. He was obviously awakening. Out of consideration, she supposed she should call back. But no. Under present crisis conditions in Homicide, there wouldn't be time. The yellowing fuzzy glassed clock on the wall read eight. In a moment the Eggplant would be roaring into the squad room, breathing fire. Things were getting worse. The night before there had been five more murders, all of them drug- and gang-related.

"There is a large Parker House roll in the bed beside me," Chappy said.

"Christ, Chappy. Stop being so literal."

13

"So why am I prescient?"

"Polly Dearborn did Chester Downey this morning."

"Poor bastard."

"You called it, Chappy. That day at the races. You said it wouldn't matter. Remember how cozy she was with him that day. Made no difference."

"Never does."

"Bottom line is that Chester Downey, our erstwhile Secretary of Defense, once you cut through the bullshit, is a bit of a rogue. He apparently hid his assets from his wife during their divorce and she suggests that he favors a certain company for defense contracts. His son just happens to be an executive there. And that's just part one. First of three."

"More than enough already for the dry rot to begin its work."

"She does her homework."

"You mean her incantation. The 'Witch of Watergate' is doing her thing again. She's whipped up an impression, recorded it for all time. Now it's in data banks, clipping services, libraries, a commodity for instant information retrieval. Old Chester will have to live with it, of course. It won't be enough to topple him now. But it will dog him forever, kill him slowly, foreclose on any other public ambitions in the future."

She let him spend himself, waiting for the pause. He had apparently worked himself fully awake.

"Call me after you read it, Chappy."

"Sorry, Fi. I can't bear it. To read her always depresses me. There, by the Grace of God, went I. My inclination is to call the man and commiserate. Poor bastard is now a piece of bait. The so-called media feeding frenzy begins once again. Only part one, you say. The man will be nibbled to death." He cleared his throat. "Let he who is without sin cast the first stone."

"Kind of early to be biblical," she joshed.

"You woke me. Now I have little choice."

She was confused.

"If you'll excuse me I will attend to this Parker House roll beside me. It is my intention, if you will allow me to be biblical again, to go in unto her."

"You're incorrigible."

"How would you know?"

He had barely hung up when the Eggplant's shadow loomed over her desk.

"I'm happy to see that you, FitzGerald, have enough time on your hands to read that rag. In their eyes, we are incompetent fools responsible for making this city the murder capital of the U. S. of A."

He was in his usual foul mood and his milk-chocolate complexion was grey with exhaustion. Pressure and frustration were taking their toll.

He had called a meeting of everyone for eight-thirty. Such meetings had become routine, angry sessions to vent frustration, blow off steam. His harangues were often bitter and rambling, products of a growing siege mentality that had rolled over them like hot lava. These morning meetings had become a painful experience, a kind of group therapy gone awry that did little to improve motivation and morale. She finished her coffee and sticky bun, folded the paper and put it in her desk drawer.

She looked toward the door. The men and women on her shift had straggled in, anticipating, like her, another agitating experience. Cates, her partner, had not yet arrived. She hoped he wouldn't be late. God help those who scampered in while the meeting was in progress.

15

They crowded into the Eggplant's "conference" room, a forest of mismatched chairs surrounding a long, battered rectangular table. The pictureless walls were painted a grim vomit green that was especially hell on dark complexions, the possession of the overwhelming majority of those present.

Seen together, as Fiona observed, they were a motley crew, mostly black, male and ungainly in suits that bulged with fat, muscle and firearms. Although they generally competed and covered with banter and sarcasm their various antagonisms, they had been miraculously bonded by the crisis of recent events.

There was one other woman in the room, a recent transferee from Burglary, a severe-looking black woman who in the week that she had been on the squad had, to Fiona's knowledge, never smiled or made a single friendly gesture to any of the others. Her name was Charleen Evans.

The air in the badly ventilated room was filled with smoke. Rules that applied in the civilian world were not applied here, not now in this atmosphere of siege and despair. The Eggplant puffed deeply on his panatela, expelling smoke through both nostrils like a raging dragon. His bloodshot eyes squinted through the smoke, scanning the somber faces in the room.

"Last night makes the record," he rasped hoarsely. "We're numero-uno, number-one in the whole fucking country. We are the cutting edge of the scythe that is mowing down American society." He had, Fiona noted, obviously been thinking deeply on the subject, searching for words that might describe his rage and convey it to the squad. "I am..." He paused and again scanned the faces in the room. His eyes were heavy-lidded, tired, pitying. "...I am disgusted by my fellow man. The conduct of these people defies rationalization."

He was conveying another message as well, especially to the blacks present. It was essential that he make the moral separation between the brothers, since it was, however it might be disguised, the good brothers ranged against the evil brothers. Fiona sensed the painfulness of his having to imply such a condition and she felt embarrassed for him and the others, especially since it had to be implied in front of her, a white woman, a minority in this place, further separated by privilege and class distinctions, a reality that she detested but could not deny.

"Under ordinary circumstances," he continued, his words cascading on a flume of smoke, "the performance of this division would be the envy of any department in the world. Wherever. Nairobi, Bombay, or Tuscaloosa. Our apprehension record is, bar none, the top of the line. We're making our cases stick. You people . . . I'll say this once . . . then forget where you heard it." Small grunts of knowing snickers rippled through the room. ". . . Are the best homicide cops anywhere. The fucking best." He drew in a deep puff, mostly to mask a surge of sentiment. Out of embarrassment few eyes confronted him directly at that moment. Then his voice boomed out. "But, ladies and gentlemen, we are shoveling shit against the tide. We are being overwhelmed by numbers. And we are manpower short by half. The bad guys are winning. For the moment. Maybe forever. Who knows. They tell us help is on the way." He made it clear by facial gestures in what contempt he held that promise. "Nevertheless, our job is to plow ahead, and since we are captive to a frightened and de- manding establishment and an outrageous media we must follow the priorities that they create."

She wasn't sure what he was driving at, glancing at Tay- lor, the Eggplant's number-two, for clarification. Taylor shrugged and lifted his eyes to the ceiling. He was white

17

and near retirement, an old hand who had seen it all. To the Eggplant he was a point of reference between the old days and now.

At that moment Cates came into the room. As always, he was immaculately groomed and attired, looking distinctly out of place in this company of mostly males of nondescript appearance.

"Well, well, Sergeant Cates," the Eggplant said, bringing the full force of his general animosity into specific focus on its unwitting target. Actually, having seen public humiliations done on numerous occasions by the Eggplant, Cates' only defense was to lock himself behind a facade of scrupulous nonreaction. "We are talking here of priorities. Apparently your priorities are not consistent with the rest of the group."

"I'm awfully sorry, Captain..."

"Sorry? Sorry, Sergeant Cates? We are all sorry. That is the subject of this meeting... sorriness. We are sorry for all the killings, sorry for all the havoc, all the dead cops, all the wasted lives. We are the collectors of human garbage, the harvesters of shit..." He paused, glared for a moment silently at Cates, then directed his attention back to the group as Cates dived for a chair behind a line of beefy cops.

"Priorities are as follows. From here on in, we do it this way." He counted off the order of battle on his fingers. "Gangs and drug-related. Double or triple teams if necessary. We have been assured uniform backup. Everyone on that beat in vests. Capish?"

A wave of mumbling rippled through the room, quickly preempted by the Eggplant. "The domestic bloodbath is strictly in second place, along with naturals and suicides. Of course, we do them. Like always. But it will be strictly skeleton crews. The name of the game is drug-related, especially the gangs. And they're armed and dangerous. The bitch is we've got to get enough to make the cases, get the bastards off the streets."

"Fat chance," someone whispered behind Fiona, reflecting the general disillusionment with the criminal-justice system.

"It's not going to be business as usual," the Eggplant continued. "There will be changes. New partnering and, what is worse, transient partnering. It flies in the face of the way we have operated for years. But we have no choice. Not now. We're in the midst of one fucking dangerous trench war. For us it's a prescription for disaster. Understaffed and overworked. In wars that's when people die." He paused and rolled his eyes. "Things could change . . . if help ever comes."

"You don't believe that, do you, Captain?" one of the men asked. It was a question posed with deference by one of the less loquacious of the group, a detective named Harding who had recently been laterally transferred from Bunko.

"There is value in hope, Harding," the Eggplant shot back. He panned the group once again. "The fact is, make no mistakes about it, we are in heavy combat."

"For which we get no combat pay," Harding muttered.

"Nobody is twisting your arm, Officer," the Eggplant retorted with a sneer. The man brooked nothing less than dedication.

The remark prompted some to exchange glances, obviously seeking allies in anger. One of the men, Robinson, a black twenty-year veteran, flat nostrils quivering with indignation, took out his piece and put it on the table.

"They got automatic widowmakers. We got peashooters."

"And I got three kids," Alberts said. Like Taylor, he was

one of the few white men still putting in his time.

"We're cops, not soldiers, Captain," someone said, followed by a chorus of approvals.

To Fiona there was another, more ominous implication. The notion of combat carried with it the idea of female inequality. Women, in the fighting services, were still barred from combat. It was a notion that carried over to the police, although it was not official policy. A not-so-subtle change was taking place. Things were going to get a lot more physical in the streets. As they, the men who ran things, saw it, being physical was still a man's game.

She detested the idea. From her perspective it was an erosion of her rights as a police officer. Besides, she could be as physical as any man.

The Eggplant shook his head, still contemplating the piece being exhibited on the table.

"We are the law," he said quietly, raising his eyes to confront the man making the challenge. "The thin blue line."

The statement had all the drama of simple but powerful eloquence, and it quieted the recalcitrant rumbling. Robinson took his piece off the table and replaced it in his holster. Oddly, the gesture seemed one of satisfaction, as if the Eggplant's remark had miraculously settled the question.

Despite all the secret ridicule and mimicry, some deserved, Captain Luther Green did command respect. His ambition was naked, his ego at times overbearing, his Machiavellian manipulation and bluster often heavy-handed, but under fire and in the logic of police reasoning, he was always the consummate professional, a leader who had the true trust of his underlings. He knew his trade and he absolutely believed, a notion not without merit, that he would make the perfect Police Commissioner. It was a goal toward which all his waking energy was devoted.

"The bottom line is that all assignments are being shuffled," he continued, now that he had recovered his sense of domination. "Those on drug-related are to continue. Most of you on domestics and naturals will be reassigned to drug-related."

"Cannon fodder," a detective named Thompson blared. It was more an observation than a protest.

" 'Fraid so, boys," the Eggplant said lugubriously, confirming her worst fears. So this was one for the boys, she thought, turning to exchange glances with Charleen Evans, who avoided looking at her. Her face seemed like sculptured granite, carved forever in a fixed, unblinking, unemotional, no-nonsense expression. Her transfer had, in fact, deprived Fiona of her position as the only female on the squad, although she retained the title as the only "white" female.

During her week on the squad, Charleen Evans had barely acknowledged Fiona's presence. Even the bonding possibilities of their meeting in the ladies' room had not opened up any communication, merely the barest grunt of acknowledgment. Only the forceful sound of her ablutions in the closed toilet booth hinted that she did, after all, have human qualities.

So far, Fiona had found no common ground between them, not even on the grounds of gender. To be fair, no opportunity had arisen for that kind of alliance. Until now.

"We're posting new assignments for most of you," the Eggplant said. He stood up and stamped out his panatela in the overflowing ashtray in front of him, then moved out of the room to his office.

Chairs squeaked on the scuffed wooden floor as the squad filed out. There were few smiles. One couldn't, Fiona felt, quite characterize these meetings as pep rallies, but they did reinforce the sense of bonding and determination that was needed to continue their operations in the face of the new reality.

"Looks like splitsville for us," Cates said. Having been partnered with a woman, he, too, had understood the implications.

"I'll raise holy hell," Fiona said, hissing through clenched teeth, anger pumping up her adrenaline. "My badge is like yours." She slipped it out of her purse and showed it to him. "See any balls on it?"

"Nobody wants it, Fi," he muttered, keeping his voice down. "You heard him. Combat."

It was obvious that he did not like being a party to this particular confrontation.

"Well, I want it on principle," Fiona said.

She debated whether or not to jump the gun on what she was dead certain was coming. She had not long to wait. With the exception of her and Evans the entire squad was assigned to drug-related homicide. She and Evans were to continue tracking naturals. This was a prime responsibility of Homicide, checking out every death in the District of Columbia, mostly a routine task, confirming death certificates, culling data from hospitals and funeral parlors, eyeballing suspicious corpses.

"Hope you're not going to take this, Evans," Fiona said.

"Take what?" Evans snapped, not looking at Fiona. Her inquiry seemed surly, her attitude standoffish and sour. Fiona was not sure whether this demeanor was actually meant for her or was simply Evans' regular attitude.

"This macho-pig bullshit," Fiona said. "They start this separating crap, you know where it ends."

"They got two bathrooms, lady," Evans said between tight lips. Although her skin was dark, like bittersweet chocolate, her features were delicate, more Caucasian than

22

Negroid, and her hair was cut in a tight helmet of curly hair, peppered by premature grey. She seemed to be Fiona's age, mid-thirtyish, but it was difficult to tell.

Her clothes fit well on her long frame, a solid navy blue suit with a red kerchief carefully placed where her decolletage hinted at an ample bosom tightly in check. She wore tiny gold earrings but no rings or bracelets. Fiona had already noted that her legs were shapely and muscular and she was sure that under her clothes was a tight, muscular and well-exercised body.

Everything about her—voice, speech and carriage—announced her formidability. Fiona speculated that she was the kind of castrating black woman that scared the shit out of black men. At least that was the persona that she presented.

She had noted that the men on the squad treated her with deference, and she had been, up to then, paired with a grey-haired, soft-spoken, black homicide veteran affectionately nicknamed "Pop" Herman, who held a hard-won reputation as a man who could charm a rabid dog into submission.

So far they had appeared to get along efficiently, if not warmly. To put it mildly, Charleen Evans could not strike anyone as warm and friendly.

"It's wrong, Evans," Fiona persisted. "He's deliberately putting us out of the mainstream."

"His prerogative," Evans snapped.

"I can handle myself, be as physical as any man," Fiona said. She studied Evans with deliberation, her glance washing over her body. "And I have no doubts about you."

Charleen Evans barely moved a facial muscle. Fiona noted that her brown eyes were flecked with yellow.

"Sorry, lady. We got different agendas," she said firmly, turning away. She moved to her desk, sat down and reached for the phone. Fiona followed her and stood beside the desk. She was tempted to reach out to still the hand that was punching in numbers. Instinct told her to abort the gesture. The moat that Evans had constructed around herself brooked no contact.

"They get away with this, other things will erode. We'll have to reinvent the wheel, go back to the regs and the statutes. It's fucking discrimination, Evans." In trying to regulate the decibel level of her voice, Fiona's words came out as a wet hiss.

With careful deliberation, Charleen Evans replaced the telephone and stopped punching in numbers. She looked up at Fiona, her eyes narrowing, her stare intense.

"Do you wish to discuss discrimination, Sergeant FitzGerald?" she said with contempt.

"Well, well," Fiona said. "One of those."

"Those? A black bitch, you mean."

"We are not dealing with race here, Mama. Only gender." She watched the woman's eyes glaze with growing anger. *You test me, I'll test you, bitch*, Fiona decided.

"Well, well," Evans said, unsmiling. "One of those."

"Put away the pussy-whip, Evans. It won't work on me. Be an ally or an enemy. That's your choice. I don't give a rat's ass. I've told you my position and I intend to articulate it with or without you."

Fiona wanted to say more, but she held off and turned away instead. This was one tough, arrogant, fearsome black broad with a big chip on her shoulder and no visible softness. She felt her eyes burning into her as she moved toward the Captain's office. Most of the others in the squad room had scrambled, gone into combat.

The Eggplant was on the phone. He looked up when she came in and waved his hand to shoo her out.

"I've got to see you, Captain."

"Later."

"It's rather important," she said, raising her voice.

"Can't you see I'm up to my ass?"

"I want to lodge a protest," she said, her voice cracking, suddenly conscious of a growing feeling of impotence. He barked into the phone. Had he heard? She wasn't sure.

"I'm not going away," Fiona said, her feet feeling as if they were encased in cement.

"Then stay," he shouted. "Who gives a shit? I've got more crap on my plate than any homo sapiens can handle. Two more this morning. You got it. Drug-related. Gang motivated. What the fuck have you got on your mind?"

"It's important," she mumbled, but her resolve was waning. She was losing heart, feeling compassion for his dilemma. Her own concerns seemed suddenly trivial.

"Please, FitzGerald. I appeal to your better nature. Whatever it is, put it on ice. I promise we will discuss it. But not now. Not fucking now. I beg of you."

There was little she could do. She felt helpless, a sense of weakness. The timing for protest was all wrong. Turning, she went back to the squad room. Charleen Evans had surely heard everything. Was she gloating? She was speaking on the telephone and did not look up.

Fiona slumped at her desk, slightly disoriented, nursing her wounds, trying to salvage some self-respect. Worse, she felt defeated by this woman. Yes, pussy-whipped by her aggressive self-assurance. Fiona's antagonism should have been directed against the Eggplant, against the male macho bigotry. Instead, it seemed concentrated in her feelings toward Charleen Evans.

Suddenly a file slapped the desk, startling her. She saw a shadow hover, then recede. She knew it was Charleen Evans and she fought the urge to look up, lock glances. She reached for the file, but did not open it. She knew what it was, the overnight list of hospital deaths. No, she decided, patting the file. She will not intimidate me. Finally, she looked up, turned and confronted Charleen Evans.

She was talking into the phone, but her eyes lifted when she saw Fiona's face. It was then that she raised her middle finger, punching the air. Fiona flushed and turned away. No split decision here. Fiona FitzGerald had lost the first round.

3

THROUGHOUT THE NIGHT, Fiona revolved like a top in her bed, ruffling the sheets with each crease feeling like a razor's edge cutting into her flesh. She was fully conscious, as if unable to shake a caffeine high, but try as she might she could not find her lost courage.

Reliving yesterday had all the earmarks of a nightmare. She had spent the day trying to sublimate her anger and humiliation, finding words she might have spoken, but didn't. It only added to her misery to know how badly she had handled the situation.

She had, she decided, been a fool not to insist on making her protest, despite the Eggplant's problems, if only to put her complaint on the record. The record was essential. At the least she should have started to create a paper trail. In dealing with the bureaucracy a paper trail was essential.

It was not trivial. It was a matter of bedrock principal.

Through the slats of her drawn blinds, visible through the sheer curtains of her bedroom, she waited for the lightening of the world. Perhaps in the new day she would find her courage. She wished she had the arms of a male to comfort her in this moment of her lost confidence, an irony that was not lost on her. But she was currently undergoing a time of shortage in that regard, some of it self-generated. There were peaks and valleys in the rhythm of her desires. She was now in a long, dry, barren valley of sexual disillusion, lustless and unfeeling. It was a time of questioning, which always left her vulnerable. Was this single life her subliminal choice? An exercise in self-protection or self-deception? Like her love life, the maternal instinct also ebbed and flowed, usually in inverse proportion to her emotional involvement. When she loved, she felt threatened by the idea of marriage and motherhood, but when she was meandering through the dry valley, she felt as if she had been abandoned by life, the womanly role of wife and mother sorely missed.

However convoluted the trail of self-pity, the full focus of her anger was directed against Charleen Evans, the castrating black ballbuster. She could identify now with the horror experienced by the black male when confronted with such a menace, the humiliation, the fear.

This was the monster that caused them to cup their balls for self-protection and reach for their "johnsons" for self-assurance. These black overbearing bitches, like the African honeybadger, were out to tear off their genitals, rendering them useless as performing males.

Charleen Evans' message was loud and clear. Fiona could identify it all right. In a mysterious gesture she reached for her own crotch, seeking her own reassurance, finding none.

Through all this self-pity and angst she heard the rasp of the telephone, boring into her consciousness like a metal drill. She reached for it with an unsteady hand as if she were awakening with a hangover.

"FitzGerald?"

The voice was instantly recognizable. Fiona shot up to a sitting position. Her. The voice of the damned. She pinched her cheeks to be sure she was not dreaming.

"Yo," Fiona replied, determined to be casual.

"Officer Evans," the voice said.

Fiona squinted into the red digital numbers of the clock on the dresser. It was barely five in the morning.

"He just called," Evans said, oddly tentative.

"Who?"

"Captain Green."

"He called you?"

Fiona could not contain her indignation. She was the senior detective. Why call Evans first? A Homicide rookie to boot. It was, she knew, petty and egocentric to think such thoughts, but she couldn't stop it.

"He wants you to pick me up as fast as you can and get us over to the Watergate."

"The Watergate?"

"You won't believe this. But there's a woman hanging from a balcony."

"A suicide?"

"We'll soon know, won't we?"

There it was, the incipient arrogance. But somehow it had the opposite effect. Fiona had more homicide experience. In that area the woman was a real tenderfoot. Nor would she want to fuck up for lack of experience. The worm turns, Fiona thought, banking the fires of her indignation. Just like the Eggplant to call Evans first. He wouldn't want to go through any protest shit. Not now. Not with a woman hanging from a balcony of the Watergate, soon to be fully visible to an awakening Washington.

"Give me directions to your place, Evans," Fiona barked, taking charge. Evans gave them. "And call Flanagan and the tech boys."

"I already have, Sergeant FitzGerald."

"*Ain't you just wonnerful,*" Fiona told herself silently.

29

"Meet you outside, Officer," Fiona snapped.

"I'll be there...Sergeant," Evans shot back.

Fiona hung up.

"Black bitch," she muttered, jumping out of bed.

They could actually see a woman dangling over the tooth-shaped cement balcony of the tenth floor of the Watergate South Building, like a broken puppet on a string, flapping in the breeze, her pink satiny dressing gown catching a phosphorescent glint from the meager predawn light.

They stood on the river side, squinting upward along the building's white curved facade from the vantage of the greening lawn that separated the building from Rock Creek Parkway. Cars did not slow since the body was too high up and it was too dark for a clear visual shot.

Three elderly people in robes stood in a cluster a few feet from Fiona and Evans looking upward as a doorman in uniform described the event of the discovery. Fiona figured him for about fifty, a cut above the ordinary variety of doorman.

"Got this call from Mrs. Epstein in 1H," the doorman said, pointing to one of the two grey-haired ladies, her complexion white and pasty in the dull light. "Said she walked out on her patio. I'm used to it. Lot of older folks here. They see things, hear things. I check them all out anyhow." He looked at his watch. "Forty minutes ago. You people are fast."

Mrs. Epstein sensed that they were talking about her and moved closer.

"You could have knocked me over," Mrs. Epstein said.

"Have you been up there?" Fiona asked the doorman.

"Hell no," the doorman said. "That's your job." He

looked up and pointed. "You can tell from here the lady's dead." He was right, of course.

"I don't sleep very well," Mrs. Epstein said. "Sometimes I come out here on the patio in the middle of the night. I just happened to look up."

"That was when?" Evans asked, poised, pad and pen in hand.

"Just about an hour ago, I'd say. Wouldn't you, Howard?"

"Just about," the doorman said, nodding.

"Better lead the way," Fiona told him. She turned to Evans. "Get her statement. I'll take scene." She saw the hesitation in Evans' eyes, the brief debate of dominance, then the surrender. Cop professionalism was taking over. Fiona was by far the more experienced in these matters and Evans knew it.

"Before Mrs. Epstein's call, did you sense anything in the building that seemed different?" Fiona asked the doorman as they went up in the elevator.

"Same as always. Wish I did."

"Why so?"

"Hell, this is Watergate, Officer. This could get me famous like those others." He smiled, showing his yellowing teeth.

She followed the doorman to the service door of the apartment and waited as he found the right key.

"Apartments here have a main door and a service door," the doorman volunteered.

Fiona put out her hand and he placed the passkey into her palm. He seemed disappointed by the silent request as if they were shunting him aside and he was seeing fame slip away.

"Could be on security," he grumbled. "They got these

31

systems, but people forget to activate them."

"Apparently, this one did," Fiona said, carefully turning the key, feeling the locking mechanism retract. Wrapping her hand in a handkerchief so as not to spoil the prints, she opened the door. It opened to the kitchen and they walked through a dining area into the living room.

It was getting lighter now, throwing shadows along the walls and on the carpet, which was thick and well padded. There was art on the walls, large splashy canvases. A break-front, looking very much like a real antique, in which numerous ceramic figures were displayed. Dresden, she observed, remembering her mother's penchant for them, delicate human figures in groupings, the women in long gowns, the men in stockings, tight pants and powdered wigs. Low bookcases lined the inner walls.

The outer walls were floor-to-ceiling windows and a sliding door that led to the terrace. With the wrapped hand, she slid open the door and stepped out. The view was panoramic, the slate grey Potomac waiting for the glint of sunrise. She could see the three bridges that crossed over the river to the Virginia side. To her left she saw the Jefferson Memorial, and straight ahead the high-rise skyline of Virginia and a sprinkling of window and street lights.

The terrace was shaped in a half-moon lined with plantings along its edge. A rope was wrapped around a cement tooth, held fast by a complicated professional-looking knot.

Two potted evergreens in wooden tubs lay on their sides as if they had been deliberately toppled to make room for someone, a body, to scale the low terrace wall. On the inside edge of the terrace, just beyond the sliding door, were two pink slippers placed casually parallel to each other.

Peering over the edge, Fiona saw the female corpse

swinging gently in the breeze, a pale ghostly apparition in a pink dressing gown hanging from the end of about eight feet of rope.

"People downstairs will get one helluva surprise when they wake up and see Miz Dearborn's body swinging up here," the doorman said as he looked over the terrace wall.

"Dearborn?"

Fiona suddenly remembered Chappy's remark referring to "the Witch of Watergate."

"Not Polly Dearborn?"

"That's her down there. Make no mistake," the doorman said, proud to be back in the game again.

"Big stuff," Fiona said, thinking of the Eggplant and his allocation of manpower resources. Can't avoid this one, she thought, wondering if she could persuade him to give Cates back to her. At least it solved the matter of her protest, put it on the back burner.

"Rotten way to do it," the doorman said, continuing to peer down at the corpse. "She should have just jumped, got it over with."

"What makes you think it's suicide?" Fiona asked, leaving the question in the air as she turned to face the oncoming Flannagan and his band of technical people. They fanned out. Cameras flashed.

"Crazy," Flannagan muttered as he looked over the terrace. More pictures were taken, then the body was hauled up and laid on the tiled floor, over which the men had placed a body bag.

Although these people had done such a thing many times before, Fiona was always surprised at the almost reverent regard for modesty with which the body was handled. In this case, the woman's dressing gown, worn over her nightgown, was stretched taut and tucked tightly behind her calves.

They could, of course, do nothing about the neck, which was askew and reddish blue where the rope, to which it was still attached, had cut into the flesh. The woman's head was permanently cocked to one side. The protruding eyes and extended purple tongue were part of the classic death mask of a hanging victim.

"It's her all right," Fiona said to no one in particular as she studied the corpse's face then kneeled to inspect the knot, which appeared to be a well-constructed, obviously efficient hangman's noose. "Polly Dearborn of the stiletto pen."

"Polly Dearborn, the writer?" It was Charleen Evans' ejaculation of surprise as she came through the door to the terrace. Evans looked down at the body as if the identification needed corroboration.

"Used to be," Fiona said.

Evans kneeled beside the body. She reached out, pulled at the upper part of the dressing gown. The dead woman was wearing a metal device of some sort around her neck.

"We'll need that," Evans muttered.

"What is it?"

"The key to her computer," Evans said, fingering it. "Custom job. I was wondering why her computer didn't work." She looked up at Fiona. The key was on a gold chain. "It's that important," Evans said.

Fiona nodded. With strong agile fingers, Evans loosened the rope and lifted it over the woman's head. She did the same with the gold chain, inspecting the key.

"I'll see if it fits," Evans said, going off to the bedroom.

The men began to bag the body, which they lifted and placed on a stretcher. Two men carried it out of the apartment. The doorman followed, perhaps reasoning that his potential notoriety was now directly proportional to his proximity to the body.

34

"Through the garage, please," Fiona barked as the men passed through the door. In sensitive high-profile cases like this one, the Eggplant's caveat on the media was always operative. Only one voice speaks for Homicide. His. The object was to keep things under wraps until the Eggplant was "apprahzed."

When the last of Flannagan's technical team had gone, Fiona stood in the center of the living room, inspecting the immediate vicinity, while Evans roamed through the other rooms.

Always when she was working scene, she needed a single moment of calm reflection, a time to concentrate. Suicide or murder? This was the overriding issue here.

Beware the obvious, she cautioned herself, although the visible evidence clearly bespoke suicide. Death had offered its blandishments and become the operative choice at the historic moment of bedevilment, the so-called wee hours when the imagination fixates on the worst-case scenario.

She carried the idea further in her mind, letting it take hold in her imagination. Depression, like a spreading oil spill, would have soaked into the woman's psyche, crowding out all optimism, leaving death as the only alternative to a life of guilt and the pain inflicted by ghosts and goblins.

For whatever reason, fame, money and power were no longer a palliative against real or imagined outrages. Death as a temptation had become tantalizing.

A rope lies waiting. Earlier the woman had chosen it as the weapon of choice, a common idea with a familiar history. It has lain in readiness, coiled like a snake, the hangman's slipknot awaiting its weighted prize.

Then suddenly, at the appropriate moment, the bewitching hour, the reaction takes place, the explosion that prods the mind to take action. The woman reaches for the coiled rope. This she has done before, many times, perhaps fitting the noose over her head, pulling it taut around the neck, waiting, summoning the courage that had not come. Until now.

She fastens the unknotted end around the cement tooth of the railing. It has already been rehearsed, tested, imagined. She lifts the hoop of rope over her head yet again, pulls the heavy knot against the vertebrae of her neck, makes a path by upending the two potted trees, then rolls over the side. Hardly a gurgle upsets the balance of the soft night.

"No note in sight," Evans said, interrupting Fiona's thoughts. She had come back from the bedroom.

"The computer key?"

"It fits. Custom made. She had her own method of computer security. Has two hard disks instead of the usual slots for soft ones."

"What's your assessment, Evans?" Fiona asked in her most official manner. She knew she had interrupted Evans, who was on the verge of saying more about the computer. It was a deliberate deflection and Evans complied.

"An obvious conclusion. Murder by hanging is statistically rare."

"You've studied it, have you?" Fiona asked.

"The better informed, the more options available," Evans said, exhibiting a self-proclaimed superiority that embellished her arrogance.

Smartass, Fiona thought, longing for Cates whose humility, which often infuriated her, now seemed refreshing.

"Note the slippers," Evans said, pointing to the slippers placed just outside the terrace door. "The woman walked to the terrace, took off her slippers, put the rope around her neck, anchored it and jumped."

"That's the way you see it, do you?" Fiona asked. Evans

had offered a perfectly logical explanation. It was the hasty conclusion that irritated Fiona.

"For starters, yes," Evans said through tight lips.

Fiona offered only a grunt in reply and started to explore the apartment. In the bedroom, she inspected the bed. It was turned down, but too neat to be slept in. On one side of the bedroom was an alcove with a desk, a computer and bookshelves. Where she worked, Fiona assumed.

"This the computer?" Fiona asked.

"That's it," Evans said.

Fiona nodded and turned her attention elsewhere. She studied a forest of pictures on the bureau: Polly with familiar faces, Polly with youngsters, Polly with Harry Barker, the Editor-in-Chief of the *Post*, Polly with Mrs. Grayson, who owned the paper. "To the best in the business," an inscription at the bottom of the Grayson picture read, and a signature, Sally Grayson. No Polly as a child, Fiona noted. No sign of Polly with parents.

She carefully opened drawers, looked in the closets, the bathroom. Where had the rope been stored? Fiona wondered. The closets were exceptionally neat, carefully compartmentalized: dresses, slacks, blouses, belts, shoes, were all carefully hung on identical wooden hangers.

In the drawers, underwear, panties, bras, pantyhose, all folded as if awaiting a military inspection. There were no signs of a man, not even the hint of a toilet article nor a sign of the sex act, not a vestige of its contemplation, like a dial of birth control pills, a diaphragm, condoms, spermicides, the safety equipment of the sexually active.

Evans held up a plastic case that she had discovered in the cabinet under the vanity, hidden behind boxes of tampax, tissues and a mound of toilet paper.

"She got it off with this," Evans said, holding up a red dildolike vibrator of generous size.

"What does that tell us, Evans?" Fiona asked with a deliberately patronizing air accompanied, she hoped, with a sneer of sarcasm. At the same time, she detested her own attitude. But the woman, her manner, her humorless demeanor, her blatant arrogance, her superior airs, was, to Fiona, aggressively offensive.

"It tells us..." Evans paused, raising a pugnacious chin toward Fiona as her eyes narrowed. "It tells us that the lady was..." Again she paused. This time her lip seemed to curl in contempt. "... An independent, self-contained."

"What the hell does that mean?" Fiona snapped, wanting to hear it said aloud.

"She did not need men." She held up the vibrator as if it were a weapon. "She pleasured herself."

"Mistress of herself," Fiona snickered. Tells me a lot about you, Evans, Fiona thought. To characterize the possession of such an instrument as a total substitute for men was revealing. Fiona owned one, but it was strictly an alternative, not a first option.

"Maybe she didn't want complications," Evans said, confirming Fiona's speculation.

"Lot of good it did her."

Evans activated the vibrator. A muted whirring sound cut the air. Then she shrugged, cut it off, replaced it in its plastic box and shoved it back where she had found it.

They inspected the other rooms. Next to the bedroom was an alcove, also neat as a pin, with everything in its place. There was a computer and a printer on a desk and various plaques and prizes hung on the walls, including a Pulitzer Honorable Mention.

"Seems uncommonly neat for a journalist," Fiona said.

"Not for this lady," Evans said.

"How so?"

"She was obviously controlled, obsessively organized,

tightly focused, compulsively tight-assed and secretive."

You must know the turf, lady, Fiona thought.

"Did you know who she was?"

"I read the papers."

At that moment, there was a sound at the door and the Eggplant strode in, looking surprisingly chipper, dressed to the nines in the dark tan suit he wore for television appearances. He sported a beautiful blue paisley tie on a light blue shirt and his shoes were mirror-shined.

"What have we got, ladies?" he asked, his eyes flitting from one face to another.

"Polly Dearborn," Fiona said crisply. "Female, about forty, Caucasian, prominent journalist. Looks like death by hanging."

"Self-imposed?"

Fiona exchanged glances with Evans, who had remained silent, deferring to Fiona, following the protocol of seniority.

"Maybe," Fiona said hesitantly, quick to sense what a bonanza this case meant for him. It could serve as a decoy, force people's attention away from the killing fields of the drug wars. The deceased, after all, was a prominent newspaperwoman who had thrown more people of prominence into the garbage heap than any journalist around. In that respect, she was the champ, the numero-uno nutcutter, a world-class investigative reporter. Her death, any which way, had the makings of a media feast.

The method of her demise was compellingly bizarre, the image vivid. The bitch goddess of Journalism hanging from the balcony of fucking Watergate, for chrissakes. Fucking Watergate, the physical place and the genre, symbols of corruption and cover-up, the biggest political story of the century, bar none.

This eclipsed mere drug-related gang wars. This was

whitey's turf. No wonder the Eggplant looked as if the weight of the ages had been lifted from his breast.

"No note?" he asked.

"None."

"Any sign of foul play?" he asked hopefully, looking around the room. His gaze rested on the overturned potted trees visible on the terrace.

"She could have done that herself," Fiona said. "To get over the wall."

"Or they could have fallen when she was thrown over," the Eggplant said. From his point of view, murder would give the story more legs.

"This is a lady with a lot of enemies," Fiona said, deliberately feeding the Eggplant's hope.

He began to pace the living room floor. By now the sun was poking above the horizon, throwing glints along the slate surface of the Potomac.

"Somebody might have bit back," he said. He suddenly stopped pacing and looked around the room. "Lady lived the good life here. That's real money on the walls and you can't knock the view. Are you dead certain there's no note?"

She looked toward Evans for some support to buttress the fact. She was used to Cates interjecting himself when the Eggplant interrogated them. There was a faintest hint of a smile on Evans' lips, one of those secretive cryptic Madonna smiles. But the woman kept her silence.

"Unless one shows up somewhere," Fiona replied. "She might have mailed a note to someone."

He stroked his chin while she tracked his logic. Without a note, a judgement of suicide could be merely a subjective call. An investigation, on the other hand, would stir up the media, create a mystery good for a running story of many days' or weeks' duration. A note would preempt such a possibility. If they flushed out a true murder so much the better. If they solved it? Bingo.

"Barring such a note, I'd say we have our work cut out for us." His exhilaration bordered on ecstasy. "Considering all the big shots she's shot full of holes, I'd say we'd have a suspect list as long as an ape's arm."

"Lots of grist for the mill, Captain," Fiona said. No point in being coy about it. More fun in it than doing naturals. Again, she looked at Evans, who had maintained her Madonna smile. Of one thing Fiona was certain. She felt no comraderie with this woman, no sense of sharing or partnership. She debated asking him at that moment for Cates, but held back. No sense raining on his parade.

"We'll run a tight ship on this one, FitzGerald." The statement was barked out as an order, setting the parameters. His eyes shifted to Evans, then back again to Fiona. "We three. No outside verbalizing." He pronounced it "verbalahzing." She took the hint.

"You'll be apprized of every detail, Captain." She pronounced it "apprahzed."

If she was voting at this moment, she'd vote suicide. But that was too pat. She'd been through that before, only to be fooled. Clever killers could make things look like a suicide. Unless an autopsy revealed that the woman was dead before she went over. That would be another ballgame entirely.

The Eggplant started to pace the room again. She could tell he was still mulling it over, considering possibilities.

"You found no sign of a struggle?"

"Only that." She moved her head in the direction of the overturned pots.

"Any theories come to mind?"

"Not yet," Fiona said, turning once again to look at Charleen Evans. She seemed to be watching and listening to their exchange with detached bemusement.

"They hear she died, they'll be dancing round the flag-pole," the Eggplant said. He reached into his pocket and pulled out a panatela but he didn't light up. "I've asked Doc Benton to do the autopsy himself. Considering the traffic, I'd say that was an accommodation."

"He's that kind of a man," Fiona said. Dr. Benton, the Medical Examiner, was her friend, mentor and confidant. No one could learn more from a corpse than Dr. Benton.

"This is your turf, FitzGerald—I want you to really give this one a ride." For the first time in the conversation he turned to Evans. "And a real opportunity for you too, Evans. Let's show them what the girls can do."

Shit, Fiona thought. Why go and spoil it? Here she was playing the game exactly as if he had scripted it himself and he goes back to the macho-pig business. She pulled a face to show her obvious displeasure. If he saw her reaction, he didn't let on. Instead, he looked at his watch.

"I'm going to hold a press conference downtown in a couple of hours. Meantime I want everything you can get ...without, I repeat, without spilling the beans on the lady's identity. Not till we've had our say. I want those bastards to understand that they're dealing here with a first-class police department. Capish?"

"You'd better put a lid on the doorman," Fiona said. "He's a real glory hound."

"Him? We've got him on ice downtown. Taking his statement. Loves to talk."

When he was purring, the Eggplant was, most of the time, a step ahead of her.

"And the old folks downstairs?"

"Likewise."

In his sly way he had bounced it against her for confirmation that he was taking his best shot. She knew why he was waiting the two hours, but saw no harm in it. It would be at least two hours before the reporters and TV crews would be up and running. He was an old hand at media manipulation and public relations and he knew how to work it out for his benefit.

So fortune has smiled, Fiona thought. She could see his reasoning. Throw them a nice tasty bone to keep them all occupied in another direction. Made sense. She'd go along up to a point. Could she honestly search her intelligence and her gut and still find room for doubt about a suicide? Stay with maybe, she decided. Murder would be a lot sexier. No doubt about that.

With a look of satisfaction, the Eggplant lit his panatela, inhaled and puffed smoke out of his nostrils. He nodded and his mouth formed a broad sunny smile. She hadn't seen him do that for months. He started toward the door.

"I don't think it was murder, Captain," Charleen Evans said quickly, before he was out of earshot.

The Eggplant stopped, cocked his head, but did not turn.

"It's a clear case of suicide, Captain," Evans said. "Any objective analysis will tell you that hanging is the weapon of choice for a certain pattern of suicides. It is quite common. This is a textbook case. We check hard enough we'll find the place where she bought the rope and where she stored it in this apartment. Hanging is the rarest form of modus operandi for a murder. There actually hasn't been a murder by hanging in this city for nearly three decades."

She paused for a moment and the Eggplant turned and glared at her.

"Also," she continued, her chin jutting out, throwing Fiona a glance of clear contempt. "There probably is a note."

"You found one?" Fiona asked, on the verge of a blowup. This was a real lethal lady, she thought. A hard case.

"No, but I think I can and I know where and how to look for one."

Smug bitch, Fiona thought, exchanging glances with the Eggplant, whose complexion had turned to the grey tone displayed at the morning meeting.

"Do you now?" the Eggplant asked, offering his familiar grimace of intimidation.

"In the computer, Captain. If it's anywhere it's there."

The veins reddened in his eyes. Fiona saw the great effort he was making to repress his anger, knowing that his perception of her as a castrating female was far more menacing than her own.

"Would you like to hear my theory?" Evans asked.

A nerve twitched in his jaw as he studied her.

"You got two hours, Mama," he said.

With a man in his command, he would have exploded in rage. In this case, he turned quickly, bottling up his agitation as he stormed out of the apartment.

4

"YOU'VE GOT A problem, Evans," Fiona said after the Eggplant had left. Any remote hope of allegiance on gender grounds had totally evaporated.

"So it seems," Evans responded. "He would have been better served to hear me out."

"It's not that, lady. You've got a piece missing in your character." It was, Fiona decided, a fully justified frontal assault.

"Do I?"

Evans was unfazed, her features a mask of indifference.

"It's called insight," Fiona pressed. "Plus a screw loose on timing."

The woman's eyes studied her, betraying nothing that was going on behind them.

"You want my theory or not?"

Fiona shrugged.

"How can I avoid it?"

Evans nodded, then crooked a finger, as if coaxing a recalcitrant child to follow. Assuming that her gesture was enough of a summons to Fiona, she moved into the bedroom. Capping her exasperation, Fiona followed, more curious than obedient.

Evans stood facing the computer on the desk in the bed-room alcove, her back to Fiona. Fiona looked at the computer screen perfectly centered on the desk. Behind it was a long shelf of programming handbooks. Beside the screen was a laser printer and on the shelf below a fax machine.

"You know computers, FitzGerald?" Evans asked without turning to face her. Fiona caught the insult in the condescending words, tone and position.

"Apparently you do."

She bridled at her own childish response, feeling inadequate to the occasion, knowing that the woman was about to flaunt her superior knowledge. Fiona's experience with computers was rudimentary, just enough to service the basics.

"Note the passion for neatness evident everywhere," Evans continued, her voice flat, but with a teacher's earnest surety. The woman was lecturing now. "This is the working space of a journalist, an important journalist. There is not a piece of paper visible. The books on the shelf behind the computer are all programming handbooks, most of them very sophisticated. My guess is that this woman was a computer expert." Still not turning, she put a palm on the monitor. "It's also obvious that the computer is her principal tool. Everything has to be in there. Notes, research, first drafts, everything. Which suggests that she was fully computer literate."

Evans sat down at the desk, put the key in the computer and switched it on. Strings of amber words, numbers and symbols marched across the monitor screen. Evans seemed totally at home, her brown fingers flying swiftly over the keyboard keys while amber symbols raced across the screen. She said nothing, intent on her work.

"There," Evans said. "She's hooked into a large number

of data banks." She pointed to the screen, which rapidly scrolled lists as Evans repeatedly hit the space bar. "This is a menu of data banks. There are scores of them. Anything a journalist might want to know about anybody. Could even be some computer violations if we really looked."

"Nobody is private any more," Fiona muttered, irritated by her resort to sarcasm.

"There's a gold mine here if you want to get something on someone."

"That was her business. No question about that."

Fiona waited as Evans worked her fingers over the keyboard, intensely watching the screen.

"Okay, I'm impressed, Evans. You're a whiz. Now what about the suicide note?"

"If it's here, I'll find it."

Her fingers raced over the keyboard.

"Talk about confidence. You left the impression with the Egg..." She stopped herself. The familiar nickname was too private and affectionate to be shared with this alien. Without insight, it was impossible for Evans to understand the kinship of respect and ridicule many of her squad mates had for the Chief. "...with the Captain that you were dead certain. You posed the idea almost as a conclusion, not a theory." It was Fiona's turn now, although she knew she was setting herself up for a crow's feast if Evans was right, which seemed a distinct possibility.

"Just exercising logic, FitzGerald, which is the heart of this instrument."

"I'll stick with the human variety, the one influenced by emotion, subtlety and insight."

"Of which you believe I have none."

"If the shoe fits."

Fiona heard a sound come from Evans, a cross between

a chuckle and a harumph. She stood over her shoulder, watching the screen, which moved too fast for her understanding.

"Takes a while to dope out her system," Evans said, as she swung her pocketbook off her shoulder and laid it beside the computer. She seemed to be settling in for a long, intense stay. "I'll get it."

"You've got two hours," Fiona said.

"You needn't stand there watching me," Evans said, dismissing her. It was infuriating. Fiona stood there, rooted to the ground, angered and embarrassed, unable to concoct a response. At that moment she heard a faint muffled sound.

"What the hell is that?" Fiona asked.

"What?"

It seemed to be coming from somewhere in the vicinity of the computer. Evans stopped beating on the keys and listened. Then she opened a drawer.

"Answering machine," she said. A telephone stood beside the computer, but it hadn't rung. "She's got it silenced."

They watched the machine until the sound had stopped and a red numeral one began to flash. Evans reached into the drawer and pressed the button of the instrument, setting off the rewind mechanism. When that stopped she pressed another button. Again she seemed to be deliberately flaunting her electronic wizardry. But this time it triggered in Fiona a grudging respect. Fiona would have wasted time trying to figure out how the machine worked with predictably mixed results.

"Polly," a high-pitched, young-sounding voice said. "Sheila here. Mr. Barker is still not happy with the last Downey segment. As I told you last night, I have a feeling that he is being pressured by Mrs. Grayson. He seems to be having second thoughts and wants to discuss it with you. I also have the impression that there are lawyers involved. I told him I'd get you to call immediately. He says it's real urgent." There was a short pause. "Seven-ten and I'm still home but will be heading to the office in a few minutes. I wouldn't have bothered you so early if I didn't think it was important."

"Eager beaver," Fiona said.

"No modem," Evans said. "Interesting."

"What's a modem?"

"Put it in your computer you can send something over the telephone wires. She chose a printer and a fax instead. Tells you something."

"What?" Fiona asked.

"That she guarded her computer. Wouldn't even connect it to her office. That's why she has two hard disks, one for backup and dupes. Afraid someone might copy things onto floppies. Harder to do otherwise. You need another computer to receive the dump."

Fiona was confused, but wouldn't dare admit it. Evans returned her attention to the computer.

"There," Evans said, pointing to the screen. "This is her memo file. Apparently Sheila is her assistant. Woman's name is Sheila Burns."

Again Charleen Evans' fingers raced over the keyboard. At that moment they heard a tingling sound from an open shelf below the computer. It was the fax machine. They waited for the paper to roll out. Evans tore it off and handed it to Fiona.

"A message from Harry Barker." Fiona said. Harry Barker was the editor of the *Post*, a household name in Washington. "Jesus. He's hot." She read it aloud. "Tried calling you last night. No answer. Sheila says she can't get hold of you this morning. Better stop ducking me, Polly. This last Downey piece still needs work. We don't hear from you soon, I'll get out the old blue pencil. This is not what we agreed. I'm pissed. Harry."

"I'm afraid Polly has ducked Harry Barker permanently," Fiona said. She remembered him as a reporter. Years ago he had been to the house to interview her father and she would meet him occasionally at Washington social events. Handsome leathery face, athletic body, tough-talking. He posed as a rough-cut diamond, but he didn't fool anybody. Under it all he was Ivy League to the marrow.

These days, as editor of one of the most important papers in the country, he was a national powerhouse, a celebrity.

"Looks like the lady left some unfinished business," Evans said.

"We've got some ourselves," Fiona said.

"The man gave us two hours," Evans snapped.

She worked the keyboard again and went back into her computer trance, staring at the screen. By now the media had been told about the press conference, but not the subject matter. Fiona left Evans to her search, went into the living room and continued to poke around.

No question, she decided, the woman was organized, neat, everything in its place. She stood in the center of the room, trying to imagine herself as Polly Dearborn, to feel like her, to understand what might have been going through her mind. Maybe she was having second thoughts about herself, the role of destroyer, killer journalist. Perhaps she was having a fit of conscience, an attack of self-revulsion. Considering the ruined lives in her wake, she might have decided that there was little left for her but judgement day.

How long had she been doing these pieces? Ten years or more, Fiona calculated. Her style was always witty and sophisticated and she seemed to believe that she was presenting a balanced assessment.

Always, Fiona recalled, the stories dealt extensively with the subject's achievements. This was the good news and it always came first, a setup for a fall. The better the good news, the worse the bad news. Such was the reader's expectation.

Because she had the ability to wield so much power in a place where power was the only criteria of true achievement, Polly Dearborn was deeply feared and coveted by those who thought that ingratiation might somehow cause them to escape her clutches.

The memory of Polly Dearborn cozying up to Downey at the races gave the lie to such an idea. Her media killing was business, not personal. She was like a hit man, emotionless and uninvolved, who could blow a man's brains out and the next moment provide succor to the victim's mother.

Perhaps that was the way it was done to her. An uninvolved hit man responding to orders. Kill the lady. Make a statement. Of course, the discovery of a suicide note would put an end to such speculations.

Apparently Barker was referring to the third Downey piece, the one that was evidently going to run tomorrow. It occurred to Fiona that, because of the early summons to the Watergate, she had not even read the second installment.

She found the paper in the corridor in front of the apartment's front entrance. As the *Post* had done yesterday, they had run the story on the front page of the Style section. Considering the importance of the revelations, Fiona wondered why it had not been begun on the front page. Hell, it accused the Secretary of Defense of malfeasance in office and cast a long shadow over his character.

She began to read. In yesterday's story Dearborn had made her accusations. In part two she was embellishing, expanding, going into the court records of Downey's divorce, comparing Downey's present financial statement, filed when he was appointed Defense Secretary, with the testimony of the divorce case and the settlement agreement with his ex-wife.

The accusation of hiding assets verified, Dearborn's story concentrated on the accusation that Downey favored one defense contractor over others. There was a chart showing how much business this company, Interplex, did before Downey became Secretary with how much they got after he took over the Defense Department. The jump in contract totals was more than two thousand percent higher. But it wasn't until the very last paragraph in the installment that Dearborn turned the knife.

She wrote: "There is always the argument that the reason Interplex got the business was because it was the best company for the job. Did the sudden upsurge in orders have anything to do with the fact that Downey's son, Robert, had become a vice-president of the company three months after the elder Downey was appointed Defense Secretary? More on this tomorrow."

The article ended on this note. Fiona shook her head. Poor Chester Downey. Poor Robert Downey. Investigated, convicted and hung in three days. Was a massive attack of remorse the reason for Polly doing herself in? She shook away the idea. Not now. Not yet.

Fiona looked at her watch. More than an hour had passed since the Eggplant had given them their deadline. Fiona went back to the bedroom. Evans was where Fiona had left her, tranced out in front of the computer screen, fingers dancing nonstop over the keyboard. Deep frown lines had engraved themselves on her forehead. Obviously, her search was not having the results she had imagined earlier.

"Anything?" Fiona asked, forcing a neutral tone.

Evans grunted, concentrating on the amber symbols moving like soldiers in formation across the screen.

"And you still think you're right about the note?" Fiona asked.

Evans ignored the question. Fiona had to prod her.

"You could be dead wrong," she said.

"I'm not ready to concede yet," Evans said through clenched teeth. At that moment the sound of chimes erupted. Fiona made no effort to move.

"A suicide wants a note to be found. One would think it would be more obvious," Fiona said.

Evans cut a quick, almost surreptitious look at her watch.

"Will you please leave me alone?" she snapped, her irritability accelerating. The chimes started again, persistent now, as if someone were keeping a finger on the button. "Why don't you answer that?"

Fiona shook her head and left the bedroom. She looked through the glass peephole. She saw a woman's face distorted by magnification. The eyes seemed anxious, the look confused. The chimes continued, embellished now by a banging on the door.

"Polly, what is it? Is something wrong? If you don't answer I'll have to call somebody, maybe the police. Please, Polly, answer the door."

Fiona waited. The woman's voice grew louder, the knocking more persistent. Finally, Fiona felt she had little choice. She opened the door.

The woman looked up, startled. She was a short, stocky woman with black curly hair framing delicate sculpted features. Her complexion, without makeup, was dead white. Large brown eyes seemed to gaze out with mordant curiosity as they studied Fiona's face then darted around her to search the apartment.

"Where is Polly?"

Fiona stepped aside as the woman moved past her into the apartment. Fiona remained silent, watching her.

"Who are you?" Fiona asked.

"What difference does that make? Where is Polly?"

The woman turned her head from side to side, rustling her head of tight black curls. She started toward the bedroom. Moving swiftly, Fiona planted herself in front of the woman, barring the way. The woman stopped, looked up into Fiona's eyes, her gaze an obvious query.

Fiona opened her purse and showed the woman her badge.

"I'm Sergeant FitzGerald." She was about to say "Homicide" but checked herself. "Metropolitan Washington Police Department."

"Police?" The revelation had the effect of making the woman retreat a step. Fiona saw her nostrils quiver. "Where's Polly?" The question was barely audible.

"She's not here," Fiona said. "May I ask who you are?" By then Fiona had suspected the woman's identity.

"I'm Sheila Burns, Polly Dearborn's assistant," the woman said in confirmation. A reedy tremor had crept into her voice. "Something is wrong, isn't it?"

"Afraid so, Miz Burns," Fiona said, watching the woman's eyes move to follow the sound coming from Polly Dearborn's bedroom. A moment later Charleen Evans emerged from the room, obviously curious.

"Detective Evans, this is Sheila Burns."

Evans nodded. She seemed distracted.

"Not there?" Fiona asked, finding it hard to keep a gloat out of the question. Evans shook her head.

54

"Still searching," she muttered, straightening her shoulders and lifting her chin pugnaciously as if she were compensating for her disappointment by buttressing her defenses.

"Maybe Sheila can help," Evans said, deliberately vague. Then she went back to the bedroom.

"Would you please sit down, Sheila," Fiona said gently.

"It's Polly," Sheila said, sucking in a deep breath. "She's, she's..." Sheila's hand groped for support, reaching for the armrest of one of the living room chairs. But she did not sit down.

"She's dead, I'm afraid," Fiona whispered.

Sheila's eyes widened in confusion.

"Polly...dead?...That's, that's impossible," Sheila said with more belligerence than disbelief. She seemed too overcome to say more. Tears welled in her eyes and a sob erupted in her throat. "But how...?"

Fiona ignored the question.

"Can you think of any reason why Polly Dearborn would commit suicide?" Fiona asked, cutting a quick glance at Evans.

"Suicide? Polly? I don't know." She moved to one of the chairs and sat down, visibly shaken. "I can't believe this."

"You see any signs of depression recently? Anything askew in the way she conducted herself? A suspicion, a feeling you might have had?"

Sheila shook her head, apparently unable to find words. It was beginning to hit her. She seemed on the verge of fainting. Fiona rushed into the kitchen and came out with a glass of water. Sheila took it between two shaking hands and sipped, then gave the glass back to Fiona.

"I'm so sorry," she said in a small voice, barely above a whisper. For a moment, she stared through the terrace

55

windows, as if lost in a trance. Fiona waited through the pause.

"She was always so strong, so sure and confident, on top of everything. It was hard enough keeping up. No. I saw nothing different in her. Nothing at all."

"Maybe something in her personal life was bugging her," Fiona suggested.

"Personal life?" Sheila's retort seemed too swift. The corners of her mouth turned up with the faintest hint of a smile.

"A disappointment of some kind," Fiona pressed. "A lovers' quarrel perhaps. Something deeply affecting."

"Polly? Her life was her work. As far as I know, there were no special men. No. No men at all. Polly Dearborn was a very dedicated person."

"Maybe the pressure of the work got to her," Fiona said. Almost immediately, Fiona rejected the idea. That possibility meant a sudden crack-up. If this was a suicide it was not a sudden decision. The method implied planning, calculation, the deliberate creation of a public statement, an advertisement of death.

"The Downey article seemed to have stirred up a lot of flack," Fiona said. Sheila nodded, showing no surprise.

"All her articles stirred things up. Above all, we prided ourselves on accuracy." Fiona noted the collective pronoun and, as if Sheila had sensed that an explanation was needed, she said, "Polly checked things out. The bottom line on everything was truth. Polly Dearborn was the most thorough journalist in America."

"No matter who got hurt," Fiona said quickly, thinking suddenly of Chappy. And the others. Sheila Burns showed no sign of irritation at the accusation. Undoubtedly she had confronted such criticism before.

"Our job was to find the truth. The mythbusters, that's

what Polly called us. We got behind the image and the P.R. We got to the heart of the matter."

Considering her recent shock, she was being militantly defensive.

"Do you think that her death..." Fiona paused and looked toward the bedroom where Evans was, undoubtedly, still playing with the computer. Fiona shook her head in disgust. Cates would have jumped in at that point, offering additional questions. Fiona looked at her watch. Time was running out. "...had anything to do with the Downey article?"

Sheila frowned, then looked at her hands.

"I can't imagine why."

"Pretty rough stuff," Fiona said. "A man's career down the chute. Has to take its toll on the perpetrator as well."

"The perpetrator?"

"In a journalistic sense. Could Polly have had a sudden bout of remorse? Something that pushed her over the edge?"

"A very farfetched idea," Sheila said with a touch of indignance. She appeared to have regained her composure. "We've been through this before. Nobody likes to see their bubble busted. We concentrated only on those who served the public and betrayed their interests."

Sheila had the look of frailty and vulnerability, but underneath Fiona sensed bedrock layers of blind faith. No, Fiona decided, responding to gut instinct. Remorse was not a motive for death in this case. Polly Dearborn was a zealot, a crusader, and Sheila Burns was a disciple.

"And Harry Barker, what was he after?" Fiona asked.

"He was questioning some points in the article, the piece that is set to run tomorrow."

"What points, for example?"

A cloud seemed to pass over Sheila's face. She grew

hesitant and looked down at her fingers. After a moment, she raised her head.

"Mr. Barker rarely discussed these things with me. I'm ...I was only Polly Dearborn's assistant." Fiona detected a touch of resentment. "He dealt with Polly on matters that he deemed very sensitive."

At that point the telephone rang. Fiona picked up the instrument.

"FitzGerald?"

Fiona was surprised to hear the Eggplant's voice.

"Not yet, Captain," she said, looking at Sheila, who bowed her head. Her hands were clasped on her lap.

"There's more spin on this than I figured."

He had lowered his voice but could not conceal its upbeat tone. A faint click told her that another phone had been picked up.

"That you, Evans?" Fiona said. "It's the Captain."

"Yes sir," Evans said.

"No note?" the Eggplant asked.

"It's going to take longer than I..."

"No time for that anymore," the Eggplant said. "I want your asses over to 2101 N Street. I'll hold off the uniforms for ten minutes more. Don't want this on the police radio yet."

"Got it, Captain," Fiona said. "There's someone here. Hold for a second." She addressed Sheila.

"Thank you for your help. We must ask you to leave. We'll talk later."

Sheila rose. She seemed relieved.

"It's terrible, isn't it?" she whined, again on the verge of tears.

"Yes, it is," Fiona agreed.

Sheila turned and, beginning to sob, moved quickly out of the apartment.

"Dearborn's assistant," Fiona explained. "She's gone now."

"Chief?" It was Evans. "I'm taking the hard disk. I need more time. That okay?"

There was a pause.

"Just get the fuck over to N Street, ladies. *Now*, please."

"Who is it, Chief?" Fiona asked.

"Thought you'd never ask, FitzGerald," he said in a teasing tone. "Chester Downey's maid just called. Apparently he just blew his brains out."

5

"CLASSIC," FIONA SAID as they entered Chester Downey's study. The body was sitting upright in a high-backed leather chair behind an antique desk. The gun, a .38 Wesson, was still locked in the man's hand, which rested in his lap. He was dressed immaculately, obviously having chosen his exit clothes with great care: a fresh white shirt, pressed dark pin-striped suit, paisley tie, spit-shined shoes.

He had shot himself through the right temple, and the left side of his head was soggy with oozing red matter. On the desk in front of him were two envelopes, one addressed in a flourishing hand "To Whom it May Concern." The other to Robert Downey, his son.

Outside the door to the study, they could hear the housekeeper's whimpering. It was she who had found the body and called the police.

Holding the edges of the envelope marked "To Whom it May Concern," Fiona took out the neatly handwritten note on a single sheet of plain white paper. Evans looked over her shoulder as they both read it silently.

> I am of sound mind and I take this step after careful consideration. Please see that my son gets the letter

addressed to him. He is fully aware of all arrangements made in connection with my demise. I apologize for any inconvenience and I hope any controversy surrounding my action will be quickly resolved.
                                    Sincerely,
                                    Chester Downey.

"No doubt about this one," Fiona said. "Suicide. Open and shut. Agreed?"

She turned to Evans, who nodded. Suddenly, they heard a commotion outside the den and two men rushed in.

"Feds," Fiona whispered.

They were tall, officious types, tight-lipped and unsmiling. There seemed only one distinguishing factor to separate their identities. One was bald. A kind of cloning, a scrupulously maintained neutrality of personality, was the unmistakable sign of a federal agent, any federal agent, regardless of gender.

"What you see is what you get, gentlemen," Fiona said. She pointed to the two suicide notes. "All down in black and white. Our jurisdiction, I'm afraid." She showed her badge and gave the man her card. Evans followed her lead.

"A national-security matter," the bald man said, flashing his credentials.

"CIA?" Fiona snapped, turning to Evans. "The bully persons."

"He was the Secretary of Defense, for chrissakes," the bald man said. The other man opened the note and read it. He moved to the side of the room and whispered into his wrist.

"They love their toys," Fiona whispered to Evans, who nodded. For the first time since they had been partnered, Fiona could sense the first fleeting signs of alliance. "Everybody will be in on it, all the initials—FBI, DIA, NSA."

Probably the Secret Service, too, alerted for a possible conspiracy to assassinate the President. "Now you see it. The power of the media. Our little Miss Dearborn writes her story." She looked around the room. "Then this."

Suddenly, they heard a commotion outside the den. Through the open door, Fiona could see other agent types. Footsteps could be heard on the floor above. The Feds were "securing," searching the premises.

An agent came in with a camera and started to take pictures.

"Who's he?" Evans asked.

"Company man," Fiona shot back. "Local procedures get fuzzy around the edges when something likes this comes up." Besides, she had already reached her conclusions. Cut and dried. Unassailable. The man blew his brains out. Polly Dearborn's legacy. Fiona cut a glance at Evans, who looked confused.

After the photographer, a group of tech boys came into the den, all business, inspecting the premises. Her instinct was to protest the usurpation of police power, but she repressed that. The Eggplant would have raised hell. But this was, after all, bigger than a mere suicide. There were implications beyond police jurisdiction. Downey could have been, what did the Brits call it, a mole for a foreign power. A traitor. The Feds had to contend with these issues, conspiracy, the fate of the nation, establishment paranoia.

The bald man and his partner conferred out of earshot, then talked into their wrists again. After a while, the bald man came back and addressed Fiona.

"We're in touch with your superiors. The body is going to the MPD medical examiner." Fiona watched as the weapon and the notes were put in Ziploc plastic pouches. "We'll be sure you're copied on these."

Two men with a folding stretcher came in and began to

bag and load the body, leaving a trail of blood and matter along the carpet.

Fiona looked at her watch. The Eggplant's press conference would be in full swing. In moments, the two deaths would be connected. The media circus would begin. To the Eggplant, Downey's death would be a bonus, as if he had been granted his fondest wish.

"Truth kills," Fiona said, looking at Evans, wondering if she fully understood.

They moved through a sea of agents and MPD uniforms as they followed the body to a waiting ambulance. Press and television reporters were already on the scene, taking pictures, attempting to question agents, who rebuffed them with stony silence. A reporter who knew Fiona yelled a question at her. She put a hand over her mouth, signaling her response.

In the car, with Fiona driving, they headed back downtown.

"You let yourself be intimidated, FitzGerald," Evans said as Fiona swung the car into the M Street traffic. The tone was accusatory.

"It's a joke, right?" Fiona said.

"No joke at all. That was our jurisdiction. You let them push us around."

"Where were you?" Fiona snapped. The woman was infuriating.

"This is your turf," Evans said. "You're the experienced operator." Evans turned and looked out of the window at the streets of Georgetown, the heavy street traffic with few black faces, the trendy restaurants and boutiques.

"What does that mean?" Fiona said.

She knew exactly what it meant. To Evans, Fiona was the honky princess who specialized in all the fancy white crimes. It had been said often enough by her colleagues, always articulated with sarcasm and resentment.

Fiona understood it, of course. The establishment, high society, the power elite, had nurtured her. This was her natural milieu. Homicide detectives with that background were nonexistent. The squad knew that. They also knew that, if called upon, she could deal with Washington's underbelly, it's scummier side. But that didn't prevent some from secretly resenting her, her gender, her color, her education, her background, her contacts, her money. The best she could hope for was respect, which had to be won many times over. With newcomers, it was harder. Especially if she wasn't motivated. Like with Evans.

Evans did not answer Fiona's question, which just hung there now, a sail flapping helplessly in the wind.

"You've got a real attitude problem, Evans," Fiona said. "You don't like the way I handled things, bring me up on charges."

"No way. They'd laugh. Call it a cat fight."

"So what's the point of bitching?"

"The point is that I'm on to your kiss-assy little game. Doesn't mean it's right. Means it's expedient. You backed down because you didn't want to upset the Eggplant's show. A fight with the feds wouldn't look good just now."

"Which side are you on, Evans?"

"My side—and don't you forget it."

Cantankerous bitch, Fiona thought, letting her anger simmer. She took a stab at trying to analyze Evans' hostility toward her. Some deep-seated race and gender thing, as if Fiona's very presence and persona provoked agitation. Fiona supposed, if she worked at it, she might crack through, reach common ground. Professionals compromised, repressed, accommodated.

Why bother, she decided. Whatever was bugging her, this was Charleen Evans' problem, not Fiona's. When they

64

got back she'd ask the Eggplant for Cates. The Eggplant understood the delicate chemistry between partners. He wouldn't refuse, not with a high-profile case in the making, not when he might be needing her.

She pushed Evans out of her mind. She'd have Cates back and Charleen Evans would be history. She forced her thoughts back to Pamela Dearborn. They had said good-bye to Sheila Burns, locked the apartment and dashed over to Downey's house. Yet something lingered in her mind, some vague discomfort nagged at her.

If Polly Dearborn was murdered, a distinct possibility in the absence of a suicide note, they would have to start blazing a trail through thickets of suspects, meaning everyone the woman's cruel pen had skewered. This implication of numbers made her think of Polly Dearborn's computer. All in there, Evans had said.

"What was on that computer?" she asked Evans, trying to keep her tone indifferent and professional. She was surprised when Evans answered her, adopting a similar tone.

"Lots of things. It's going to take hours to get through. She was hooked into scores of data banks. There was also a Rolodex containing hundreds of names and private numbers, dates and times of contact, personal comments, opinions. In hard copy it would have filled filing cabinets."

"But no suicide note?"

"I didn't say that." There it was again, that attitude, the touch of arrogance. "I only said I hadn't found it yet." She jerked a thumb toward the rear seat. "That's why I took the hard disk."

"And if it doesn't turn up, then what?" Fiona asked. Evans shrugged.

"It was a good shot, win or lose," she muttered.

"This isn't a contest, Evans."

"Then why make it one?"

At that point one of the more macho of her colleagues might have said, You wearing the flag, big Mama? She felt herself on the verge of mimicry, but desisted. Instead, she prepared her own retort.

"I'm not going to plumb your depths, Evans. I'll leave that for your shrink."

"Good. Stick to your last, Sergeant. And I'll stick to mine."

"And if you don't find a note, will you concede it might, just might, be murder?" Fiona asked.

"Maybe," Evans conceded.

First words out of her mouth when she got downtown would be "Give me Cates!" The Eggplant would ask why and Fiona would talk about the sensitivity of the case and the need for teaming up with an experienced partner. She wouldn't mention the attitude problem or the woman's self-righteous arrogance. Leave that to others to find. She'd stay with the experience part. He'd see through it, of course, maybe give her a bad time at first. That was his way. In the end, she knew, he would give her Cates.

She navigated Washington Circle, turned down 23rd Street, hung a left past the State Department and headed toward Constitution Avenue.

"And if it is murder," Evans said as they neared head-quarters, "then that computer will tell us who did it."

"That's what I detest about you most, Evans," Fiona said through clenched teeth. "Your sense of certainty."

They sat in the Eggplant's office, where she heard the death knell to her idea that she might be able to rid herself of Charleen Evans.

"I've got two of my best people on this, Amy," the Eggplant said into the phone, his chair angled, his spit-shined shoes resting above a pile of thick folders on his desk. He puffed deeply on his panatela and blew perfect smoke rings, a sure sign of his satisfaction. "Two women. Detectives FitzGerald and Evans." He was silent for a moment as he listened to a voice on the other end. He smiled and nodded and put his hand over the mouthpiece of the instrument. "I hadn't thought of that." He winked at them. "Amy Perkins, New York *Times*. Likes the idea of women investigating the death of a woman."

"Verisimilitude," the Eggplant said, his hand off the mouthpiece. "I like that. Sure, Amy. Anytime." He hung up and took a deep puff on his panatela. "Always darkest before the dawn." His eyes scanned the faces of the two women who sat before him.

They had briefed him, Fiona doing most of the talking, putting everything in perspective. Evans said nothing, wearing her favorite neutral expression. He was exhibiting too much goodwill for them to show him the ugly side of their relationship. Nor was the Eggplant in a badgering mood. He had not brought up Evans' failure to find a suicide note. At a less amiable time, he might have excoriated her for her apparent certainty. And Evans hadn't expressed her opinion about Fiona's quick jurisdictional surrender to federal agents, although Fiona had alluded to it herself.

"Why get into a pissing contest with the feds?" the Eggplant said. "Unless an autopsy comes up with surprises, I'd say Downey's suicide is unassailable."

"It doesn't absolve him as a suspect," Fiona said, cutting a glance at Charleen Evans. At least Fiona had kept that theory to herself. It probably had never even crossed Evans' mind. But now she needed to gain ascendancy over Evans with the Eggplant.

Yet, Fiona was far from ready with theories. Even the

idea that Downey was Dearborn's killer was premature. Nor had they ruled out without a shadow of a doubt that Polly Dearborn had committed suicide. Evans might find a suicide note in the computer, which would eliminate Downey as perpetrator. And there was still the autopsy.

"Downey a suspect?" the Eggplant mused, tapping his teeth.

"I don't see it," Evans interjected, rushing into an explanation. "If he was planning to kill himself anyway, why go to such elaborate lengths to kill her? A bullet or a knife, even a garroting, would have done the job very well. Think of what hanging requires. The purchase of the rope, bringing the rope to the scene, researching the fine points of hanging, constructing the right knot, not only the one around the noose but the one around the cement pylon of the terrace. Not to mention that there is no evidence to suggest that he was there."

"So far," Fiona pouted.

"I'll grant you..." Evans paused, throwing a smug glance at Fiona, "...that anything is possible. Downey's note to his son, for example." Again she paused. No question, she had their attention. "That letter to his son could have been a confession."

"What letter?" the Eggplant asked.

"Downey's letter to his son," Evans said. "His personal suicide note. Along with the other. The ones the feds confiscated." She looked pointedly at Fiona.

"You let them take it?" the Eggplant said, directing the question to Fiona.

"They invoked national security," Fiona muttered.

"You didn't read it?" the Eggplant asked.

"No, I didn't," Fiona answered. "I'm not certain we could do that." There was, of course, the legal issue of privacy. But that was a cop-out. The fact is that they should have beat the feds to the confiscation.

"I'm sure the feds had no such compunction," Evans said, troweling the blame onto Fiona.

"We can still confront the younger Downey," Fiona said defensively, feeling herself nakedly vulnerable on that point. "On the question of murder, he would also be a suspect. Along with everyone else she had wronged." She thought suddenly of Chappy and his threat. Undoubtedly, there were many more who had the same violent wish.

"I'd say that the term 'wronged' is inaccurate," Evans said. "It implies the people she wrote about were innocent. 'Exposed' might be more apt."

"That's because you've never been on the receiving end," Fiona snapped, remembering how her father was excoriated by the press when he made his antiwar stand. She glanced at the Eggplant. "The fact is, we're all on the receiving end now. Like it or not."

The Eggplant nodded, but he did not pick up the cudgels to dispute Evans. At the moment he wasn't happy with the media, especially the *Post*. But when they made him a hero, publicized his exploits, he was the first to embrace them.

Evans was like most people not in the power loop. They loved to see someone, particularly a person from the so-called power elite, impaled in the press. It was a favorite Washington sport, like watching a bullfight. Many were quick, eager, to pass a guilty judgement, especially if the person impaled was a "have" as opposed to a "have not." Seeing these mighty "haves" fall was to many, especially to a woman with an obvious chip on her shoulder like Charleen Evans, an exhilarating experience. Clearly, the root of her hostility was putting Fiona in the category of the "haves," then bashing her.

Although Evans never spoke the words, Fiona imagined that she could hear them loud and clear: "The apple never falls far from the tree." Be on guard, Fiona cautioned herself. This woman wants to cut your heart out.

"However defined," Fiona began, tackling the issue of "wronged" versus "exposed." Avoiding any show of weakness, she had to repress any sign of animosity. "A media attack, deserved or undeserved, provides grounds for a motive. On that basis alone, the woman had legions of enemies."

"No question about that," the Eggplant agreed, determined not to take sides between them. It was obvious that he wanted them to stay partnered. He rubbed his chin and took a deep drag on his panatela. "Good thinking on getting that computer material. Might be something in it."

"I can't take any of the credit on that one, Chief. We're lucky to have someone as computer literate as Officer Evans." Fiona looked toward the recipient of her compliment, hoping that her patronizing tone was rankling. Evans' expression remained neutral, showing neither pleasure nor pain.

The phone rang on the Eggplant's desk and he picked it up routinely.

"Greene here."

After a brief pause, he straightened in his chair, a gesture that signaled that someone very important was on the phone. Despite the macho pose to his underlings, he could appear groveling when it suited his purpose, a performance that assuaged any guilt in her use of the term "Eggplant."

"We're not a hundred percent certain, Mr. Barker," the Eggplant said after listening for a few moments. They could hear the muffled voice on the other end. "An autopsy might tell us something." There was more talk at the other end. "Yes, we do have our hands full. But we're on this one.

You can be sure about that." More talk at the other end.
The Eggplant lifted his eyes and looked at them, first one
then the other. "Yes. We do appreciate that, Mr. Barker."
The Eggplant looked at his watch. "We can be there in
less than a half hour. I'm sure it would be helpful. Yes.
See you then."

The Eggplant hung up the phone and bashed out his
panatela. He was smiling, his change of attitude abrupt,
showing them he was merely playacting.

"The man himself," he said. "This Dearborn thing's got
him rattled." The Eggplant rubbed his chin in contemplation, then he stood up and paced his office, lost in thought.
"Offered carte blanche to the investigation. That's exactly
his words. Carte blanche. Who could blame him? They
start knocking off his reporters for writing their shit, who
knows where it ends?" He shook his head and stomped
his foot in a kind of dance of joy. "Harry Barker himself.
Shit. He wants in. Needs *us* now."

As editor of the vaunted Washington *Post*, Harry Barker
was the single most powerful person in Washington. At
the paper, his word was law, absolute. He had the ear and
the complete confidence of the paper's owner, Mrs. Grayson, who, along with most *Post* employees, worshipped
him or appeared to do so. He was, as they say, a legend
in his own time and he enjoyed the role.

Except for that one time as a young reporter when he
had interviewed her father, Fiona had not seen much of
him. He was rarely on the social circuit and was apparently
very reclusive outside the office. Who could blame him?
He had enemies. He had made the paper, in his thirty years
as editor, the voice of indignation. He had toppled Presi-
dents and poseurs with the power of the word. The trail
of busted careers and ruined lives was endless. Most, Fiona
supposed grudgingly, were justified. Others were clearly

marginal. But one thing was certain. If anyone got entangled in the net of Harry Barker's system of media justice, he was, if not doomed, damned to banishment from the national control tower.

"Let's roll. We can strategize on the way," the Eggplant said, starting for the door. He looked toward Evans.

"Better keep working on that computer search," the Eggplant said.

"Maybe that note will turn up yet," Fiona said, smiling. Evans said nothing, but Fiona could detect the flash of hatred in her eyes. "If it's there, Evans will find it."

"Be a damned shame, wouldn't it?" the Eggplant said as he and Fiona dashed out of the office. Fiona cut a final look at Evans. Unhappy hunting, she wanted to say. She hoped her eyes conveyed the thought.

6

HARRY BARKER'S OFFICE had a glass wall through which he could see the vast expanse of the paper's city room. His legions of editors, reporters, researchers, secretaries and copy persons could also see him, which seemed the object of the configuration.

He sat on the flat side of a conference desk shaped like a fat half moon. Around the rim of the rounded part of the desk were chairs for six people. These people faced Harry Barker and the window, which looked out on 15th Street. Harry Barker faced his visitors and his city room.

"I really appreciate this," he said politely in his gravelly voice, standing up to shake hands. There was a brisk courtliness about him and a firm sense of command. His face was like old cracked leather, his eyes watery blue, his hair a neat steel grey with a perfectly straight lefthand part. He wore a light blue button-down shirt with a striped blue-and-red tie, and when he stood Fiona noted that his waist-line was small, boyish. He reminded her of some Hollywood image of an old sundried cowboy dressed in strange clothes who had wandered into this place by accident.

Yet Harry Barker had presided over this city room for

more than thirty years and, from the look of him, he seemed determined to preside here for another thirty.

He leaned back on a big leather chair and lifted his thick-soled smooth-topped military-style shoes to the desk, his feet crossed at the ankles. The introductions had been cordial and they had been given coffee in cups and saucers of good china.

"Been a long time, FitzGerald," Barker said. "Wouldn't have figured you'd wind up as a cop." He turned to the Eggplant. "I interviewed her old man, the Senator. Helluva guy. What was it, twenty-six, twenty-seven years ago? You were a kid. I remember the Senator asked if it was okay for his daughter to sit in."

"And you said, 'Sure. She looks like she can keep a secret.'" The recall had suddenly become vivid.

"What a memory. He was quite a guy, your old man."

He watched her for a moment, made a clicking sound with his teeth and focused his watery eyes on the Eggplant, who was waiting patiently for the formalities and small talk to be over.

"Polly Dearborn was a stiff pain in the ass," Barker said. "But one helluva clever reporter. The 'Witch of Watergate,' they called her. Tougher than hardtack." He shook his head and said "shit" through clenched teeth. "I'll say this, if she did kill herself, which is doubtful, that's the way she'd do it. Something bizarre like that for all to see, hanging there in the breeze." He chuckled. "Maybe with a broom between her legs."

"There wasn't any broom," Fiona said, surprised by her retort. She was also surprised at Barker's attitude. For some reason she had expected it to be different—if not grieving, at least respectful. Polly Dearborn was, after all, his ace investigative reporter.

"We think she was murdered," the Eggplant said flatly,

then hedged: "Not that we're ruling out suicide, but it's become more and more doubtful."

"I think you're right, Captain," Barker said. "If you do rule out suicide then the ramifications for us are enormous. Let's face it, the obvious conclusion is that she would have been killed because of something she did on the job. Nothing like that has ever happened to any of our reporters. Not in my memory. It has the stink of terrorism. I'm not saying she was murdered by anyone she wrote about. But I'm sure you're not going to rule that out. There's also a bigger picture here. Like she might have been murdered to intimidate us, to serve as a kind of warning. What do you think, Captain?"

The Eggplant rubbed his chin, took his time. He had apparently decided how he wished to appear to this powerful editor. Fiona watched him transform himself into the wise old darkie, the philosopher who had seen it all. He was trotting out his garb of dignity.

"We rarely theorize about the obvious, Mr. Barker. Not that everything you say might be correct. We've barely begun our investigation. The victim also had a personal life, a life away from the business. That, too, must be explored."

"Personal life?" Barker said. "Not Polly. She was always working. I never knew her to have a boyfriend. She had escorts." He looked toward Fiona. "You know what I mean. No love interest. Not even a girlfriend. Aloof. That was Polly Dearborn. A loner. As far as I know, few people were ever invited up to her pad in the Watergate. 'The witch's lair,' the wags called it. Not that she didn't go out. She went out a lot. She could put it on. Be social, gregarious, sometimes funny. But she never fooled me. Nor did she try to. Her kind of work required obsession, dedication."

The day's paper was on the desk near his elbow and he slapped it with the palm of his hand. "She couldn't do what she did without that kind of focus. You could see it from the beginning, the moment I saw her. I hired her fifteen years ago. She had worked on a paper in South Carolina, had this sweet drawl, innocent face." He shook a finger in the air. "Didn't fool me. I knew a nutcutter when I saw one."

"I seemed to have formed the same impression from her stories," Fiona said.

"They passed muster, though. Lawyers raked over her stuff. I did, too. Not that we didn't have protests. Some of the people she hit squealed like stuck pigs. We got hate mail, but we're used to that. Hell, every day I get buckets of the shit, call me every name under the sun. Threaten my life, my children, my grandchildren, my wife. Sometimes, whenever I get too smug or cocky, I read a few. Sobers you up. Lots of crazies out there."

"And Polly Dearborn," Fiona asked, "did she get hate mail?"

"Piles."

The Eggplant shot her a glance of rebuke. This was to be his show and he made it perfectly clear that she was to keep her mouth shut until prompted.

"You ever report these threats?" the Eggplant asked.

"You've got to be kidding. You'd clog up the system. In my experience, they're empty threats, sounding off by wackos. Why bother? They want to knock you off, they knock you off. No need to advertise." He looked up at them. "I'm still here, aren't I?"

The Eggplant shrugged acknowledgement then took his time absorbing the information. It carried little surprise for each of them. Yes, there were crazies out there. Yes, the media could trigger inflammatory conduct. She watched the Eggplant struggle to keep his dignified image intact.

"Has Polly Dearborn ever been threatened by the people she wrote about?" he asked.

"Horse of another color," Barker said. "Many of them bitch like hell. They protest. They threaten legal action. Imply worse. They come running to me or Mrs. Grayson and scream smear or distortion or excoriate us for printing lies. Oh, they threaten dire consequences. Say things like, 'I'm gonna getcha.' We're all used to that. We expect it. Hell, we expose dark deeds, bring down the liars, the cheats, the scum. That's our mandate. We cut through the bullshit. We've been wrong sometimes and we've paid the price. But I'll say this, Polly Dearborn didn't make too many mistakes. Go through her copy over the years, you can find lots of murder suspects. The point is, it never really happens. They think it, wish it, hope it. But, in the end, it's just talk."

"Until now," the Eggplant said.

Harry Barker nodded and lifted his feet off the desk. He leaned over and rested his elbows where his feet had been.

"You really think that, don't you, Captain?"

Fiona could see now what was in the forefront of Harry Barker's mind.

"I told you, Mr. Barker, it's difficult to theorize at this stage."

"How do you connect the Downey thing?" Barker asked suddenly. So there it was, Fiona thought.

"It's a suicide. No question. Man left a note more or less apologizing for the mess." The Eggplant cut a glance at Fiona, who nodded confirmation.

"That I got, Captain," Barker said. "What about the other note, the one to the son?"

The Eggplant showed his cynical smile, complete with the twitching nostrils of a genuine sneer.

"You've got your ear to the ground, Mr. Barker."

"One of the tricks of the trade," Barker said, but it was not meant to amuse.

"Then you might know more than we do," the Eggplant said. "We didn't read the note. The feds got it first."

"It was addressed to Robert Downey, the son," Fiona interjected. "I hope they've handed it over to him by now."

The Eggplant nodded his approval of her remark, then blinked his eyes, signaling her to remain silent.

"National security," the Eggplant said. "That's the ploy they use to preempt our jurisdiction. You can bet they've read the contents."

Harry Barker moved his head closer to them and lowered his voice with an air of extreme confidentiality.

"If Polly Dearborn was not a suicide..." Barker paused, watching the Eggplant's face. "You think Chester Downey could have done it, Captain?"

"It did cross my mind," the Eggplant said. "But we haven't found any evidence to that effect." He turned to Fiona.

"Not yet," Fiona agreed, adding hastily, "But nothing can be written off."

"It occurred to me that maybe the letter to his son was a confession," Barker said. A deep frown wrinkled Harry Barker's brow.

"A confession?" the Eggplant asked.

"It bothers the shit out of me," Barker said. He sucked in a deep breath and let it out with a sigh. "Fact is I cut out the really bad stuff in her story. I tried like hell to reach her last night and this morning to tell her that. It bugged me, nagged at me, and finally I cut it out."

Fiona had seen it countless times. Someone out on the limb of conscience, itching to let it out. Harry Barker, despite all his power, was not immune to such an urge. There was only one way to handle it: wait, listen, prod cautiously. Barker needed no prodding.

"Polly Dearborn and her computers," he sighed. It sounded very much like a beginning. "She was plugged into all these data banks. Indefatigable, that one. Never stopped. She picked up, from God knows where, this testimony of a case nearly twenty years ago. It seems that the Downey kid had got himself mixed up in a cult.

"One of the parents of a kid also in the cult kidnapped his own child, but the deprogramming didn't work and the kid, with the backing of the cult, sued his parents. Nice people. The point is that young Downey was a witness for the kid. One of the cult's bonding techniques was to have these kids confess to the group any abuses they had been subjected to at the hands of their parents. Idea was to make the kids hate their families, substitute the cult for the family.

"The Downey kid takes the stand and the parent's lawyer presses him. He testifies that he was sexually abused by his father. Didn't go much further than that. But Polly Dearborn picks it up on one of her data banks. Damned FBI never had it in their report on Chester Downey. Don't ask me how I know this.

"Okay, we've dumped on the guy for keeping his assets hidden from his ex-wife, for favoring his kid's firm. Bad enough. But this? Oh she had it wrapped up with every hedge in the book. I tell you I agonized over it, then got up this morning and said "nada." It won't be in the paper tomorrow."

He lowered his head and studied his hands. No question, Fiona decided, he was genuinely contrite.

"Did Downey, the father, think it was going to appear?"

"Polly wouldn't write it without confronting him."

"But you wouldn't tell him you had cut it out?" the Eggplant asked.

"No I wouldn't. But my deal with Polly was to let her know when we were cutting her stuff."

"Would she have called Chester Downey?"

"I doubt it. She would have been too pissed."

"Publishing that kind of information could really cut a man down. Innocent or guilty," the Eggplant said.

"Of course, he denied it," Barker continued. "Which was also in the story. The lawyers cleared it and it was ready to go. I just didn't feel comfortable with it. I didn't deny the truth of it. But Christ, it's so . . . so deeply personal and damning. Hell, it wasn't your run-of-the-mill peccadillo. Frankly, I felt it was overkill."

Fiona was surprised at his vulnerability. He wasn't as tough as he made himself out to be. The Eggplant, ever eager to exploit the slightest sign of weakness, jumped into the silence.

"I'd be curious to know how you intend to carry that story tomorrow."

"I'm on the horns of a dilemma, Captain," Harry Barker said. "That's exactly the point of this exercise. Maybe we can help each other."

"I'm sure we can," the Eggplant agreed. He was, Fiona knew, loving this.

"There is a delicate balance here," Barker said. "A tricky business. The wrong spin could give the wrong impression."

"I'm sure it would," the Eggplant said cautiously. "Considering the power you wield."

"Sometimes we get more credit than we're due. Everyone will be climbing on this story. We don't have a monopoly."

Fiona snickered to herself. Was he really expecting them

to buy that? The power of the *Post* was awesome. No single media enterprise came close. To imply that a reporter could be killed for destroying a man's career, whatever the truth of the allegations presented, was, from Barker's perspective, a dangerous idea. Punishment was a judicial function. Trial by journalism, while an old American tradition, was in danger of going out of fashion, irritating people. Fiona could understand Barker's interest.

"You do have a considerable voice, Mr. Barker," the Eggplant said, unable to keep the sarcasm out of his tone.

"What I want is to keep our lines open," Barker said, disengaging from the subject. "I've been very forthcoming here. And I want to report the facts as they are, without speculation. Others may theorize, but, unless the theory is official . . ." He raised his head and looked pointedly at the Eggplant, who, to his credit, did not turn his gaze. "I will not allow it in print. Not in this paper."

Fiona could see the deal emerging. Barker was going to downplay the notion that Downey killed himself because of Polly Dearborn's story. And the Eggplant was not going to indulge in speculation that Downey killed Polly Dearborn. Unless it was absolutely, positively proven beyond all reasonable doubt.

What Barker was attempting was to minimize the impact of the obvious, that media bashing could, one way or another, kill, that reporters could be terrorized, that great newspapers could be intimidated. He wanted to set the tone, steer the direction of the story, keep all the players in check. He knew his power, knew his manipulative strength and he knew a thing or two about intimidation.

He had cleverly shown them his human side. He seemed genuinely shaken by Downey's response to Polly Dearborn's story, although he felt absolved, to some extent, by his own self-righteous act of charity by eliminating the homosexual incest reference. He was, Fiona decided, one clever son of a bitch.

He was saying to the Eggplant, who wasn't at all dense, that he wanted to be in the loop, that he did not wish the Eggplant to mouth off theories, speculations or assumptions about these deaths to the media, a major sacrifice. In a way, he was anointing the Eggplant with his favor, downgrading the Mayor, who, by law, was the boss of the cops, and bestowing on the Eggplant powers far beyond the mandate of Homicide.

"If Polly Dearborn was murdered," the Eggplant said cautiously, "our mission is to bring the perpetrator to justice. That..." the Eggplant paused and stared directly into the editor's eyes, "...is our mandate."

"Indeed it is, Captain. Indeed it is."

"But unfortunately, Mr. Barker, we are operating under a severe handicap."

"This sudden jump in gang-related murders," Barker said, shaking his head. "It's awful. Unbelievable."

"And it doesn't reflect well on us for this city to be referred to as 'the murder capital of the world.' It also does not help us when you roast the Mayor as if it were all his fault."

"Our Mayor is a little too mouthy. Lot of blab and not enough jab. He's not doing the job. Everybody knows it."

"You certainly have made your point about him. Over and over." The Eggplant's tone was calm, almost serene.

"Well, he can't blame it all on us. The media. We have to meet that challenge. Besides, he's been indiscreet; some of his cronies are corrupt and he can't keep his pants zipper up."

"He's done some good things, too," the Eggplant said. He knew his politics and he wanted Fiona to witness his defense of the man who had the power to appoint him Police Commissioner.

On the subject of the Police Commissioner, the paper had been harsh. Unfortunately the Police Commissioner, while hard-working and intelligent, was both inarticulate and a bad administrator. His days were numbered and Captain Luther Greene was one of those favored to succeed him. The Dearborn case and its growing ramifications, Fiona knew, had the visibility that could make or break him. He would have to handle that part gingerly. In that regard, Barker would be a powerful ally.

"We have a constituency, too, Captain," Barker said calmly. "We owe it to our readers and our advertisers. A fucked-up city isn't good for business. Musn't forget that part of it either."

"And I'm not here to defend the Mayor. He's a big boy and can take care of himself. I'm just a cop trying to do my best. We're overworked and understaffed. The fact is that MPD homicide is one helluva professional outfit." He looked toward Fiona. "Sergeant FitzGerald here can testify that we have one of the best departments in the country, top professionals with great skills."

"Have we ever questioned that?" Barker said defensively.

"No, you haven't. But the implication is clear. I'm not saying it's deliberate on the part of your reporters and editors. But it only makes our job harder. More than anything, we want the killers off the streets. We, too, have our institutional image to protect."

Rarely had Fiona seen him more eloquent. He was taking his shot. He would probably never have a chance like this again. Harry Barker's eyes narrowed. They were still locked with the Eggplant's. Granted, his display of courage was grandstanding, hotdogging. But the Eggplant had calculated the odds and taken this opportunity to burn his identity into the editor's mind, show him his character, elicit his respect. From the looks of things he was doing just that.

"I see your drift, Captain," Barker said. He did, indeed, Fiona reasoned.

What the Eggplant saw, Fiona speculated, was his name in blazing headlines, a huge picture on the front page of the Style section: Captain Luther Greene, MPD'S Brilliant Homicide Chief, A Sure Bet for Commissioner.

"You see then that what we have here is a two-way street," the Eggplant said.

"Yes, I do," Barker said, nodding in emphasis.

"Worst thing that can happen is if we get surprises when we pick up the paper. It makes our job that much harder."

The contract between them, Fiona observed, was getting broader. They were forging a common front, merging agendas.

"You call us the murder capital of the United States and you keep kicking the Mayor, you undermine confidence in our city institutions." He was repeating the message, burning it in.

Barker studied him. His grin came on slowly, cracking the wrinkles of his leathery face.

"We'll do our part, Captain," Barker said.

"And we, ours," the Eggplant added. He stood up and extended his hand. Barker took it. They shook warmly. Male bonding achieved. From a box on his desk, Barker took out a card and wrote on the back of it.

"My home number," he said. "Anytime you need me."

The Eggplant took out his card and wrote his home number on the back.

"Likewise," he said, handing Barker his card.

"Guess you don't need mine," Fiona piped. Barker smiled and put out his hand. His flesh was warm, his grip strong.

"I'm glad you're on this case, FitzGerald," he said. "The Chief's got my number."

"Yes, he has," Fiona said. Then to herself, *Yes, he has.*

7

"WOULDN'T TRUST THAT bastard as far as I can throw this desk," the Mayor said, hitting the desk with the heel of his hand. The mere mention of the name Harry Barker had set him off, although he had listened patiently through the Eggplant's explanation.

Fiona sat beside him as he spoke, aware of her role. Once again she was to bear witness. She had been with him through the Barker discussion. It was now necessary for her to witness the Mayor's reaction.

The Eggplant was, of course, playing politics, forcing the circumstances to be seen his way, compelling both the Mayor and Barker, because of Fiona's validating presence, to be aware that what was being said was no old-boy back-door deal.

"Everybody has an axe to grind," the Eggplant said, as part of his summation. "Barker doesn't want it to look as if his people went too far on the one hand. And he doesn't want his people to be frightened into pulling their punches on the other. He's one shrewd bastard, I'll give him that."

"If he thinks he can control this investigation he's got another guess coming," the Mayor said. He looked fatigued and drawn. His shirt collar was too big for his neck, a measure of his weight loss, and his hair had whitened in the past six months.

The man was beleaguered and looked it. The cocky play-boy attitude had given way to the worried, embattled politician fighting for his political life. Some of his closest advisors had been caught with their hands in the till. He was rumored to have numerous mistresses on the city payroll, and although no one had accused him of financial corruption, he was a sitting duck for such allegations, especially by a frenzied press encouraged in their investigative zeal by the wave of murders, the emergence of gangs and the growing drug trade.

"He's smart enough to know that he can't manipulate the investigation," the Eggplant explained. "All he wants is to be in the loop, to have input in the way the case is presented."

"And what's the trade-off for us to cooperate with him?"

"I had the impression that he wasn't going to pile on that murder-capital-of-the-United-States shit." He paused, exchanged a glance with Fiona, then continued. "I also had the impression that he was going to let up on you."

"Fat chance. He wants me to resign. That's what's behind it all. The bastard is after me because I don't play ball with the establishment."

This was only marginally true. In his youth, the Mayor had been on the cutting edge of the civil rights movement, one of its more militant figures. He had come a long way from that point. The fact was that he was very much part of the establishment, which also had a mandate—to maintain the public order and community standards of ethical conduct. Unfortunately, the Mayor, by virtue of his office, could be faulted on both counts. Worse, he had fallen into the trap of every politician on the defensive: blame everybody but yourself, especially the media.

"They want to make it look as if a black Mayor can't run a city," the Mayor muttered. Fiona understood that attitude, sympathized with it, didn't agree, but had learned never to argue the issue.

"I think I made the point that the heat the paper was generating was counterproductive. It was my impression he understood what I was talking about and was willing to back off." He turned toward Fiona, who was expected to validate this impression. She complied.

"Seems that way. Especially since he wants something from us," Fiona said.

"Remains to be seen," the Mayor grumbled. "I'll accept the responsibility for running this city. But I resent being blamed for the gangs, the dope, the murders, the corruption around me. You can't run a city as if you were the Gestapo. The whole country is in trouble. Society is in trouble." He seemed to be starting to make a speech, recognized it, then stopped himself.

"Pamela Dearborn was one miserable bitch," the Mayor said. "When she got her hooks into you, you were dead meat. If you think about it, I guess I'm lucky. She never got around to me." He chuckled. "Nobody is going to shed too many tears over that lady."

"For us, that's not the issue, your Honor. If we rule out suicide we've got us a killer to find."

The Mayor swiveled back in his chair and made a cathedral out of his fingers.

"In that case, I hope it's connected to the work she did in blowing up people's lives," the Mayor said. "Sure Harry Barker doesn't want to see that. Make his rag look like a murder weapon. Piss people off. I can see his point. Somebody sending him a message to lay off." He paused and sat upright in the chair. "Got any ideas, Captain?"

"Some. Problem is we're so thin we can only spare two detectives." He looked toward Fiona.

"It won't be easy," Fiona said, reinforcing the pitch.

The Mayor seemed to be looking for something on his desk. He dug into a pile of file folders, slipped one out of the pile and opened it.

"You know how many cops we had in 1972?" They remained silent. They both knew the question was rhetorical. "Fifty-one hundred officers. You know what we got now? Under four thousand. You know what the police share of the budget was in 1972? Twelve percent. You know what it is now? Half that."

The Eggplant shot her a glance that told her not to respond. There was one statistic that neither of them wanted brought up. The homicide solution rate of their department was once roughly 75 percent, three out of four murders solved. It was now, this year alone, only 20 percent, only one out of five.

Sure, Fiona knew, the low percentage could be rationalized by pointing to the growing drug epidemic and gang wars. But the percentages were still ghastly and reflected on their competence.

"We'll do the best we can with what we have, your Honor," the Eggplant said. He looked toward her with an apologetic air. Just being political, his eyes told her.

Brown-noser, she answered.

8

DR. BENTON LOOKED tired and drawn. As Chief Medical Examiner, his department was literally working round the clock to accommodate the huge influx of bodies being produced in the murder capital of the United States.

Fiona watched him standing in front of a zinc basin, washing up, while yet another body was being transferred from a gurney to a work station. The smell of disinfectant tingled her nostrils.

"Seems like months since we had one of our little chats, Fiona," Dr. Benton sighed. He was her closest friend in the department, wise and cultured and full of sage advice. Often, she had sat with him in the scrupulously cared-for sitting room of his small house in Northeast Washington where he had lived for more than twenty-five years with his late beloved wife.

Amid the shrine of silver-framed photographs that constituted a record of his memories of her, Dr. Benton could always be relied upon to help Fiona through the crisis of the moment, giving her the insight and perception to, as she often put it to herself, "blunder on."

"We are encountering a new phenomenon, Fiona," Dr.

Benton said, tearing off a slice of absorbent paper from a roll on the wall and wiping his hands clean. She knew better than to interrupt his train of thought. "The automatic weapon is changing the parameters of a pathologist's time."

The idea seemed both obscure and oblique, but she knew that he would shortly reveal its logic. "Used to be that death by gunshot would involve a single entry. One bullet. Maybe two. Sometimes three, but that was rare. They come here now with an average of eight or nine. This morning I counted one poor devil with a dozen. Takes only one to kill. Imagine the waste in energy, metal and, above all, the pathologist's time. We must probe for each bullet. Because of the speed of the weapon, the killer's time is not impinged. Only us, the poor overworked pathologist. I estimate that it has increased the average time of an autopsy by twenty-five percent." He offered a wry chuckle and shook his head.

"On the other hand, the value of human life has decreased by an even greater percent." He turned and studied Fiona with his startling blue eyes, a legacy of his Louisiana forebears, the white parts now laced with lightning streaks of red.

"Are there no limits to your scientific objectivity?" Fiona chided, knowing better.

"It does keep one sane," Dr. Benton sighed. When he was tired like this, he often took refuge in philosophical concepts, avoiding the clichés of contemplating human waste and folly. He looked at the naked corpse of a young black man lying on the table. "Rule one for a department medical examiner. Never get involved in a corpse's emotional history."

"In my side of the business, it's hard to avoid," Fiona said. Dr. Benton showed a wry smile.

91

"Case in point," he said. "Your Dearborn lady. She seemed to have engendered a great deal of federal interest as well."

"They were here during the autopsy?"

"No. But they want the report faxed over immediately."

Dr. Benton started to pull white latex gloves over his hands. "She was a forty-three-year-old female in excellent health. Mostly what one would expect. Sparing you all the technical details, she did, indeed, die by the noose." He had lowered his voice, illustrating his conspiratorial alliance.

"Not before?" Fiona asked.

"Before what?"

His question took her by surprise.

"For us, the issue is murder or suicide." He knew that, of course. Sometimes he teased her this way, especially when he had concocted some theories of his own. "You're saying then that she died by no other means than hanging."

"I didn't say that. I said she died by the noose."

"That's exactly what I thought you said." She paused and noted a mischievous air about him. "Is this a riddle?" she asked.

"Yes, I suppose it does sound that way." He smiled benignly and patted her cheek with his gloved hand. "I wish we had more time to work it out together." He looked at the body on the table. "But duty calls." He expelled a long breath, then turned back to look at her. "Again sparing you the technical jargon. You'll see it in the report. Actually, from what I can see, the moment of death came when she went over the side. But she was dying when she got there."

Fiona was getting the picture now, creating a scenario in her mind as Dr. Benton spoke.

"The physical evidence, faint abrasions on the back and buttocks, the location of the abrasions on the neck, finding wisps of carpet in her hair, her dressing gown and the backs of her heels. We've sent it to the lab, but I've seen enough to be certain."

"That she was dragged across the carpet," Fiona interjected.

"By the rope. With the noose around her neck," Dr. Benton said. "A theory, of course. But the evidence is strong. The noose was slipped over her head from behind, as if she were sitting in a chair. It was pulled taut. The woman fell backward. She was then dragged some distance..."

"...And eased over the terrace wall to complete the process, made to look like death by hanging."

"Exactly. There were also grains of soil on the back of her heels."

"The turned-over evergreens. She was dragged along the terrace as well."

He clapped his rubber-gloved hands together and bowed in acknowledgement.

"So much for suicide," Dr. Benton said.

"A good try, though," Fiona said. The murderer had probably worked things out to the letter. "Hadn't banked on the intrepid Dr. Benton."

"Or believed all the media perception that the Washington Police Department was incompetent or too overworked to figure things out," Dr. Benton said.

"Makes the juices run," Fiona said. Nothing like an outside attack to bond people together. She remembered yesterday's "negotiation" in Harry Barker's office, where the Eggplant had risen to heights not thought possible.

"Captain Greene should be ecstatic. He gets a high-profile case to take the pressure off."

"I better tell him," Fiona said. "He was kind of hoping it would be murder."

"And you, Fi?"

"It is our business, Dr. Benton. Only the knife cuts both ways. Now we've got to get our man. There's a great deal riding on it, a great deal."

"I would say so. I was an avid reader of Polly Dearborn. Unfortunately, I've been too busy over the last few days to read anything beyond medical evidence."

Something had begun to nag at her, something that Dr. Benton had said. Her mind raced to find the source. Then it came to her.

"You said mostly, Dr. Benton. You said 'mostly what one would expect.'"

Dr. Benton tapped the table with a gloved finger.

"Yes. Of course. I did say that. Keep me on my toes, Fi. Not as young as I used to be." Fiona waited for his thought to resurface. "Yes, I remember now. It was most unusual."

"What was?"

"The woman's hymen. It was still intact."

9

FIONA WAS UP at five-thirty. She had stood in the open entrance to her house in her nightgown, waiting for the *Post* delivery boy.

"Up early," he said, handing her the paper and ogling her body through the translucent nightgown. She slammed the door, opened the newspaper and sat down on the stairs to read.

There it was, the stuff of books and movies. She quickly read the two major headlines on the front page. They had carried the Dearborn murder and the Downey suicide as separate stories, a not-so-subtle attempt to keep the connection separate.

Both stories were written with an eye toward scrupulous neutrality, designed to discourage the reader from making rash speculations, an impossible task. Barker was leaving it to others to draw conclusions.

Speculation, however, was inescapable. There was absolutely no way to read the stories without forming a theory or an assumption that connected the two tragedies. Indeed, one only had to read the third installment of the Downey piece to draw conclusions.

They had begun it on page three and jumped it to the

front page of the Style section. The evidence of Barker's editing was easily apparent, probably shortening the story by half. There was no mention of the cult trial testimony, although there was more on Downey's hiding assets from his wife in their divorce battle and some background on Robert Downey, his son.

In fact, the stories provided something for everyone to chew on—media bashers, police lovers or haters, armchair detectives, mystery novelists with hyperactive imaginations, Fed gumshoes, whether they were CIA, DIA, FBI, NSA or whatever other initials were appropriate to describe those involved in the intelligence community.

The Eggplant was also quoted in the story. Polly Dearborn was murdered, he had announced. "We are following up numerous leads." They had printed his picture on the jump page.

Fiona did not begrudge him the glory. It was a respite from the drumbeat of death he got each morning. Last night there had been six more gang murders. Fiona noted that Barker had kept his word on this as well. The story was buried in the back of the local section, told straight, without hysteria or innuendo. There was not a word about the Mayor in any of the stories or in the editorial.

The Eggplant called her at six.

"Looks like we're in it up to our eyeballs," Fiona said.

"Kept his word. That's the important part," the Eggplant said. "He buried the murders. No more murder capital of the United States. No more Mayor-bashing."

"Not today anyway," Fiona said.

"It's a biggie. The Mayor has given us carte blanche. You and Evans have now got to find me that killer."

"Evans?" She had forgotten. "Yes, of course." She had been on the verge once again to request Cates. Again, she had reconsidered, but for different reasons. Charleen Evans knew computers, an absolutely essential ingredient in this case.

She called Evans' number and got no answer after numerous rings. That was odd, since all homicide cops were supposed to have answering machines.

Fiona dressed quickly and drove to Charleen's apartment in Southwest Washington. However she felt about the woman, Fiona could not conceive her to be irresponsible. She was too tightly wound, too proud, too controlled to show weakness.

When she didn't come to the door at the first ring, she kept her finger on the buzzer. Then she noted that the *Post* was still on the doorstep. She picked it up and resumed her attention to the buzzer.

After a few minutes, she heard movement and had the sensation of someone peering at her through the peephole, then the door swung open.

A bleary-eyed Charleen Evans stood in the doorway in a flannel nightgown. "I was dead," Evans said.

"We got to get us a killer, Evans. The world is watching."

She carried in the *Post*. Evans looked at her briefly, then, leaving the door open, dashed inside the apartment and disappeared. Fiona came in and shut the door behind her. She heard a shower running from somewhere inside the apartment.

She stood for a moment in the center of the living room contemplating the surroundings. The room was as neat and orderly as anyplace she had ever been. There was a couch, chairs, family pictures in shiny frames, an oriental rug of intricate design, an abstract painting on one wall.

On the opposite wall were floor-to-ceiling bookcases. She noted the titles—books on criminology, pathology, psychology, computer sciences. No novels or biographies. Charleen Evans was the kind of woman who made every spare moment count.

Oddly, the atmosphere reminded Fiona of Polly Dearborn's apartment. It had the feel of being inhabited by someone who was intense and obsessive as to order, neatness, cleanliness, function. Only the abstract painting on the wall hinted at another dimension to Evan's personality.

Fiona wandered through the kitchen, where pots and pans hung in ordered sequence on a punch board. Here, the same passion for neatness prevailed. Fiona heard the shower stop and wandered into the bedroom. Even the bed in which Evans had slept seemed barely used. The blanket was still tightly tucked under the mattress and the pillows were barely indented. It was as if Charleen Evans had simply inserted herself into a tightly made bed.

Off to one side of the bedroom was a computer and printer on a clean-lined Scandinavian-type desk. Beside the desk, piled neatly on the floor, was a stack of papers.

Charleen Evans emerged from the shower in a white terry-cloth robe. Her short curly hair was wet and shiny and her skin darkly attractive against the white of the robe. With barely a glance toward Fiona she removed her robe, showing a tight, muscular and not-unattractive body. Turning her back to Fiona, she began to dress quickly.

"Worked on the computer all night," Evans mumbled as she dressed.

"No note, right?"

"No note," Evans said.

Fiona walked around her and held up the *Post*. As she dressed, Evans read the stories on the front page.

"Because it's murder, that's why," Fiona said. "Beyond a shadow of a doubt."

"I was wrong. I admit it," Charleen said, zipping up her skirt.

"No sweat, Charleen," Fiona said, deliberately using the woman's first name, hoping that might crack the ice between them.

"But I'm glad I took the hard disk," Charleen said. She buttoned up a white shirtwaist with a bow, fastened the leather strap that held her holster and put on her suit jacket.

"We're in something big, very very big," Fiona said.

"Bigger than you think, FitzGerald," Charleen said. She looked toward the stack of papers on the floor. "I printed out five hundred pages of hard copies. It'll blow your mind."

Charleen stooped and picked up the sheaf of papers.

"Stuff here on lots of people, potential victims. She's cross-referenced scores of data banks, searched legal records, testimony in trials, credit reports. You name it. She's even busted into some files that are probably verboten. I'll tell you this. What she's got is worth its weight in gold."

"To who?"

"The media, the CIA, anybody who deals in information. I can't prove it but I swear she's been in and out of the FBI and CIA files. I don't know which. But there's stuff about some of these people that could only come from there."

"And it's all in that stack?"

She nodded."

"You really know your computers, Charleen."

"Yes I do."

Fiona could spot the pride, but still no softness, no real pleasure in Fiona's compliment.

"Problem is we're tracking a killer, not bringing down the government." Fiona could not hide her irritation.

"I'm aware of that, Sergeant."

"Have you any ideas, any suspect?"

"Yes I do, Sergeant."

"Come on Charleen, loosen up. Make it Fiona."

"Downey for one. Father or son. One or both. Take your pick. You can't imagine what she had on them."

"Yes I can. Barker told us. He cut it out of the story today."

"That doesn't rule them out," Charleen said.

"No it doesn't," Fiona agreed. She had turned and now looked directly into Fiona's eyes.

"There's another suspect," Charleen said.

"Who?"

"The one she was getting ready to do. She's got more than enough to do him. Not a pretty picture, I'm afraid."

"All right Charleen, you can stop with the games."

"Our mutual boss. The Mayor."

"He had one conviction for possession, one for peddling."

"The Mayor?"

"When he was a kid, living with his grandmother in South Carolina. He used his father's name then. Later he changed it to his mother's."

"Did he go to jail?"

"Not for that."

"Jesus."

"He did six months for attempted murder. When he got out he was picked up for rape, then released when the woman changed her story."

"How long ago was all this?"

"All before he was twenty-one. When he got out he changed his name to his mother's, went into the civil rights movement. He was arrested for demonstrating, but we both know that doesn't count."

"And it's all there?" Fiona pointed to the stack.

"That's just the printout. It's on the hard disk."

"They use it, the Mayor is done," Fiona said. "All validated?"

"Chapter and verse," Charleen said. "It has all the earmarks of truth. Burns me up, too. Oh how they'll run him down. Here is a rehabilitated man. Doing his best. Maybe he's not the greatest Mayor in America. But he's been straight for more than three decades. And just because they'll want to dump on this black Mayor, they'll use it, all these things he did as a kid."

"Must it be a racial thing, Charleen?" Fiona said gently. "The Downeys are white."

Charleen shrugged and turned away. She began to thumb through the papers.

"So what do we do with it now?" Charleen asked.

"It's evidence," Fiona replied, but halfheartedly.

"It's more than that, Sergeant. It's a bomb."

"That's not for us to decide," Fiona said. Suddenly an idea began to emerge. "You think the *Post* has this?"

"No, I don't," Charleen said. She reached into her blouse and pulled out a key attached to a gold chain. Fiona recognized it.

"That's also evidence," Fiona said, suddenly remembering that there was another hard disk still in the machine in the apartment.

"I know," Charleen said.

"Can they get to it without the key?" Fiona asked.

"Doesn't matter. I went back and got the other hard disk."

"But you can't be certain no one else has this material," Fiona said. It was, she decided, considering Polly Dearborn's passion for secrecy, a good bet that they didn't have it. Not the *Post*. Not anyone. It was out there, of course, but someone would have to dig for it.

"If it's evidence, we have to bring it downtown," Charleen said. "Goes there, then somebody will fish it out."

"Then what the hell do we do with it?"

Charleen Evans shrugged.

"We've got to let the Captain know," Fiona said.

"You want the fox to guard the chicken coop."

This was one complex woman. Brilliant, in fact.

"What would you suggest?"

Charleen was deliberately, infuriatingly silent. The message was clear.

"Burn it, right?" Fiona asked.

"You said it," Charleen Evans snapped.

Fiona again looked at the stack of papers. Her throat went dry.

"We have no right..." Fiona began.

"Hell, we've been living without rights for years."

"Christ, Charleen. You're fucking impossible. What is it with you? Bottom line is we're cops. Not saviors of the world. We can't take these things on our own shoulders."

Charleen Evans sucked in a deep breath. Then she lowered her head and studied her hands.

"Don't you think I know that?" She pointed to the stack. "I've seen that stuff. Read it. I already know more than I should. I'm trying to cope with the damned system..." She turned away and paced the room. "I do have an attitude problem. I am tight-assed and I don't open up or trust people. It works for me. I've been on my own since I'm twelve." She stopped abruptly. She shook her head, as if to say "enough." She grew silent.

"I appreciate that revelation, Charleen," Fiona said. "It will guide me in our relationship. I'm different than you.

True, I don't trust many people. I'm a cynic and skeptic and can only act tight-assed. When it counts I can be hard. Like you, I chose this job. I love it and I'm good at it. I'll grant you this. You know a helluva lot that I don't. But you're an amateur when it comes to human behavior. We could be a great team, if you'll just loosen up a little."

"I'll try," Charleen said. It was, Fiona decided, a legitimate attempt at sincerity.

"We have to call in the Eggplant," Fiona said.

"You're the human-behavior expert," Charleen said.

Fiona pulled a face. "You're going to drive me up the wall, Charleen."

"I know it. I'm working on the problem."

10

IT WAS LATE. The material on the Mayor was more than a hundred pages. There was trial data, the testimony of witnesses. Polly had found and talked with both the victims of the attempted murder and the attempted rape. Neither had been reluctant to talk and neither knew that the man in question was the Mayor of Washington, D.C. It was incriminating stuff, sure to make great copy. It would finish his political career.

They had been at it for two hours. Charleen had gone out to bring in pizzas, the remains of which were still in their grease-stained boxes.

"See what I mean?" Charleen said, addressing the Eggplant. She had repressed her cantankerous side for most of the evening, although there was one moment of tension when she had requested that he not smoke. To Fiona's surprise, he had surrendered gracefully.

Fiona supposed it was some deep-seated black cultural thing, some element in Charleen's persona that commanded respect in black men. If Fiona had asked him to do the same, he would have lit up immediately. This could not happen on his own turf, not in his office. There, no woman, of whatever color or sharpness of tongue, could command him to do anything.

"Reads like a rap sheet," the Eggplant said. "Pisses me off. The guy rises above it and they'll use it to splatter him."

"Boils down to this," Fiona said. "It's not our business."

"It's our fucking boss woman," the Eggplant said.

"What about all the others she's got stuff on?" Fiona asked. She sifted through the papers, held one up. "Like medical records. Take this. This is her dossier of the Chairman of the Joint Chiefs. The goddamned Chairman. At thirteen years of age a Cook County hospital diagnosed him as schizophrenic. Imagine that. The Chairman of the Joint Chiefs. Does it say it was the right diagnosis? Does it say where she got the information? But it can, in the hands of someone with mean intent, bring the poor bastard down."

"And the one about the clap in the Army?" the Eggplant asked. "Who the hell was that?"

"Secretary of Human Resources," Fiona shot back. "It's bizarre. Medical records, court records, scholastic records. The Vice President's academic record is a disaster, including a flunk for cheating."

"And these goddamned police records." He pushed away a batch of paper in disgust. "Rap sheets. Juvenile records." He held up one of the papers. "Here's one." He looked at the name on it. "State Department. Deputy Secretary. Wife had an abortion in 1979."

"In today's climate that could be a zap," Fiona said.

"Goes on and on," the Eggplant said, shaking his head.

"Nobody's perfect," Fiona said.

"If it wasn't so serious, I'd be laughing," the Eggplant said.

"Like the Downey business," Fiona said.

"Especially the Downey business," the Eggplant said.

"You think Barker knew the extent of Dearborn's files?" Charleen asked. They had filled her in, debriefed each other.

"He sure knew the extent of her obsession," Fiona said. "No boyfriends, he said. Her own body confirmed that. A virgin at forty-three. Dear Polly went through the sexual revolution without leaving a trace."

"A real nutcutter, Barker told us," the Eggplant said. His eyes were heavy-lidded and bloodshot and he needed a shave.

"Her and her damned computer. That's another thing Barker said." Fiona patted the stack. "I really don't think he knew how deep she went."

"And if he did?" Charleen asked. "That's his business."

"He'd eat it up with a spoon," the Eggplant said. "Hell, he let her go at it all the way."

"Not quite," Fiona added. "Even he pulled back on the Downey story."

"Think it was conscience?" Charleen Evans asked.

"No way," the Eggplant said. "Not that bird. He's just watching his own ass. They go too far, they get a backlash."

"Still," Charleen pressed, "he would run that stuff on the Mayor."

"In a minute. That's for damned sure," the Eggplant said, shaking his head. "Wouldn't want my dirty wash hung out for everyone to see. We don't think about it much. Somewhere tucked away in a data bank is stuff about us." He cut a glance at Fiona. "Got any dirty little secrets, FitzGerald?"

"Mucho bytes-worth, Captain," Fiona said. An image of her mother flashed in her mind. She also heard the sound of her voice. "God knows everything. He knows all about

106

you. Don't you ever forget that." A cold chill passed through her.

He had turned to Charleen, but, for some reason, did not pose that question. Fiona was certain he had it in mind. Then he quickly asked another.

"You believe only one person did this?"

"No big deal. It's out there. You have to gain access. All that takes is know-how and money. Not a lot, either. It also takes dedication, hard work, long hours. Then there's this business of getting into secure files. That took some doing. Like outside help. There's always someone who takes a fall for whatever reason. Sure, one person could do this." She paused, studying their faces, deliberating. "I could do it."

Suddenly the Eggplant stood up and paced the length of the room. It was a living room/dining room combination. One wall of the living room was filled floor to ceiling with books. Fiona had noted the titles: mostly detective fiction, spy stories, suspense novels and technical books on crime. The Eggplant stopped for a moment to peruse the titles then came back toward them. He had thrown his coat on the back of one of the dining room chairs. He stopped and looked at it, then he slipped a panatela from an inside pocket.

"I won't light up," he said to Charleen.

"It's okay, Captain. You probably need it."

He struck a match, lit up, then, before fanning it out, he looked at it for a moment.

"There's an idea in that," Fiona said.

"Don't even think it, FitzGerald. We're here to find killers. In this case, the killer of Polly Dearborn. Destroying evidence is a felony."

"Granted," Fiona said. "Then what do we do with this stuff?"

"I know what we don't do with it," the Eggplant said. They were sitting around Charleen's dining room table. The Eggplant stood up and stretched. "We don't give it to Barker. No way." He looked suddenly at Charleen Evans.

"Especially not to him."

"Who, then?" the Eggplant asked. It was a question for both of them.

"Not the feds," Fiona said. "You let the bully boys get something on the pols, you got big trouble. Remember how Hoover kept his job."

"And our people?" the Eggplant asked. He puffed deeply on his panatela, held the smoke, then pushed it out of his nostrils. For him a great deal was at stake. If the Mayor went down, his hopes of becoming Police Commissioner went down with it.

"Damned if we do, damned if we don't," Fiona said, leaving unspoken what was obviously the central idea nagging at them. They could, after all, edit the material, remove the Mayor's dossier. But that would mean establishing a bond between them that was fraught with pitfalls and dangers.

The Eggplant took one last puff, then smashed the panatela out on a slice of cold pizza. He did not press the issue.

"Who needed this?" he said.

They were silent for a long time. Finally the Eggplant sat down and looked at the papers strewn across the table.

Fiona reviewed the options in her mind. They could bring the evidence in, hard copies and hard disks, and check it in to headquarters as evidence. They could remove the material about the Mayor, then bring it in. Technically, that would be tampering with evidence. They could destroy it completely. That would be both self-protective and logical, except that they would then share a secret between them, encroaching on their individual independence. Or they could simply put it back, wipe it from the slate. That could mean that Barker would get it.

"What happens if somebody turns on the computer?" Fiona asked.

"Gonna get a big surprise," the Eggplant said.

"Withholding, tampering, now burglary," Charleen Evans sighed.

"A multitude of sins," Fiona whispered. She glanced toward the Eggplant. "It's your call, Captain." She knew, of course, what he wanted them to do.

"Thing is," the Eggplant mused, "will it help us find Polly Dearborn's killer?"

"It could help make a case," Fiona said. "Once you write off the ones we know she wrote about."

"That would leave the Mayor a suspect, along with all the others," Charleen said.

"A motive isn't hard evidence," the Eggplant argued.

"If we don't declare it as evidence, then it's stolen goods," Fiona said. "We have no business with it. Technically it still belongs to the estate of Polly Dearborn."

"You want me to put it back?" Charleen asked.

"I say let's put it on ice for a while," Fiona said.

"Leave it here? In my apartment?" Charleen asked.

"There's still an ongoing investigation," Fiona said, turning to the Eggplant. "We declare it evidence. Bend procedures."

"We nail things down first then use only what's pertinent to the case?" the Eggplant said. "Is that it?"

"More or less," Fiona agreed. They were all a party now to constructing a credible evasion.

"Then what?" Charleen asked.

"We cross that bridge when we come to it," the Eggplant said.

Double-talk. They all knew it.

They exchanged glances and did not speak for a long time. Finally the Eggplant took his coat from the back of the chair.

"Let's all go home and get some sleep." He slipped into the jacket and straightened his tie. "And tomorrow let's get us a killer."

11

THROUGHOUT THE NIGHT, Fiona turned over in her mind the events at Charleen Evans' apartment.

A conspiracy had hatched between them, despite every effort to prevent it from happening. Moreover, she wasn't sure who was manipulating whom.

She and Charleen Evans had less to lose than the Eggplant if the material fell into the wrong hands. The Mayor, while he was still in power, could orchestrate their harassment, but they had recourse to departmental review, and since they were women they had the tacit support of women's groups both within and without the department. But that kind of a fight left a sour taste. They would be branded as troublemakers, hassled in a hundred ways.

If the Mayor was forced to resign, which was more than likely, people in the department would remember what she and Charleen Evans had done. A black man gone wrong in his youth who had rehabilitated himself and achieved a measure of success was a favorite hero of black mythology. Fiona and Charleen would be looked upon as spoilers, whatever the political consequences. Another black male would take the Mayor's place, but they would always remain spoilers, the not-to-be-trusted.

111

The Eggplant's dilemma was more complex. Although she could not be certain, she suspected that the Eggplant had received some message, some assurance, that he was high in the running for appointment by the Mayor as the next Police Commissioner. Everyone knew that the present Commissioner was on the verge of making a graceful exit. The narcotics problem and the gang murders it was spawning were putting pressure on the Mayor to relieve the Police Commissioner. Clean house. Find a replacement.

To Captain Luther Greene that appointment would be like reaching Valhalla, the culmination of a lifetime's ambition.

How far would he go to get it?

Fiona squirmed over the idea. Ambition was a powerful stimulant. The Eggplant understood Machiavellian manipulation. But was he willing to risk all by making a direct quid pro quo deal with the Mayor? Would he trade the Police Commissioner appointment for silence and the destruction of the material on Polly Dearborn's computer?

But such a move would put him at the mercy of Charleen Evans and Fiona. He could, of course, pay them off by moving them into positions of importance under him as Police Commissioner. But he would lose his authority over them.

Knowing the kind of man he was underneath all the bluster and histrionics, Fiona decided that, for him, it would be too much of a price to pay, although she could not be certain. There was also the matter of her own willingness to go along with the scheme, which was actually out of the question. She could not speak for Charleen Evans.

On the other hand, to deliver the material to the department, no matter how it was sequestered, was no assurance of privacy. Leaks were endemic, in this case a dead certainty. That could finish off the Mayor. A new Mayor would put the Eggplant and his ambitions back to square one, forcing him to do a whole new ingratiation number, which may or may not be effective.

It was highly unlikely, too, that the Eggplant would consent to turn the material over to Harry Barker. That kind of ingratiation might not work. He couldn't trust Harry Barker to keep the damaging material on the Mayor under wraps. And how would the public destruction of the Mayor help his chances to be Police Commissioner? Nada.

So what was she to do? Refuse to go along? Demand that the material be put back in Polly Dearborn's computer and let the chips fall where they may? And suppose it did get into the hands of the feds? What then? Innocent people could be used and abused, pressured, even blackmailed. Less-than-innocent people could be harmed far out of proportion to their so-called indiscretions. Cynical politicians and bureaucrats could use it to settle personal scores, especially on those whose guilt was indisputable.

By dawn her ruminations were losing their logic. She hadn't slept. The sheets were rumpled and she was uncomfortable. She wished she had a partner who was more forthcoming, more communicative and understanding. Like Cates. But she couldn't discuss this with Cates and it was utterly impossible to bring him into the case at this point. The Eggplant would never stand for increasing the circle of knowledge.

It was times like this that Fiona derided her single state. She wished that she were in bed with a trusting man, a life's companion, a friend, a lover, someone to share her thoughts and fears, to help with the hard decisions, to soothe her.

The emergence of self-pity, which she greatly feared, jolted her to action. She clambered out of bed and rushed into the shower, forcing herself to endure icy cold water. When the cold lost its shock value, she turned on the hot water until that ran its course. The process calmed her.

She was just getting out of the shower when she heard the chimes. It was still dark. Throwing on a terry-cloth robe and wrapping a towel around her wet hair, she rushed down the stairs, nearly slipping on the marble in the foyer. Charleen Evans was at the door.

"I've been ringing," Charleen said, stepping into the foyer.

"I was in the shower."

"I've got eyes."

"Christ, Charleen, it's too early in the morning for sassy bullshit." She turned and walked toward the kitchen. The timer on the coffee maker was set for seven, an hour from now. She put it on manual and the water quickly began to bubble and heat.

Charleen leaned against the wall and watched her.

"It's a bitch, I know," Fiona said.

"I put them in my car last night, the printouts and the disk. I was going to dump them in the river. Take everybody off the hook. It's what he really wants. I didn't do it. Instead, I rode around most of the night."

"You think that's wise, Charleen? Leaving them in the trunk of your car?"

"I didn't."

She bent over and reached into the front of her blouse, pulled out the gold chain with the computer key. There were now two keys on the chain. Fiona recognized the type of key used in baggage storage compartments.

"You've seen too many movies, Charleen," Fiona said.

"Union Station."

"The feds could crack into that with no sweat," Fiona said.

114

"First they've got to find it."

"I'm sure you gave it a lot of thought," Fiona said.

"I did. I considered the downside all night," Charleen said. Fiona turned to observe her. Her dark face was grey with fatigue. "An hour ago I was ready to turn the stuff over to someone, the feds, Barker, the department, anything to get it out of our hair."

"Why didn't you?"

"I don't trust any of them."

"That's the root of your trouble, Charleen," Fiona said, despite agreeing with her. She was feeling irritable, needing her coffee.

"You got it right, FitzGerald."

"I suppose it goes for me, too," Fiona said. "And the Eggplant."

Charleen shrugged. Her eyes roamed the kitchen, avoiding Fiona's deliberately steady stare.

"I've got no choice on that." Charleen said.

"I'll buy that, Charleen," Fiona said. "You're stuck with us. Tight-ass Charleen Evans. Sorry about that. The fact is, Charleen, that sometimes people actually do have to trust each other. Even support each other."

"I've managed so far, thank you," Charleen shot back.

"There are other people in this world besides Charleen Evans," Fiona said, turning to the coffee machine. Impatient for the coffee, she removed the glass pot and let the coffee drip directly into her mug.

"Not as far as Charleen Evans is concerned."

"Tough shit," Fiona muttered. "Like it or not, we've all got shares in each other. You, me and the Eggplant."

"I find that name offensive," Charleen said.

"A racial put-down, right?"

"Among other things."

"For a self-control freak, you are one mass of contradictions. Are you saying now that you trust him?"

"As you said, do I have a choice?"

"That means you have to trust me, too."

"I'm afraid so."

Fiona took a swallow of the coffee. She knew she was off on a tangent, less than rational.

"Ergo, I have to trust you as well," Fiona muttered. A thought occurred to her suddenly. "Poor Charlene," she said, "must hurt like hell to give up some of your sovereignty."

"It's not easy," she sighed, showing the tiniest glimpse of vulnerability. The last drip of coffee gurgled through the machine. Fiona put a mug before Charleen and poured.

"Now that we got that out of the way, you might say we're sisters," Fiona said, deliberately sarcastic.

Charleen spoke words, but revealed very little of her inner feelings. Fiona had always detested that trait in others. It made it seem as if she were missing half the meaning.

"You think we should tell the Captain?" Charleen asked, as if even a tiny bridge of intimacy had been crossed and was now behind them. The first shot of caffeine seemed to chase Fiona's irritation.

"He may not want to know."

"He's part of it," Charleen said.

"He could always deny we told him."

"So could you," Charleen shot back. She patted her chest. "I'm the one holding the key."

"Like handing power over your life to somebody else," Fiona said, cutting directly to the heart of Charleen's dilemma. It was also Fiona's dilemma. An image of her father flashed in her mind, his decision to oppose the war when it was politically dangerous because it was the right thing to do, because his conscience demanded it.

For the first time since they were paired together, Fiona

understood the commonality between Charleen and himself. It had nothing at all to do with gender. It had to do with values, conscience, doing the right thing. What Polly Dearborn had on her computer endangered people, some of whom may be innocent. Fiona likened it to circumstantial evidence, which sometimes was responsible for convicting innocent people in a courtroom.

This was a homicide detective's nightmare, condemning the innocent. Polly Dearborn murdered people in different ways, by embellishing facts, grafting gossip and innuendo on events in their lives, by making early mistakes seem like irrevocable sins, an albatross for life. It was true that public officials were servants of the people, subject to a higher standard, but the question was who was to set these standards. Polly Dearborn? Harry Barker? Some holier-than-thou politician or power-mad bureaucrat?

Of course, there were guilty parties among the innocent. A patently illegal and immoral offence in the conduct of doing the public business was fair game for exposure. Unfortunately, Polly Dearborn gave them the wheat with the chaff. The bottom line on all this was that neither Fiona nor Charleen wanted to aid and abet that behavior, however it was rationalized as freedom of the press.

Human endeavors, Fiona knew, were governed by responsibility, and the whole system hung together by trust. Heady thoughts. But thinking them gave her a sense of participation on the basis, not of self-interest, but of knowing right from wrong.

There was only one conclusion to that reasoning.

"We're both crazy to do this," Fiona said. It was, she decided, better to avoid any mention of nobility of purpose. Charleen could never admit to that. Fiona wasn't sure she could.

"Probably," Charleen said.

12

"I WOULD HAVE killed her gladly," Robert Downey said. He was sitting in his father's study, on the very chair in which his father had sat when he killed himself.

Chester Downey had been buried just hours ago at Arlington Cemetery with all the pomp and ceremony accorded to a man of his high office. The President had spoken and presented to Robert the flag that draped Downey's coffin.

Fiona and Charleen had waited until all the guests had departed before entering the house. They had already contacted the maid, the same one that had discovered Downey's body. She had told them that the younger Mr. Downey would be willing to see them.

He was a tall red-haired man, with bushy red eyebrows and small light hazel eyes that were set deep behind knobby cheekbones. His skin was a mass of freckles. His coloring offered a sharp contrast with the shiny brown leather of his father's desk chair.

"We haven't even entertained that possibility, Mr. Downey," Fiona said, offering a pleasant smile. The fact was that they had, indeed, entertained such a possibility.

"Are you saying what I think you're saying?" Downey asked. He had sat bolt upright in his chair.

"We've ruled out suicide," Fiona said.

"Well, then there is a God in heaven," Downey said. He did not smile.

"It was an elaborately staged event," Fiona said. "The killer was making a statement."

"Good for him. I wish I had had the guts to do it," Downey said, holding the thought. His blazing eyes and the fierce set of his strong chin told them that he was deadly serious. He shook his head. "I hope she suffered much before she left this earth."

"We understand your personal animosity, Mr. Downey..." Fiona began, but he still had not run out of steam.

"She wrote lies about my father, lies about me. Deliberate malicious lies. Oh yes, there are the laws of libel. But my father was a public figure. He didn't have a chance. He was a man of enormous pride and courage. You can be sure he did what he did because he could see no way out, only further disgrace. The woman murdered him."

He sat back in his chair, lowered his eyes and studied the backs of his hands.

"She did her best to finish me off, too," he sighed. "Unfortunately, I do not have my father's courage." He paused and shook his head. "He did not play favorites with my company. I have never taken part in contract negotiations with the Pentagon. Contracts were awarded to our firm because we were the best engineering consultant group in the area. Now I'm a pariah. My colleagues look at me as if I did them in. And there's some truth to that. My association with the firm will be the cause of these contracts being canceled. Good, talented people will lose their jobs."

His face grew flushed and he moved his lips, issuing

inaudible but unmistakable curses. Fiona guessed he was not a man ordinarily given to rages. But the presence of the two detectives gave him the opportunity to vent himself.

"Too late for Dad," he said. "Me? I'm still comparatively young. I've got to go on living with this." An involuntary sob shook his chest. To mask it he coughed into his fist. Recovering his calm, he said, "I'm sorry. I'm still shook up."

"If you'd rather we come at another time . . ." Fiona said. It was, she knew, a ploy at ingratiation. She and Charleen had determined that they must not let this case drag on. She also knew that there were rough moments ahead for young Downey in their interrogation.

He gestured, mimicking a traffic cop's stop hand signal.

"No. It's all right. I'd rather get it over with. I'd rather get everything about this behind me."

"You do realize that it's our job to find Polly Dearborn's killer," Fiona said, looking at Charleen.

"I hope you never do."

Fiona and Charleen exchanged glances.

"We understand, Mr. Downey. But it's still a capital crime to deliberately take another life."

"Not in this case," Downey snapped.

"Believe me, Mr. Downey, we understand your feelings. But we do have to ask some questions. Then you can forget about the whole thing." From the corner of her eye, she could see Charleen nodding.

He appeared to mull it over.

"You think I'll ever forget what that woman did to us?"

"Poor choice of words," Fiona added quickly. "I'm sorry."

"Okay, let's get the damned thing over with."

"We greatly appreciate that, Mr. Downey," Fiona said

in a further effort to placate him. "We'll try to get out of your hair quickly."

Although they had not discussed any joint interrogation strategy, Fiona noted that Charleen was letting her lead the way, a good sign. There would be moments where she would welcome her interruption, although such times had not yet arrived. Cates had a sixth sense about such things and, once again, she regretted his absence.

"Were you and your Dad on good terms?" Fiona said, deliberately using the word "Dad" to convey warmth and ingratiation.

"Excellent terms. We were great friends."

"And saw each other often?"

"Not as often as we both would have liked. He was quite busy and so was I. I lived over in Dupont Circle, just a few blocks from here. We managed dinner together once or twice a week."

"Ever stay over?" Fiona asked, studying him.

"Sometimes," he said crisply. "Not often. I told you. I had my own place."

"But you did talk on the phone?"

"A few times a week," Robert Downey said proudly. Fiona detected in him a touch of defiance. "Not once did we ever discuss my firm's participation in defense activities. In fact, we both made it a point to avoid such matters."

"Did your Dad ever mention that he knew Polly Dearborn?" Fiona asked, hoping to convey an air of innocence.

"Knew her?"

"Socially, I mean. Did he ever say anything about her that indicated he might have met her?"

She watched his face. He obviously did not have the ability to hide his feelings.

"My father was enormously gregarious, a real social person. Yes, he did say he knew her."

"Did he say he knew her well?"

"That's the irony of it. When all hell broke loose and he got wind of her story, he told me that he had actually considered her a friend. Some friend."

"Did you ever meet her?"

"Never. Dad and I did not travel in the same social circles."

"Did you ever talk with her?"

"Yes. She called me." He mumbled under his breath. "Bitch."

"You spoke?"

"She asked if I had anything to do with getting Pentagon contracts for my firm. You know how they do things obliquely. Subtle. Soft southern drawl. Butter would melt in her filthy mouth. I told her that her implications were a lot of bullshit." He was starting to wind up again, knew it, and seemed to make a genuine effort to hold his rage in check.

"So she called you that one time?"

Robert Downey turned away suddenly. The knobs on his cheekbones flushed.

"Makes me livid to think about it."

"She called you again, then?"

"Oh yes. But she called Dad lots more times. He discussed these conversations with me. At first he told me he was very forthcoming, very. Open and honest. That was him. But when she started asking about the divorce from Mother, he got his back up. Oh, he expected controversy, expected to be vetted. He was an old pro and he knew what kind of stuff that woman did. I told him to stay away from the bitch. Too late by then. Maybe he thought he was above it all. That was a mistake. No one is safe from

122

the Polly Dearborns of this world. No one."

"Did your Dad have any girlfriends?"

"I never discussed that aspect of his life," Robert Downey said flatly, without emotion.

"But he did date women?"

"Yes. Many. Part of the game. The bachelor condition is a two-way street. Washington is a pair town. Everything in twosies. An uneven dinner party counts as a disaster."

Fiona knew she was dancing around a delicate theme.

"You sound like you know the drill, Mr. Downey?"

She could detect a flash of defensiveness.

"I do. I'm a bachelor."

She caught the tiniest edge of aggression.

"Did you discuss the Dearborn inquiries with your father?"

"Yes, I did. We were both appalled at the turn it was taking. How do you combat stuff like that? Also that part about the divorce with Mother. She failed to mention that they were divorced in California, which is a 50-50 settlement state. Of course, he tried to protect his assets. You don't know my mother. Where was Dad's comeback? He had to grin and bear it."

"Did you see today's story in the *Post*?"

His eyes glazed, as if he had suddenly turned inward, searching inside of himself for a way to answer the question. Fiona was certain that he had seen it.

"I never want to read that paper again. Never. As long as I live."

She exchanged glances with Charleen. The question had to be asked and she searched her mind for some easy way to approach it. In Fiona's mind the abuse issue was surely the one that kicked Chester Downey over the edge.

"Did she ask you about the cult trial?" Fiona asked, as gently as possible.

Downey frowned. His lips tightened and his eyes seemed to reflect the animal's fear of the predator. His guard was definitely on alert.

"We know you left something out, Mr. Downey," Charleen said suddenly. The timing of the question seemed all wrong. Downey reacted swiftly.

"I don't believe I want to go on with this interview," he said.

"Neither do we," Charleen said. "Not on this basis." She looked toward Fiona. Dumb, insensitive bitch, Fiona thought, trying to mime a severe rebuke. This interview had to be salvaged.

"We know it's a touchy subject, Mr. Downey," Fiona said. "We also know that your Dad attempted to get Harry Barker not to run the cult trial material. As you see, he didn't. Perhaps if he had known that it would not run, he would not have taken such drastic action. Unfortunately, we, as investigators, can't avoid discussing it."

"It's a pack of lies. Even Harry Barker must have thought so—" He checked himself, then shrugged.

"We have to assume that you and your Dad did discuss the matter," Fiona pressed, hoping to tamp down his agitation. She was furious with Charleen for disrupting the interrogation with her blatant insensitivity.

Fiona waited through Robert Downey's long silence. Charleen, too, remained silent. Perhaps Fiona's look had sent its message. Downey studied his hands with great intensity, as if he were searching there for a way to confront the issue. Finally he spoke. A hoarseness crept into his voice.

"We talked about it, yes. It was depressing for him, but I never thought this . . . this would happen."

"Did he tell you he spoke with Barker?"

124

"Yes, he did. Barker said it was on the record, that the Dearborn bitch had checked it out. Something about Dearborn using data banks on her computer, that she had the testimony on her computer. But Dad did say he was not going to take it lying down."

"Did he say what that meant, what he was going to do?"

Again, Robert Downey's eyes glazed over.

"Well, did he?" Fiona pressed.

Downey shook his head.

"Did you threaten any action?"

"Yes," he said, his eyes clearing, suddenly alert as a ferret.

"Like violence on the person of Polly Dearborn?" Charleen interjected. Again Fiona was infuriated with Charleen's interruption. Her sense of timing was totally awry, counterproductive. And her choice of words, antiquated legalese, was horrendous.

Downey gurgled a hysterical chuckle that was more eloquent than words.

"What was your father's reaction?"

"He begged me not to do anything foolish, that I was still young, had lots of things ahead of me." Another sob broke through, which he could not mask. Instead, he took deep draughts of air to tamp it down. "I told him that I thought it was worse to stain his distinguished reputation as a public servant. I told him, yes I was young enough to rise above it. But for him it was a travesty. I told him..." He seemed to be having trouble getting himself under control.

Suddenly he held up his hand with the same traffic-cop gesture he had used before.

"That's about all I care to discuss on this matter," he said.

Fiona hesitated, exchanged glances with Charleen.

Once again he had wanted this interview to stop, but he made no overt move to retreat.

"I was just a kid, nineteen years old. Twenty-one years ago..." he began, then shook his head and did not go further.

"But you did testify at that trial?"

The subject itself seemed to loom as such a monstrous taboo in his mind that she feared a more specific reference would end the interview once and for all. He was now running on inertia, but he would have been well within his rights to throw them out and get himself a lawyer.

"Yes, I testified for them," he said with an air of resignation. "I was brainwashed by the cult. Explaining that to you people would be like reinventing the wheel. I was coerced to lie, mentally forced to discredit my father."

"Did you explain that to Polly Dearborn?"

"Of course I did," Downey said belligerently. Rage was rising in him now. "Oh, how self-righteous she was. Said she was only reporting what was on the record, not drawing any conclusions. That's a laugh." He drew in a deep breath. His nostrils quivered with anger. His hands gripped the arms of the chair in which his father had died. "She's the one who pulled that trigger."

"The issue here, Mr. Downey, is not how your father died, but how Polly Dearborn was killed." Fiona said the words slowly, determined to convey the real message of their conversation.

"You think he killed that bitch, don't you?"

"There's not enough facts to draw that conclusion," Fiona said.

"Or me. Maybe you really believe I did it."

"Or together," Charleen snapped. Fiona couldn't fault her on that intervention.

"Yes, together. That would be rich."

"You certainly had the motive. Both of you," Fiona said. There were others, too, that Polly Dearborn had destroyed, but this one was too recent, too compellingly topical, to be ignored.

"Bet your ass on that," Downey muttered. He got up from the chair and strode across the room, looking idly at a row of books on their shelves. Then he turned suddenly.

"But you have no evidence," he said pointedly.

"Frankly, no, but that doesn't foreclose on the possibility that maybe you have."

"Me?"

"The note he left you," Fiona pressed.

"It's none of your business. His last words to me were for my eyes only."

"When was it given to you?"

The question seemed to confuse him momentarily.

"It was hand-delivered to me at the funeral parlor. I thought it was from the police."

"Wasn't us. Federal agents were on the scene within minutes of my getting here. They took charge of the letter."

"All I want to know is whether there was anything in it that suggested that your father might have been the person who killed Polly Dearborn."

"A confession, you mean?"

"Yes."

"If that was so, why would the federal agents have returned it to me?" Robert Downey asked.

"They have their own reasons for everything. Their agenda is not that of the Metropolitan Police Force. They have other priorities."

He appeared to be thinking it over.

"Nobody will ever see it now. I've destroyed it."

"Why did you do that?"

"I don't have to explain that to you."

"No, you don't," Fiona agreed. "But it is possible that what you destroyed was not the genuine article. You'd be surprised how accurately they can create authentic-looking correspondence."

Her imagination was soaring into the realm of spy fiction, CIA shenanigans, dirty tricks, conspiracy and double-cross. Give her a little time and she might construct a logical scenario. Chester Downey, America's Secretary of Defense, was a former KGB mole or somesuch. Lots of people around who would bite on that apple.

"All right, Mr. Downey, then I'll ask you—do you believe that your father murdered Polly Dearborn, then killed himself?"

Downey smiled and bit his lip. The knobs of his cheekbones were beginning to turn scarlet.

"If he did, he would have done it that way. A public hanging. That's what was symbolically happening to him. He appreciated things like that."

Despite his grief, Downey appeared fascinated by the interrogation. Suspects, guilty or not, often enjoyed these cat-and-mouse games, especially those with a vaunted opinion of themselves, where matching wits with their pursuers represented a life-or-death challenge.

"Yes," Downey said slowly, shaking his head in the affirmative. "Why not proceed on that theory?"

"We are," Charleen snapped. "Is there something you can offer us that might help?"

"I wish I could," Downey said, offering a bold smile.

Despite the sardonic challenge, Fiona sensed that it was probably unlikely that Downey senior would have told his son that he murdered Polly Dearborn. As an allegedly loving father, he would not wish to complicate life for his son after his own death. It was time to switch gears.

"Where were you on the night Polly Dearborn was murdered?" Fiona asked abruptly. She had hardened her approach now. For his part, Downey showed the first signs of caution.

"I was in bed, I suppose," he murmured.

"Were you alone?" Charleen asked abruptly. Fiona cut her another glance of rebuke.

"Alone?" He seemed to recoil from the question.

"Just looking for corroboration," Charleen said.

"Yes," he said after a long hesitation "I was alone." His answer did not carry much conviction.

"Too bad," Charleen said. "A witness would have disposed of the matter quickly."

"I think it's time that I disposed of both of you quickly." He strode to the door of the den, opened it and stepped aside. They had apparently invaded his boundaries. He was being conclusive now and Fiona sensed that it was not the time to press forward without more evidence. She started to cross the room. Charleen hung back.

"Were you sexually abused by your father?" Charleen asked Downey. The question seemed to freeze him. He looked at her for a long moment.

"Not my day for the kindness of strangers," he said, puffing his cheeks, then expelling the air. Fiona knew the reference from the Tennessee Williams play. They were definitely transgressing now. He would, Fiona knew, be prepared to defend that boundary with his life.

"I think we've taken enough of Mr. Downey's time," Fiona said, shooting a cutting glance at Charleen.

"But we haven't finished here," Charleen said.

"Yes we have," Fiona said. She grabbed Charleen by the elbow and ushered her out of the room.

Back in the car, they were silent for a long time. To Fiona's surprise, it was Charleen who broke the silence.

"He was wide open," she said. "We could have run a truck through him."

"For what purpose?"

"There was a compelling reason here. A motive with teeth."

"You really think he did it?"

"He or his father. Or he with his father."

"That's a conclusion without evidence."

"Then we've got to find the evidence, don't we?"

"That's a dangerous way for a homicide detective to think," Fiona said, as she drove. She could feel Charleen's eyes boring into her.

"The guilt came out of him like sweat."

"Which guilt was that?"

She waited for Charleen's answer.

"I have an advantage over you, Sergeant FitzGerald," Charleen said.

"Fiona. Make it Fiona, Charleen. The formality seems, well, hostile. Now what's the advantage?" She had pointed the car toward M Street. They had told Sheila Burns that they would meet her at the *Post* sometime after lunch.

"I read Downey's trial testimony in the hard copies. You and the Captain hadn't got to it. But I read it and it disgusted me."

"Doesn't make a case, Charleen. Sexual deviation is one thing, murder another."

"Sometimes you're so patronizing, Sergeant Fitz— Fiona. It's galling."

"Can't you just remove the damned chip, Charleen?"

She was silent for a while, then she spoke.

"He testified that his father seduced him at twelve on a camping trip in Yosemite National Park, and that it happened many times after that."

"Did the father confirm or deny it?"

"Denied it. Said it was the cult's doing. That they came up with the most horrible thing they could devise to tear father and son apart."

"And the verdict?"

"Hung jury. Young Downey went back to the cult."

"All this was in Polly Dearborn's computer?"

"Everything. Apparently he drifted out of the cult himself about a year later, went back to college and, you might say, reconciled with his father."

"What's this, 'you might say'?"

"Dearborn had a comment on her computer. She suspected that this affair was a lifelong thing, that it was still going on."

Fiona felt a sudden stab of rage. Self-righteous Polly Dearborn, a sexaphobe, afraid of the dick, a virgin after forty. How dare she judge the sexual propensities of others? She cast a sidelong glance at Charleen Evans. And you, she asked, silently, imagining tight-assed and controlled Charleen impaled on some big black dick. No way, she decided, remembering the obsessive order of her apartment. Nothing ever out of line for old Charleen.

"Okay, so what if they were still having an affair? We're still talking murder."

"It's one strong motive," Charleen said. "Imagine having your deepest secrets splashed all over the papers."

"She's done it before. There are others who have also been brought down."

"Not like this. This was more than an ordinary career-breaker. This was ten points on the psychic Richter scale."

"Not bad, Charleen," Fiona said. "The part about the Richter scale."

"Now it's ridicule," Charleen harumphed.

"You and your attitudes. I'll try to ignore it. The bottom line is do you seriously believe that one or the other Downey or both killed Polly Dearborn?"

"Let's say that the possibility should be seriously considered."

"You want to bring it to Captain Greene?"

Charleen was silent as she looked out of the window. A warm sun had brought out early lunchers who brown-bagged on Farragut Square and filled the sidewalk tables of restaurants.

"Not yet," Charleen said. "But I think we missed something at the apartment. I don't know what. But something."

Fiona headed the car toward 15th Street, then made a right into a parking lot adjacent to the Washington *Post* building.

"Okay. I offer you my expression of support. After the Burns woman we go back to the witch's lair."

"There it is again," Charleen said.

"I hope so. Ridicule, was it?"

"Sarcasm," Charleen replied. Fiona took it as a good sign. Charleen was loosening up.

13

THEY FOLLOWED SHEILA Burns to her office.

"You'll never find it without me," she had said cheerily over the telephone at the reception desk in the lobby. A few moments later, she was beside them, a small woman with white skin framed by ringlets of jet black hair. She shook hands and led them to the elevator.

"They've got me in this Siberian hole," she said after the elevator had stopped at the third floor. Fiona noted that the editorial department was on the sixth floor. They followed her through a maze of corridors until they came to an unmarked, door which Sheila opened with a key.

They entered a narrow room with a computer work station at one end and a long shelflike overhang covering the length of the room. On the shelf were newspapers, reference books, a coffee maker and a mismatched cluster of coffee mugs. Next to the computer were four oversized, thickly stuffed manila envelopes.

Aside from the computer desk chair, there were two others made of shaped green plastic on chrome legs. Recessed ceiling lights cast an orangey glow over everything. It was not a flattering color, especially for Charleen. There was a window in the room, but the blinds were drawn.

On the walls were a series of photographs. A young Sheila Burns with ex-President Reagan. A somewhat older Sheila Burns with former Defense Secretary Casper Weinberger, with Maureen Reagan, with Justice Sandra O'Connor.

"My rogues gallery," she said, seeing Fiona eyeing the pictures.

There were other pictures as well, personal pictures. Sheila Burns running in the Boston Marathon. Another of her skiing. Another showing her and others with a group of elephants. Still another of her rappelling up a mountain and another with a group of people, some of whom looked quite foreign, Filipinos, perhaps. An inscription read: Nepal, 1985. Ghurkas probably.

"I'm an outdoor girl," she said, apparently pleased at Fiona's and Charleen's interest. Her height belied the evidence. She stood near the coffee machine.

"Coffee?"

"No thanks," Fiona said. Charleen shook her head.

She poured a mug for herself and motioned them to sit down on the plastic chairs and turned the desk chair toward them. Then she sat down, placed her legs Indian style on the chair and faced them. Reaching out, she patted a small pile of thick manila envelopes.

"Clips of Polly's stories. Ten years' worth. Mr. Barker wanted you to have them. Ten years' worth of Polly's stories. I'm not sure you've got as many suspects as you think," Sheila said.

She lifted one of the envelopes from the pile and read from notes she had written on it.

"Note that most of our subjects were either rich or powerful. She didn't go after the little guys, only the big boys. And no one ever got to her legally. She was scrupulously accurate."

"You think it's possible that one of them did her in for revenge?" Fiona asked.

"You've got them. Judge for yourself. Polly believed that she was performing a public service, rooting out the liars, the hypocrites and the cheats. No question that she hit them hard. She called them broken-field runners. When her stories stopped them from going one way, they went another. I did a little checking. Most of them came up with a pretty good afterlife."

"It's possible. Revenge has its allure," Fiona said.

"Seems so." Sheila sighed.

Fiona looked around the small office.

"This the best they could do?" she asked. "Doesn't look like the office of a hotshot columnist."

"It's not," Sheila replied. "It's my office. Polly has never been here. Never will, either. In fact, I don't know how long I'll be here."

"Will they replace her?" Fiona asked.

Sheila hesitated. Her eyes moved from Fiona's face. She shifted her body in the chair and clasped her hands in front of her. The clasp, Fiona could tell, was tight, a gesture of resolve.

"They don't tell me much. Mr. Barker said I should just hold down the fort for the time being. So I'm holding it. I've been talking only to those people Mr. Barker has authorized me to talk to. Like you. Not to any outside media. Notice how quiet it is. Only internal calls get in here. And I'm living at the Hilton across the street to keep out of the way of the other media. The paper is moving lots of copy on it. And this thing with Chester Downey. Very strange.

"It's a first," Sheila added.

"A first what?" Fiona asked.

"A first suicide. Not one of Polly's other subjects did that. Even those that eventually went to jail."

"Maybe she was rougher on Downey than on the others," Fiona suggested.

"Not really. A number of those she wrote about got in trouble for being too nepotistic," Sheila replied. "But they didn't blow their brains out."

"Somehow," Fiona said, "I think the other, the sex thing, might have set him off."

"It never ran," Sheila said.

"But Downey thought it might," Fiona countered.

"Might be worth pursuing," Sheila shrugged.

"You think so?" Fiona asked.

"I'm not alone. It's all over the television news. People speculating that Downey killed Polly, then killed himself. The media loves quick and easy solutions."

"Anything surface on the sex business elsewhere?" Fiona asked.

"I haven't seen anything on it," Sheila replied.

"You think it will stay under wraps?" Fiona asked.

"In this town?" Sheila emitted a long throaty laugh. "Even dust particles send messages."

"Have the feds been here?" Fiona asked.

"Oh yes. I talked to them for hours last night."

"What did you tell them?" Fiona asked.

"Everything I knew, of course. Mr. Barker sat in."

"Did he?"

"After all, he was her employer. Mine, too. There were also two lawyers there. And a stenographer with one of those machines."

Can't be too cautious with the feds, Fiona thought. Of course, Barker had the Eggplant in his pocket. No need for caution on that score. Above all, Fiona hated to be taken for granted. She exchanged glances with Charleen and, for the first time, she sensed that they were on the same wavelength.

"What exactly did you do for Polly Dearborn?" Fiona asked.

"I guess you'd say I was her everything. Mainly I was her person at the paper. Simple as that. I did all the easy research, relayed messages, picked up material around town, answered all her calls at the paper, was a kind of conduit between Polly and Mr. Barker. You see, Polly worked out of her apartment. Never came to the paper. Sometimes she would query me to find out this or that."

"Were you plugged into her computer at the apartment?" Charleen interjected in a deliberately benign and gentle way.

"She sent her copy in by fax."

"I was referring to access," Charleen said. "Could you get into her files with your computer?"

"Absolutely not." She smiled and stared directly at Charleen. "You have to understand Polly. She was a control freak. Also paranoid about her material."

"You did say you did general research," Fiona said.

"Oh yes. I researched where all the data banks were. Also where new ones were coming up. She was a fanatic on data banks. That's where she claimed she got most of her backup material. Right there in some data bank. I was never authorized to go into one of them to search out something. She never did give me the access codes. Polly did all that herself. She was a whiz at computers. I'm kind of a dumbhead when it comes to them, although I'm okay with word processing, but Polly was—" Sheila paused, then shook her head in approval of what she seemed about to say—"well a real computer whiz. Would you believe that she was plugged into nearly fifty data banks?" She leaned forward on the chair and lowered her voice a few decibels. "There's no privacy anymore. None at all. For Polly getting the dirt she did was like falling off a log."

"Did you ever operate the computer in her apartment?" Charleen asked.

"Polly would have chopped my hands off," Sheila said. "No way. I did meet with her there for an hour or so three times a week. We would go over the mail, invitations, things to do, the usual. As for her computer, that was sacrosanct to her."

"Do you have any idea what was on the computer?"

Sheila seemed to grow cautious. She had not unclasped her hands throughout the questioning process. In fact, her knuckles had turned whiter.

"Not specifically."

"Hot stuff though?" Fiona asked.

"I can't say. I've never gotten into it."

"Could you have?" Charleen asked.

"I doubt it. I assumed she had it pretty well secured." She paused, then added quickly, "I assume she had it totally secured."

"Now that she's dead, what do you expect will happen to the information in the computer?" Charleen asked.

"Not for me to say." She raised her eyes upward. "That's for the powers that be to decide."

"Barker?" Fiona asked.

"That would be his decision."

"When is the funeral?" Fiona asked.

"Won't be any." Sheila sounded suddenly hoarse. "She's been cremated and her ashes spread over the Potomac."

"That was fast."

"She had it in her will," Sheila said.

"When was the last time you were at the apartment?" Charleen asked. She and Fiona had finally established an interrogation rhythm.

Sheila cocked her head, obviously searching for an accurate answer.

138

"Not counting when we met...three days ago," she said.

"What did you do?"

"I told you, we went over things. There were invitations to go over."

"Did she get many?" Fiona asked.

"Hundreds. And she went out a lot. Picked up lots of leads that way. Polly kept her ears open. Of course, she had to pick and choose where she went. In the kind of work she did she made lots of enemies, also contacts, people wanting to kiss her butt so maybe she wouldn't be an enemy. Lots of people called her to give her little tidbits. You know, tips. Between that and the data banks she could track things, confirm things. You know what I mean?"

Fiona knew, of course. In Washington leaks were endemic. People had secret grievances, private grudges, and the media encouraged those with axes to grind to come forward, promising anonymity to informers and gossip mongers.

"One thing about our stories," Sheila continued. Fiona noted the use of the collective pronoun. "They were the truth. Very, very rarely were we off the mark. Polly was unusually thorough in her checking. She always called those about whom she had found negative material to give them a chance to defend themselves. That was a religion with her."

"Like Chester Downey?"

"And his son," Sheila said.

"I assume you knew about the material that was cut out of the story that ran today?" Fiona asked.

"I told you that."

"When did you know it?"

"When Polly faxed it over."

"Not before?"

Sheila shook her head.

"You didn't know Polly. She only showed her stories when they were finished."

"Barker was going to discuss the third installment with Polly first, give her some opportunity for rebuttal. Am I right?"

"Yes. That was their agreement. If Mr. Barker thought something material should be eliminated, his policy was to call her. Always. In the Downey situation, when he couldn't reach her, he contacted me, and when I couldn't reach her I went to the apartment... where I met you both."

"Do you think that Polly sometimes went too far in her stories?" Fiona asked.

"Too far?"

"Like on the Downey story. The father-son incest. Do you think that constitutes too far?"

Sheila looked puzzled for a moment. A frown creased her brow and quickly smoothed.

"Not at all. The public has a right to expect the highest standards of morality and character from public officials. The media is the court of last resort. Corruption and immorality must be exposed. That was Polly Dearborn's job and she did it like no other. She was the best. I learned a great deal from her."

"You'd like to do that type of work?" Fiona asked. "Not just be an assistant, but really do it. Like Miss Dearborn."

"If Mr. Barker made me an offer..." She paused. Her hands had relaxed for a while. Now the knuckles went white again. "What's wrong with that? Anyone would jump at the chance."

"Have you put in your oar for Miss Dearborn's job?" Fiona asked.

Sheila shrugged and seemed reluctant to answer.

"You'd be the logical choice," Charleen said.

140

"I thought so," Sheila replied, swallowing the words.

"You've learned a great deal on this job, haven't you, Sheila?"

"Yes, I have."

"Did you like Polly Dearborn?" Fiona asked.

"My, that sounds almost accusatory."

"It wasn't meant that way," Fiona replied. "I'm sorry."

Sheila stared at Fiona's face. Fiona offered a broad, warm smile. It was natural for people to get paranoid at an interrogation in a murder case. Some more than others. When that happened, Fiona did everything she could to put them at their ease. Sheila Burns could be a fund of knowledge.

"I had nothing but admiration for her," Sheila continued. "She was fantastic. Aloof, yes. A loner, yes. Not very giving, but she knew her business."

"Did it bother you that people got hurt from her stories?"

"Not at all," Sheila said quickly. "That wasn't our affair. We told no lies. Public officials must be accountable. That was the way Polly thought about it and I agreed with her completely."

"Do you think that the sexual material about Downey and his son should have been printed?"

"Why not? It came from testimony of a court trial. She might have found it in one of the data banks. I'm not sure. But she had the material confirmed. I think the American people are entitled to know about a man's character, especially if he is in a key role like Defense Secretary. Why not?"

"Because Downey and his son both denied the truth of the testimony and the cult thing was mitigating circumstances."

"We are journalists, not lawyers. The information ex-

THE WITCH OF WATERGATE

isted. Polly made it quite clear that it was not something that had been dreamed up. And she hedged it as best she could."

"So you disagree with Harry Barker?" Fiona asked.

A frown passed over her forehead.

"He's the editor. Actually, Polly won most of the arguments. She would submit proof and usually Mr. Barker would bend."

"But not in this case."

"I think she died before she could make the case." Sheila shrugged. "The fact is that the information is out there if you know how to find it. It wasn't fabricated. Polly had dredged it up through hard work. I think Mr. Barker was wrong not to run it."

"You think he bowed to pressure from Mr. Downey?"

"I wouldn't begin to speculate. I have a great deal of respect for Mr. Barker. In his wisdom, he made the decision to eliminate it. I won't second-guess him."

"Does he know how you feel about it?"

"What would it matter? I'm just a peon."

For the first time since they had been with her, she grew sulky and distant. Fiona was beginning to feel a sense of enormous frustration.

"But wouldn't it have been overkill?" Fiona asked. She knew it was a deviation from the central focus of her questions, but Sheila's growing militant attitude was irritating.

"The truth is the truth is the truth," Sheila said. "A journalist's job is to present it. That's our mandate. Polly Dearborn died for that principle." Sheila's face had flushed. A bit of spittle clotted on one side of her mouth. Fiona was surprised at the sudden vehemence. She felt the rising sense of her own rage.

"In my business," she said, "getting at the truth is a tricky business. Things are not always as they seem at first.

And even when you think you have the truth and bring a case to the courts, the most vicious criminal has a right to defend himself and juries must be unanimous in their judgement, which has to be 'beyond a reasonable doubt.'

"Now I'm getting a lecture," Sheila said. "Are you saying we have to come up with the same parameters as a court of law? Come on."

"Why not?" Fiona said. "Beyond a reasonable doubt sounds like a pretty good standard for journalists."

"What about people who abuse a public trust?"

"Like Downey?"

"Sure. Like Downey. Favoring his son's company. That's abuse. Hiding assets from his wife. That's a manifestation of his character. Same goes for incest with his son. That also has something to do with character."

Fiona paused to study the woman, still sitting Indian style, hands clasped tightly as if she were holding a device to keep herself upright.

"At least I know why Polly Dearborn hired you," Fiona said, looking at Charleen, meaning for her to join in.

"You say she died for her principles?" Charleen asked.

"People do," Sheila said pointedly. "Martin Luther King, for one."

"Guess we got your dander up," Charleen said, ignoring the pandering.

"I'm committed on that point."

"Do you think that Polly Dearborn was killed by someone she wrote about or was about to write about?"

Sheila appeared to be mulling the question.

"I'm not a detective."

Charleen turned to Fiona, an obvious gesture that she had done her part and was now passing the relay stick. Fiona took it eagerly.

"Who was to be next on Miss Dearborn's hit list?"

"There it is. The raw bigotry of a true media basher."

"I'm asking only for names," Fiona said. She was fishing now, hoping to catch something on their hook that wasn't to be found in the computer material. The fact was that Polly Dearborn was gathering facts on many important people, raiding data banks, assembling material for future use. Nor was it likely that the future target knew that he or she was being researched. Or was it?

"On that point, she kept her own counsel. I never knew who she would be writing about until she had committed herself."

"Not even the barest hint?" Fiona prodded.

"Not even that."

"Would Mr. Barker know?"

"No. Their deal was that she would tell him who she wanted to write about and he would have the right of veto. As far as I know, he never turned her down. Frankly, I doubt very much that she had told him about what story she would be working on next. She trusted no one on that. Especially Mr. Barker."

"And you," Charleen said. "Did she trust you?"

Frown lines formed briefly on Sheila's forehead.

"Yes, she did," Sheila said with indignance.

"Not completely though," Fiona pressed.

"You don't understand," Sheila said with a sneer. "And I don't think I could explain it."

Fiona studied her. Yes, she could understand. Some things were just too valuable to share. Polly Dearborn was self-contained. She lived within her own bounds. That had been adequately confirmed. No one invaded Polly Dearborn, not her mind or her body. It was time to shift the perspective.

"So you don't think that her next target knew if he or she was in her sights?" Fiona asked.

"You people..." Sheila began. "You may not realize it, but there's lots of folks out there that are from the as-long-as-they-spell-my-name-right school. Most people in power kissed Polly's butt, hoping that their name would come up on her big wheel. They knew what they were in for. Many thought it was worth the risk. Even Chester Downey."

Fiona remembered seeing him at the races, his attention to Polly Dearborn eager and solicitous,

"I can buy that," Fiona said. "What I can't buy is that people would subject themselves to her scrutiny if they truly knew that they had something to hide."

"Polly once explained that to me," Sheila said. "Many people believe their secrets to be well hidden. Others have erased them from memory." She paused and looked directly at Fiona, staring into her eyes. "Hell, we all have secrets that we think are well hidden or have deliberately forgotten. Haven't we?"

"We work on a similar principle, Sheila," Fiona said.

"And when you come up with a damaging secret you don't expect to get killed for it."

"Not necessarily," Fiona countered, remembering statistics she had seen indicating a startling increase in the number of police deaths. She looked at her watch. It was getting late.

"I guess you didn't bargain for a debate," Sheila Burns said. She was smiling amiably now, obviously relieved that the interview was coming to an end. She unclasped her hands.

Fiona and Charleen stood up. Fiona extended her hand.

"Thanks for your cooperation, Sheila."

Sheila's hand felt soft and clammy. Charleen followed suit.

"It's all right, we can find our way out," Fiona said as they moved into the corridor and toward the elevators.

"Tough little biddy," Fiona said.

"Bet she'd love to have Dearborn's job," Charleen said.

The elevator door opened, but before they could move in they heard Sheila's voice calling out. They looked up the corridor and saw her running toward them.

"Sergeant FitzGerald."

She reached them, breathless.

"Captain Greene just called. He wants to see you both immediately."

"Thanks. We'll head right downtown."

"Oh, he's not downtown. He's in Harry Barker's office."

14

"FUCKING LAWYER," HARRY Barker fulminated. He was livid with rage, pacing his office like a caged lion unable to get to a lioness in heat.

Fiona wondered what cataclysm had created such an outburst. Here was this invulnerable, all-powerful editor, roaring defiance as if he were some impotent lowly Washington species. This was Harry fucking Barker, top of the heap, a world-class nutcutter. She wasn't sure whether to be frightened or amused.

They were sitting around the rim of his desk, the Eggplant, Charleen and Fiona. They had not had a chance to consult with each other. The Eggplant looked whipped and uncertain.

"Oh, how they love to take shots at the big boys. Really pisses me off."

Fiona was confused. Even Charleen's face revealed a rare show of emotion. The Eggplant did not look their way, staring instead at the raging Harry Barker.

"Guy named Farber comes to my office two, three hours ago, says he's Polly Dearborn's lawyer. Okay. No appointment. He makes a big fuss with my secretary. I let him in. Greasy guy, slimy. Pinstripe with a red rose in his lapel.

147

Stinks from heavy perfume, the kind that makes you want to throw up. Then he says that he's the executor of the Dearborn estate. I must have looked as if I didn't believe him. Then he pulls out a paper from his inside pocket. I look at the first page. Last will and testament of Polly Dearborn. So far, okay. He tells me that Polly wished to be cremated. No ceremonies, no people. Ashes into the Potomac. That's her wish, it's okay with me. He's taking care of it himself in the next couple of hours he tells me. Then he says it's also her wish that the material in her computer has to be destroyed."

Fiona resisted exchanging glances with the Eggplant and Charleen, each of whom continued to stare at the ranting Barker. A solution, Fiona thought, knowing it was in all of their minds. Manna from heaven. Providence intervening. Then she remembered that the computer contained no information, that the disk and hard copies were sitting in a luggage compartment in Union Station. Still, she did not look at them, nor they at her.

"Fact is I had been thinking about that damned computer. Polly's assistant, Sheila Burns, has been on me about that. Says that Polly had a gold mine just sitting there inside that damned computer.

"Makes a helluva case considering all those data banks Polly was hooked into and her method of operating, close to the vest, thorough, detailed, well within libel limits. Sheila figures that it's all in there—Polly's network of informants, contacts, notes, gossip, leads, the usual reporter's mixed bag of goodies. Real ballsy kid.

"She's made a pitch for Polly's job. It's a tough one for me. Move a tenderfoot like that straight up into the big leagues and I get lots of experienced people pissed off. Bad enough I had this special deal with Polly. It's tempting, though.

"But the point is that Sheila put it in my head that that computer material is valuable as hell. Then comes this sleazeball lawyer with his pitch and I can see that Polly herself must have thought that the material was so hot that she had better see that it was destroyed if she died rather than let it get into the wrong hands.

"Believe me, I don't fault her for that. Okay, she trusted me, but even I won't last forever. Better the divil you know than the divil you don't. The fact is that Polly never expected to exit the scene so soon and so abruptly. I have to believe that she wanted me to have that material if I was still around.

"Anyway, the paper did pay for that computer. We paid for all the data banks. We paid Polly Dearborn a lot of bread. The stuff in that computer belongs to us, and will or no will, Polly Dearborn can't tell me from beyond the grave what to do with it. No way."

He drew in a deep breath and continued to pace.

"No way. I told him that we'd fight him tooth and nail for that material, that he had better not take any precipitous action or else there would be hell to pay. Then he says he doesn't want to be obnoxious about it. He says maybe we could do business. Do business? I got the bastard's message fast enough. No fencing around. How much? I ask the cocksucker."

He stopped for a moment and pointed with his finger in the direction of those observing his tantrum. "I've checked the prick out. A real bad apple. Can't imagine under what rock Polly found him."

Barker shook his head in an attitude of disbelief, then continued:

"Six figures. No piker, this scumbag. Hundred thou. You're off your rocker, I tell him. He argues with me. It's probably very, very valuable, he says. Probably is. I granted him that. But I contended that we won't pay for what belongs to us.

"I ask him if he has seen the material. No, Farber tells me. He doesn't want to see it. But he does say that he will have to defend any action on the part of the paper to obtain it. That, he tells me, would cost the paper far more than a hundred thousand dollars. Then I ask him how he can simply go against Polly's will with the snap of a buck. He says he can tell the judge that the material should go to the paper for the greater public good, some legalese bullshit.

"Blackmail, I tell him. Hell, we got an army of lawyers on the payroll. We'll get an injunction. He says go ahead, but first he tells me put on my running sneakers. A real hard case, that one."

He stopped his pacing, then walked purposefully back to his desk and sank heavily into his chair, propping his feet on the rim. Fiona noted that his shoes were new, the soles and heels barely worn. His pose was rough-hewn and salty. Underneath, she was certain, he was pure Ivy League and snobby.

"I told him to get the fuck out of the office." Barker said. "Didn't faze that bastard. He gets up, hands me his card and tells me to think it over and let him know what I've decided. Then, just as he's walking out that door, Farber turns around and says: "You've got six hours." Gives me a fucking deadline. This is one hot number. He doesn't know who he's dealing with."

Suddenly he slapped his hand down on the desk, startling them. But they said nothing. What was there to say? There was more coming. Save your energy for the worst that was to come, Fiona decided, searching for ways to brace herself for the inevitable.

"I still have a newspaper to run. The whole Dearborn

mess is bizarre. Okay, this thing with the lawyer is a whole new wrinkle. I can crucify this guy, but let's face it, this is sensitive stuff for the newspaper. I've got to assume that old Polly has a gold mine in her computer. Sure we want the material, but not this way."

Harry Barker paused and scratched his head. From where she sat, Fiona could see the frenetic activity in the city room and hear the muted hum of the busy staff manufacturing tomorrow's paper. In it would be the recorded agonies and ecstasies of people forever frozen for posterity in a moment in time. Fortune or failure could hang on the manipulation of language and truth, and Barker could, by guidance or decree, shift the balance of life by a mere change of a word or phrase, a tiny adjustment in the calibration of language.

Fiona felt a strange thrill course through her. She wasn't sure whether it was the result of fear or awe, but she had no doubt it had something to do with the immensity of Barker's power. Then suddenly his pause was over and his scratchy voice began again.

"I called you, Captain Greene, as soon as I hung up from Farber. There he was on the horn two hours on the nose from when he left my office. Probably to the second. He tells me he used the key that Polly had given him when her will was signed, gone to her apartment and taken the computer and that it was now in a safe and secret place. He tells me that if we don't make a deal by noon tomorrow, he will destroy the material on the computer."

Fiona froze. There was no way that she could restrain herself any longer from exchanging looks with the Eggplant and Charleen. Providence intervening. No apparent reference to the fact that there was nothing in the computer. Of course, Farber might find that out. All he'd need was a screwdriver. Best thing that could happen was for Farber to dump the computer lock stock and barrel into the Potomac along with Polly Dearborn's ashes. Just desserts, Fiona thought, forcing herself not to smile.

Barker seemed to be studying them for their reaction. Fiona wondered how he was reading them. The Eggplant's complexion had turned grey. Charleen had crawled behind her stoic, frozen look. It was, she knew, one of those decisive moments that change the course of events. The air seemed charged, electric. Don't say, "search warrant," she begged Barker in her heart.

The Eggplant cleared his throat and coughed into his big fist. He had obviously been summoned to Barker's office on an emergency basis, adding to the impossible burdens already imposed on him.

"How did the conversation end?" the Eggplant asked. He was obviously stalling, testing Barker's knowledge of police procedure.

"Open-ended. I told him I'd have to think it over."

"And are you?" the Eggplant asked.

"I'm thinking what schmucks we were not getting to that computer before him."

Fiona felt her heart lurch.

"I'm not blaming you, Captain," Barker added quickly. "I thought your initial idea was right on target. You had indicated that one theory you were following was that Polly Dearborn might have been murdered by someone she had written about, someone who had been badly hurt by what was published. I understand your people got the clippings we provided."

The Eggplant nodded.

Fiona lifted the envelopes that Sheila Burns had placed in their hands minutes before.

"Sheila has just given us the material," Fiona said, hoping to keep the subject deflected.

"The thing is, maybe she was killed by someone who had not yet been written about," Barker said. "Someone she had been compiling stuff about, stuff in the computer."

Fiona felt her flesh grow cold.

"You didn't know who her next... her next subject would be?" the Eggplant asked cautiously.

"Our deal was to finish one story before we started on another," Barker said. "We were set to talk next week."

At least he was moving away from the heart of the issue.

"But it did set me thinking," Barker said. "Maybe we've been looking at things ass backwards. Maybe the real clue is not in what was written in the past, but what was intended. I figure it's in the computer, right?"

"It's a possibility," the Eggplant said haltingly, showing contrived disinterest.

"That's what I thought, Captain," Barker said. "And if it's a possibility then what's in that computer is evidence."

"Following that theory, yes."

An oiliness began to ooze out of the Eggplant's skin. He was, of course, being deliberately indecisive.

"That's why I called you in, Captain," Barker said. "I'm looking for ideas. I figure we both have an interest in getting into that computer."

The two men studied each other across the desk.

"We certainly should question the lawyer," the Eggplant said.

"From what I can tell, he'd stonewall. He's beyond intimidation. We need some device that moves faster."

"Doesn't give us much time," the Eggplant said, looking at his watch.

"I'm instructing my lawyers to get an injunction to prevent him from destroying the computer," Barker said. "It's a long shot though. I don't know if they can work fast enough."

A long shot. Good odds, Fiona thought. The deadline passes. Farber destroys the computer. The information that's in the luggage compartment in Union Station no longer exists officially. The Eggplant looked somewhat relieved.

At that moment, Charleen, with her infallible nose for bad timing, spoke out:

"Maybe we can speed things up. Get a search warrant and pick up the computer."

Fiona thought the Eggplant would collapse. She saw him grip the arms of his chair. Fiona felt her heart jump into her throat.

Harry Barker's eyes moved quickly to contemplate Charleen Evans.

"Now there's one smart lady," he said.

15

THE PARKING LOT adjacent to the Washington *Post* was not the best place in the world to have it out, but the Eggplant was adamant.

"Here and now," he said.

They stood by the car that Fiona had driven, a nondescript Ford from the pool, badly in need of washing. Charleen, tall, straight and unbowed, stood directly in front of him, feet planted firmly on the ground, her face wearing its most neutral mask. The Eggplant, on the other hand, wore a rainbow's worth of emotions on his dark, perspiring face.

Fiona could sympathize with him. No. Empathize, she decided.

"What's your game, woman?" he asked, between clenched teeth.

"Game? I thought I was doing the right thing," Charleen said.

"You and your right things," the Eggplant said with exasperation. He was having a hard time repressing his anger. A man passed them, walking to his car. He looked at them briefly, then moved on.

"We have the material, Chief. Not Farber," Charleen

155

said. "We find the computer, we have options."

"Like what?"

"We put the disks back into the computer," Charleen said, looking toward Fiona for help. Fiona looked away. Poor Captain Greene. Charleen was his albatross. Fiona's, too.

"Before or after Barker gets his injunction?" Fiona asked.

"He said it was a long shot," Charleen said.

"Long shots win sometimes," the Eggplant said.

"Not often," Charleen pressed. "What I was thinking was that we find the computer, replace the two hard disks. Barker doesn't get his injunction. The disks are destroyed."

"But you said it's possible that Farber does not know the disks are missing," Fiona said.

"It's possible," Charleen said. "Depends how much he knows about computers. Since I screwed the metal container back in place, he may not be aware of it. That's the point, Captain. If we get to the computer, I can easily pop the disks back in. Then we're all off the hook, whether Farber knows or not."

"Suppose you're wrong and he does know the disks are missing. We get a search warrant, find the computer, replace the disks. Farber would know somebody has jacked him around. Like us."

"His word against ours, I guess," Charleen said. She did not look too comfortable saying it. "I only said we get a search warrant. Barker loves the idea. You saw him. Who knows, we might not even find it."

"On purpose. Is that what you're suggesting?"

"We just don't find it," Charleen said. "Not officially find it. But if we do, we just replace the disks."

"And if we don't?" the Eggplant asked, pulling a face

156

of total exasperation. "And Barker gets his injunction?"

Charleen mulled it over for a moment.

"Then he thinks Farber screwed him."

"And a can of worms grows into a can of snakes," the Eggplant said. "Aside from the fact that we've made a mockery of police procedures and opened us up to enough legal violations to"—he sucked in a deep breath—"I don't even want to think about it."

Fiona could tell his level of tolerance was fast reaching the breaking point. Undaunted, Charleen pressed on.

"Farber gave Barker until tomorrow at noon. Let's say we get the search warrant. We do his office and his house," Charleen said. Her tenacity was swiftly becoming obsessive. "And we don't find the computer."

"For real?" the Eggplant asked.

"For real," Charleen said.

"I don't believe this," the Eggplant said. He was surprisingly calm, probably numb with exasperation.

"Farber sees there's no money in it," Charleen went on. "He meets the terms of Polly Dearborn's will. He destroys the computer." A profound smugness was developing in her attitude. As if she had it all figured out. The entire exchange seemed like a Ping-Pong game without end. "We destroy what we have and that's the end of that."

"But suppose he discovers that the disks are missing?" Fiona asked Charleen.

Charleen pondered the question.

"I don't think he will," she said.

"Gut instinct?" Fiona asked.

"Sort of," Charleen muttered.

"Like your theory on the note in the computer?"

The Eggplant shook his head rapidly in a gesture of despair.

157

"Shall I base my entire police career on your gut instincts, Officer Evans?" Charleen seemed at the end of her rope. She shrugged and said nothing.

"We're all crazy, you know that?" the Eggplant said. He kicked the tire of the car. "If I was smart I'd go right back in there and tell him that we have the disks, that we took them because we calculated that the material would be necessary to our investigation, that we have to keep it private until the investigation is over."

"I was hoping you would tell him that," Fiona admitted. He turned to her, gave her a look of total disapproval and pressed on.

"Now he expects us to go before a judge, get a search warrant and find the computer. Sounds simple, right?"

"That's exactly what I thought," Charleen said, grabbing this straw of justification.

"You thought," the Eggplant said again. "What do you think Harry Barker expects us to do with the computer material?"

He did not wait for her answer, which apparently was to be slow in coming. She looked utterly confused.

"He wants us to get it for him, Evans. Never mind the legal niceties."

Charleen rubbed her chin and again looked toward Fiona, who returned what she hoped was a good imitation of Charleen's best look of neutrality. She hoped it was being read by Charleen as: *You'll get no help from me, Mama.*

"I'm all confused," Charleen said, turning away, facing the Eggplant again.

"Welcome to the club, Officer Evans," the Eggplant said pointedly, cutting a sidelong glance at Fiona as if she were the judge in this dispute. "Now I've got to get us a search warrant."

Fiona clutched the large manila envelopes filled with

clippings that Sheila Burns had given them. She put one in each palm as if she were weighing them.

"And we've got a killer to find," Fiona said.

"Think you'll find him in there, FitzGerald?"

"I don't know what to think anymore."

"With a little luck maybe you could nail him by noon tomorrow," the Eggplant muttered as he opened the door of his car and prepared to slide inside.

"Maybe so," Charleen said.

He stopped in mid-motion, still doubled over to avoid hitting his head on the roof. In that position he stared at Charleen Evans for a long moment, then shook his head in disbelief and slid behind the wheel.

"You really want to stay in Homicide?" Fiona asked after the Eggplant had left the lot.

"Absolutely," Charleen responded. "I'm made for it."

16

"ALL THIS ELECTRONIC garbage," Howard, the doorman said. "Just window dressing. Anybody wants to get in, they get in."

It was the same man that had called the police and brought them up to Polly Dearborn's apartment.

"On days now." Howard explained. "After that experience, no more nights for me. For a while there I thought they might think I was the one done her in."

He stood leaning against the front desk dressed in a brown uniform. A switchboard operator of Asian extraction with a giggling high-pitched voice answered the phone and took messages, smiling at them between calls.

Through the window walls they could see the sweeping driveway and surrounding concrete structures of the Watergate complex.

It was really Fiona's idea, to go back to the scene of the crime. There was so much extraneous matter interfering with this case, that she thought it might be a good idea to go back to basics. Charleen had offered no opinion. For the first time in years, Fiona felt professionally out of control, subject to complicating political agendas and media pressures. Not to mention the pressure of coping with

Charleen Evans, which had assumed gargantuan proportions.

"What about the security system in each apartment?" Fiona asked, determined to treat the Charleen factor as an aberration to which she had to become adjusted.

"Too complicated. People forget to turn it on." Howard said. "Place leaks like a sieve. You can get in from the garage and if you're determined you can even find a way up the stairs." He waved his hand around the lobby area. "You can even con yourself in through here. None of us have eyes in the back of our heads. And Carmelita here, she has to go to the john while I'm on a call, next thing you know we got a visitor."

"Nevertheless," Charleen said, "according to our records, there have been surprisingly few break-ins." There was never any telling what homework Charleen had done.

"Psychological barriers is the secret on that." He lowered his voice. "But between us and the lampost it's an easy place in which to score."

"Miss Dearborn's lawyer was here earlier," Fiona said, casually watching the man's face. He hesitated for a moment, but it told Fiona what she wanted to know. For twenty bucks, he'd give away the store.

"He had a key," the desk man said defensively. "Said he was here to take inventory of Miss Dearborn's effects." He frowned and looked puzzled. "Okay to let him up, wasn't it?"

"Don't sweat it," Fiona said.

He seemed relieved.

"I knew the brother would be okay, too," he said.

Fiona kept her face composed. Brother? A quick glance at Charleen showed her instantly alert as well. Polly Dearborn had no relatives.

"Of course. There would be no reason not to let the

family up. I told Carmelita it would be okay to give him a passkey. He said he'd be right down. I was up in 8A helping Mrs. Parker. She's real old..."

"You remember when?" Fiona asked casually.

He looked at his watch.

"No more than an hour, I'd say. That right, Carmelita?"

"About an hour," she confirmed, shaking her head.

"What did he look like?" Fiona asked, trying to maintain her detachment.

Carmelita shrugged.

"I don't remember, except that he wore a hat. Oh, he said he was in a hurry and needed something from the apartment. Howard probably would have brought him up but he was busy. And I couldn't leave the board. When I called him at 8A he said okay and I gave him the key."

"How long did he stay?" Fiona asked.

"Oh, maybe fifteen minutes. No more than that. Howard wasn't even back yet from 8A."

"We okay on that, too?" Howard asked.

"No problem," Fiona said, confused by the revelation.

"Would you say the man had a reddish coloring?" Charleen asked. Fiona knew where she was headed.

Carmelita looked puzzled for a moment, then her face brightened.

"Maybe..." Then she hesitated. "I can't be sure."

"What about his hands, Carmelita?" Charleen pressed. "Did they have reddish blond hair? Freckles?"

"I don't know. I think he wore gloves."

"Did he have high cheekbones? Like knobs here?" Charleen demonstrated.

"Maybe," the girl said.

"Beware the power of suggestion," Fiona said.

"I'm just trying to make her recall," Charleen countered.

"Yes," Carmelita said. "Maybe high cheekbones." She

shook her head. "I think." Then she brightened. "He wore a hat. I remember that."

"Could you recognize him if you saw him again?" Charleen pressed.

"I'm really not sure about that. I was so busy."

"What about his voice?" Charleen asked. "You are a telephone operator."

"I'm sorry. I really am not sure."

"Did you ever see this man before?" Charleen asked. Carmelita shook her head.

"Not hanging around. Like on the night Miss Dearborn was killed?"

"I think you've come to the end of the line on this, Officer Evans," Fiona said, turning again to the doorman in an effort to foreclose on this line of questioning.

"Did she get many visitors?" Fiona asked.

"Very few. A maid came twice a week is all." He rubbed his chin and looked at the ceiling as if more information could be found there. "This short girl with black hair came." He scratched his head. "Maybe twice a week."

"Sheila Burns."

"Yeah. Burns. That was her name."

"When she came did she stop at the desk?" Fiona asked.

"At the beginning, yeah. Then after a while you get to know people and you just nod. Let them know it's okay for them to go up. Nice lady. Always ready with a smile. We like people to give us a smile, don't we, Carmelita?" Carmelita giggled and nodded.

"No other regulars?"

"Regulars?" He scratched his head again. "Nobody that made an impression. She went out a lot, though. People would pick her up, stop at the desk and we'd call and tell her so-and-so was waiting."

"Can you remember any names?"

"Hell, I see so many people."

"That night..." Fiona began, trying to jog the doorman's memory. "You saw nothing strange, nothing out of sync?"

"Not until I saw Miss Dearborn hanging from the balcony. I'll never forget that sight. You know the police pumped me for hours on what I saw or heard that night. Believe me, I wish I could come up with something better."

"You've been very cooperative," Fiona said. "Now we need to get back into Miss Dearborn's apartment."

"I'll take you right up," he said.

"Just the key will be fine," Fiona said.

The two potted trees on the terrace had been set straight again. Fiona also noted a different "feel" to the apartment. It already had the air of space not lived in. A thin layer of dust had begun to build on various surfaces.

Charleen had gone to the bedroom.

"Computer's gone," she said when she returned.

"Did you have any doubts?" Fiona sighed.

They stood in the center of the living room. There were times when Fiona had revisited a murder scene and quietly contemplated the surroundings. Often, she would absorb insights from such contemplation. It was almost as if the atmosphere, the air, the space, the inanimate objects, these silent observers who had borne witness to a heinous event, had the capacity to articulate these observations in a mysterious way.

The details of the deed itself seemed clear. Polly Dearborn, garroted then pulled across the floor by the rope. Rope, carpet fibers and grains of soil had confirmed that theory.

On the terrace, the end of the rope had been tied down and the woman thrown over the side.

A clearer picture of the woman had begun to emerge. For Fiona that was always a primal point. The victim was always the quintessential clue. This victim, a term which seemed excessive in this case, Polly Dearborn, was self-directed, tightly focused and carefully controlled. She was secretive and obsessed with a forum to wreak havoc, especially if her intended victim was important enough and self-deluded enough to believe that all his warts and indiscretions had been carefully buried behind the facade of power and privilege.

"Are we looking in the wrong direction?" Fiona asked suddenly, surprised that she had given it a voice. The question had been intended to be silent and rhetorical.

"Maybe the motive to do her was personal, not professional," Fiona mused. Before Charleen could reply, Fiona plunged forward. "We've been assuming that she was killed for something she had written or was going to write. Maybe this was purely personal. A man with whom she was involved. A crime of passion. Which might explain the second man."

"No," Charleen said somewhat abruptly.

"That's a pretty affirmative no," Fiona snapped, irritated, yet again, by Charleen's propensity for absolute convictions. She missed Cates' tentativeness, his willingness to debate with an open mind.

"This woman had no other life," Charleen said.

"How can you possibly know that?"

"There was no room in it for anyone else. This lady had a mission." Charleen's eyes seemed to have adopted that vague introspective look that Fiona had seen before, as if she were looking for explanations deep within herself. "Her life was her work."

Fiona had a burst of insight.

"And her computer was her lover," she said, hoping the remark would sound facetious, which it definitely was not. Alertness leaped back into Charleen's eyes.

"Something like that," Charleen said haltingly.

You're talking about yourself, aren't you, Charleen, Fiona thought. Tread carefully, she warned herself. At the same time she felt oddly relieved. She was discovering the key to Charleen's character. Since they were locked together in this bizarre conspiracy, that was no small thing.

"And the second man?" Fiona asked. "In your head, you've already convicted the poor bastard."

So far she had not conveyed to the Eggplant Charleen's theory about one or both of the Downeys as the perpetrators.

"You object to my pursuing my theory?" Charleen said with a flash of belligerence.

"Instinct, right?"

"Anything wrong with that?"

No point in confrontation, Fiona told herself, retreating. Instinct, or, as she liked to describe it, subconscious thinking, was a perfectly appropriate device. Following a hunch was often surprisingly effective. Except that Charleen's instincts seemed somehow awry, based on an irrational certainty.

"All right then," Fiona said. "Why would he come back?"

"The computer," Charleen said flatly. "When the story didn't run with the information about him and his father, he thought he might as well try to destroy the place where it was stored."

"That's taking an awful chance," Fiona said.

"People that would do a thing like that take risks," Charleen said confidently, not a doubt visible. "Then he saw the computer was gone and he left."

166

"If he was the killer, why not get rid of the computer when the job was being done?" Fiona asked.

"Because the killer wanted it to look like a suicide, remember." Charleen said smugly, offering the faintest hint of a smile. "He told us about what was in the computer. He said that Barker had mentioned it to his father. It must have suddenly occurred to him that the material existed in Dearborn's computer and that he had to get rid of it somehow."

Fiona reviewed the conversation with Downey in her mind. Maybe so, she admitted to herself, but she was still unwilling to buy Charleen's theory.

"Well, it's obvious...I'll grant that...that the man had a purpose for coming here," Fiona said. A thought seemed to come to her and she nodded suddenly. "He might have left something in the apartment."

"On the night he killed her?"

"You're talking yourself into something, Charleen," Fiona cautioned.

"I'm giving you logic," Charleen countered.

"Speculation," Fiona shot back.

"All right, what is your theory?"

"I have no theory. I'm not even certain it was Downey who came back here," Fiona said. "That telephone operator said nothing that could possibly confirm his identity. It's in your mind only." It was an outright rebuke.

"Well, here we are," Charleen said sarcastically, casting an eye around the apartment. "A stranger was here. Why?"

They had searched the place thoroughly on the morning of the murder, not quite knowing what they were looking for. It was Charleen who came the closest, opening the computer, revealing possible motives. Nothing else seemed to have relevance.

"I'm not sure," Fiona said. "But first we bring Flannagan's boys back to dust this place." She grew contemplative again, studying the apartment from her vantage point, turning in a complete circle. "Wouldn't know where to begin. That's the trouble with this case. There doesn't seem to be a starting gate."

"But it does have a finish line," Charleen said. "And that I think I can see pretty clearly."

17

THEY SAT IN the darkest corner of Paddy's, a little bar that Fiona occasionally frequented by herself when she needed the blandishment of solitude and the stimulus of alcohol.

It was after midnight and weariness had seeped into her bones. But it had been impossible to sleep and she had roamed the house like a ghost unable to find peace. She had tried to read the material provided by Sheila Burns but after a few futile tries she had put it aside.

Then she had turned on the television. But she quickly turned it off when a bulletin offered the news that four more gang murders had occurred in Southeast Washington. The news fed her anger and her agitation and added to the idea that was at the root of her discomfort. She felt the awful sense of losing control of her life, of being rootless, ineffective and unsure in the face of Charleen Evans' certainty.

Being in that frame of mind, she was not surprised by the Eggplant's call. A similar dilemma can merge agendas. He was undoubtedly involved in his own soul-searching.

"We gotta talk," he said, his voice hoarse with fatigue. She suggested Paddy's.

Now they sat opposite each other in the dark booth.

They had often put aside their rank, antagonisms and confrontations to take time out like this. Such moments, they knew, were an arranged truce, designed to cut across the natural borders of race, gender, class, background and philosophy and to meet on the common ground of humanity. They had not clashed much on this case. They had Charleen to soak up antagonisms.

A few people sat at the bar watching a hockey game. The other booths were empty. The Eggplant had sipped a scotch from a shot glass and chased it with a beer, while she nursed a white wine. His hand shook as he lifted the shot glass to his lips, spilling a few drops on the dark table. He looked up with bloodshot eyes, noting her concern.

"It's getting to the old Eggplant," he said, shaking his head. "It's a bitch, FitzGerald."

"This, too, shall pass," Fiona said, feeling genuine compassion for him. The strain on him was telling. He looked drawn, grey, pinched.

"The shame of it is we're losing the war out there," he said hoarsely. "It may not be worth the candle."

She sipped the wine, sour to the palate. Then she put it aside, having no desire or taste for it.

"It's everything piling on at once that's doing it, Captain. You haven't got a chance to step back and see what's really happening." It was the kind of advice she had been giving herself all night, without effect. It also had no effect on the Eggplant.

"I had an hour with the Mayor tonight," he said.

"You told him?"

He did not have to ask what she meant.

"Hell, no. Why add to the poor bastard's troubles? He's got everybody on his ass—the press, the city, the bureaucracy, the feds. Hell, the whole country is pointing its finger. He's the Mayor of the fucking capital of the U.S. of

A., taking the heat for every damned politician who's using the dope-and-gang-war issue to get elected. Country needs a scapegoat and he's it, so he's got to find his own scapegoat."

"The Police Commissioner?"

"I feel for that sad bastard, too."

He finished his scotch and put the shot glass back on the table with such force it made a popping sound. People sitting at the bar turned around.

"Did he offer it to you?" Fiona asked.

The Eggplant nodded. Then he motioned for the bartender to bring him another drink.

"Not for me," Fiona told the bartender. She turned back to face him. "Cheer up. That's what you wanted all along, Captain."

"It showed, huh." He smiled, showing big teeth and a half inch of pink gums.

"What did you tell him?"

"I told him I'd think about it for a few days."

"That's smart. Don't be too easy to get."

The drink came and the bartender sat it in front of him with another beer. He looked at the shot glass but made no move to pick it up.

"I'm not sure I want it."

She studied him, looking for signs of sincere reticence. She found them.

"You're not joking," Fiona said.

He shook his head.

"Do I deserve the job? Sure I do. I've got the savvy and experience. I'd do a helluva job. You know me, FitzGerald, I'll kick whatever ass I have to get it done. I won't stop all the gang killings, the dope, but we'll get a handle on it. That I can promise. Problem is..." He paused, picked up the shot glass and upended it, downing the liquor in one gulp, then chasing it with a swallow of beer. His eyes watered. "I don't feel right about taking it under the circumstances."

"Am I hearing right? You, the bottom-line man?"

"You know what I mean, FitzGerald."

Of course she knew. Suddenly, the way of the winning was more important than the prize.

"Charleen and that damned computer," Fiona muttered, feeling a sudden surge of anger. "If you didn't know what was in it, we wouldn't be having this conversation."

"That's the point. We do know and we had no right to quash it. Wrong is wrong."

"Wrong? Nothing is ever as it seems." She smiled. The line was a cliché they had often relied on as gospel. "You know what will happen if Barker gets his hands on that information. The Mayor will be tarred and feathered in the paper without a chance to defend himself. Okay, he was a bad boy years ago. People will say once a rotten apple, always a rotten apple. He'll be the perfect whipping boy. The story will hound him right out of office."

"You got it," he said. "And who is keeping that from happening? Us. And who has the most to gain by this act ...hell, call it what you want...it's a cover-up. And it's wrong. Also against regulations. We have no right to do this thing."

"No right?" She mulled over the implications, then said, "If you need balm for your conscience, then order us to turn it in."

"Shit. We'd be aiding and abetting a political murder. I'm not saying he's a saint. Point is he's no worse than most of them. I just don't like the idea of handing Barker the meat axe to chop off the Mayor's..." His voice trailed off.

"No you don't, because that's not right, either," Fiona said with a triumphant air.

"Two wrongs don't—"

"Oh Christ. Not that," Fiona said.

"Actually three wrongs," the Eggplant said sadly. "Me toadying up to Barker. I hate it. I'm ashamed of it. Trying to curry favor with him. It offends me."

"Let's say it's not exactly an ego builder. But why beat up on yourself, Captain? Accept the facts. Barker has the biggest stick in town. You're doing what any sane man would do in similar circumstances."

"Protecting my own ass," the Eggplant muttered.

"That's no crime."

"Fact is, FitzGerald, you people don't have to go along with any of it. I were you, I would turn those disks in, get out while the getting is good. I won't stand in your way."

"Nobility makes me nauseous," Fiona said, pulling an appropriate face.

"Okay, then try on self-interest. Think how it looks if it ever comes out. We deliberately cover up this information to keep the Mayor viable so that he can appoint me Police Commissioner. There's a great career-builder for you."

"Won't do much for Charleen and me, either," Fiona said.

"Evans," the Eggplant groaned, signaling the bartender for another drink.

"The ever-certain Charleen. That puts a topper on the evening." She called out to the bartender. "Make it two."

"Now there's a nightmare for you. If I take this job, I'll always have Charleen hanging there, like the sword of Damocles, ready to tell what she knows if it suits her. How the hell did I ever bring that lady into the squad?"

"I was meaning to ask you that question," Fiona said.

The bartender set down their drinks in front of them.

"She didn't tell you?"

"Tell me what?"

"Fifteen years ago Charleen Evans' parents were murdered in cold blood in Baltimore. The killer was never found. That kind of motivation sold me to take her on. She had the credentials, paid her dues on the street. We needed another woman on the squad. Bright, tough, black. Why not?"

"I've been with her a few days and I can think of a hundred reasons."

"Only a hundred."

"She's impossible, I'll grant you, Captain. And I know it will be hard for you to believe. She's infuriating, exasperating and compulsive. I also think she lacks insight and has an uncanny talent for the wrong timing. She's obsessed, overly tenacious and obnoxious. In short, she's a twenty-four-carat pain in the ass. But I don't think she's venal."

"Probably not. She's lethal."

"She's determined to make Downey or his father or both the Dearborn killer.

"Even if they're not?"

"That won't stand in her way."

"Is she onto something we don't know about?"

"That's the hard part. I'm not sure."

She told him about the man who visited the Dearborn apartment and her suspicion that it was Robert Downey.

"You don't think it was him?"

"There's no real evidence to support it. Not that that bothers her. But I can't put it totally down. She might have something. Might. Maybe. Problem is there are no mights and maybes for her."

"That's another thing. Charleen Evans is not a desirable conspirator."

"And I am?"

"We're here, aren't we? Doing the whole number."

He studied her for a long moment, then smiled. Briefly, the fatigue seeped out of his face.

"Damned females," he said, the smile slowly fading.

"Fate worse than death, eh, Captain? Beholden to two pushy broads."

"That's part of it, I suppose," he sighed, looking at his watch. Then he dipped a hand in a side pocket and pulled out a folded paper, which he threw on the table. "I got the bastard his search warrant."

Fiona touched it, but did not pick it up.

"Do we find the computer, Chief? There's nothing in it."

"You find it, there will be," the Eggplant sighed.

"You want us to put the disks back in?"

"I would appreciate that," he said. Fiona allowed him the sophistry. The chances of finding it were slim at best. It was the exercise that was important.

"Chips fall where they may?"

He nodded. Fatigue had gripped him again. Wearily, he slid out of the booth.

"On us, probably," he said. "Chances are the *Post* will get their injunction. In this town they always get what they want."

"Crazy, isn't it? Like hunting for a stuffed animal."

The Eggplant smiled thinly.

"Keep me apprized." He pronounced it "apprahzed." Then he forced a spring into his step and walked out of the bar.

18

BARKER WAS RIGHT. Even in his silk paisley robe and matching pajamas and ascot, Farber struck Fiona as a sleazeball.

He had opened the door of his townhouse on Capitol Hill himself, as if he were expecting them. It was promptly seven A.M.

"Come in, officers," Farber said, smiling broadly. "Right on time."

Fiona showed him the folded warrant. He brushed it away with a pudgy hand.

"No need. My house is yours."

"We'll do the office later," Fiona said.

"I have a summer home in Nantucket," Farber said, continuing to smile. "When will you do that?"

Fiona had often seen bravado mask anxiety. His attitude did not foreclose on the possibility of finding it.

Farber's house was well furnished. He apparently had a passion for soft leathers and ultrasuede. Most of the furniture and backgrounds were done in these materials. On the walls were a collection of etchings depicting early days in Washington.

"Shall I show you around?" Farber asked.

"That isn't necessary," Charleen said.

176

"It's a big item," Farber taunted. "You shouldn't have much trouble spotting it."

He followed them as they moved through the house, opening drawers and closets, all of them knowing that it was an exercise in futility.

"We can play 'hot and cold,'" Farber said, chuckling. "At the moment you're both sojourning in the Ice Age."

"We're just doing our job," Charleen said. Fiona shot her a look of rebuke. The first of the day. Fiona detested this cliché of absolution. They hadn't said much on the way over to Farber's house, a five-minute ride from headquarters.

They moved through the downstairs portion of the house into the kitchen, where Charleen opened the oven.

"Baked computer. It's the latest rage," Farber said. He wanted to bait them and was enjoying the process.

They went through the basement, then upstairs on the bedroom level. Farber obviously was doing quite well financially.

"Any leads yet on who did Polly?" Farber asked in a mock serious way as they went through his bedroom. He was obviously single and indulgent of himself. A neuter, Fiona guessed. Also shrewd and devious, the kind of attorney that Polly Dearborn might choose.

After forty-five minutes, they stopped. It was a thorough search.

"Just close the door on the way out," Farber said. "I've called my secretary at the office to make you feel welcome. It won't be easy."

"Cocky son-of-a-bitch," Fiona said when they were back in the car heading toward Farber's office in the National Press Building.

Fiona had not told Charleen about her meeting with the Eggplant. The need for commiseration would be difficult

177

for Charleen to grasp. But that didn't foreclose on her mentioning what the Eggplant had told Fiona about Charleen's past.

"I want you to know, Charleen, that the Eggplant told me about your mother and father," Fiona said. She did not place the revelation in the context of time or place. Fiona was driving and, therefore, did not have to see Charleen's reaction.

"He shouldn't have discussed it with you," Charleen said after a long pause. Surprisingly, Fiona did not get any sense of Charleen's indignation.

"Come on, Charleen," Fiona cajoled. "Loosen up."

"My private life is my private life."

"Touché," Fiona said, taking her hands off the wheel for a moment to emphasize her frustration. They drove on in silence. Then minutes later, as if on a cue known only to herself, Charleen suddenly began to speak.

"I was seventeen. We had this house in Baltimore. You know the kind. Flat front with a stoop. My Dad was an inspector for Bethlehem Steel. Mom taught school. Good people. Made it on their own. I was going to be a doctor. I had a scholarship to Johns Hopkins." She was paying out her lines in a flat staccato. "I was upstairs reading. I heard sounds coming from downstairs. I thought Mom and Dad had visitors. Then I heard these pops. I had never heard gunfire before, and, therefore, I felt no sense of urgency. I should have rushed down there. Maybe I would have got a glimpse of the fleeing gunman. Not that it would have helped Mom and Dad. They were both shot in the back of the head, gangland style. The Baltimore Police said it was a mistake, a gang hit gone awry."

She paused and sucked in a deep breath.

"I accepted that notion but not their subsequent actions. They did little or nothing, contending that a hit man was anonymous and almost impossible to trace. I didn't buy that and I vowed, at that moment, to become a homicide detective in any department but Baltimore. Washington was the closest one to where I lived and I joined the MPD ten years ago."

Her response had been workmanlike, bloodless and efficiently lean. Yet it seemed without heart. Emotional paralysis, Fiona thought, confirming her earlier diagnosis. Poor Charleen, doomed to keep searching for the killer of her parents. Truth or pop-psych, Fiona wasn't certain, but somehow the woman's story, cold as it was, touched her heart. It also helped explain Charleen's lack of objectivity, a fatal flaw in a homicide detective.

"Tough luck," Fiona said. The sketchy confession had given her some insight into Charleen, but had not bridged the gap between them. Fiona waited, but nothing more was forthcoming.

"Think we'll find it?" Charleen asked.

"Doubtful. But if we do, he told me he wants us to put the disks back."

"So he's taken my advice," Charleen said.

"Guess so."

Fiona did not tell her about the Mayor's appointment offer to the Eggplant.

"And if we don't?" Charleen asked.

"Chances are Barker's lawyers will find a way to get it," Fiona said. "Then the court case begins. Injunctions, arguments, the works. All fighting over a computer without information. Sooner or later the wind will blow the stink our way."

"Will Farber fight it?"

"Depends on how much is in Polly Dearborn's estate."

They parked in the garage of Farber's office building and started up the elevator.

"And if we do find the computer and put back the disks we're throwing the Mayor to the wolves," Charleen said suddenly. A chill rolled through Fiona.

"Not our business," Fiona said.

"I don't like it," Charleen said.

"Not yours to like," Fiona said, her stomach churning. "Either way it stinks."

They entered Farber's office and were greeted by a pretty receptionist.

"Mr. Farber called. You're to get the cooperation of the entire office."

This consisted of a middle-aged secretary and Mr. Farber, who would, no doubt, be on his way. Charleen and Fiona began their search. They looked through drawers, file cabinets and inspected the two computers in the office to see if one of them might be that taken from Polly Dearborn's apartment.

They were thorough but not hopeful, knowing that Farber would soon arrive to ridicule their efforts. They did not have long to wait. Farber arrived in a pin-striped suit with a red rose in the lapel.

"Any luck?" he said pleasantly. They had just completed searching Farber's personal office.

"You could make it a lot easier on us," Fiona said. "Maybe on yourself as well."

"On myself? Don't be silly. I have a solemn obligation to the last will and testament of Polly Dearborn."

"And what is that?" Fiona asked. This was as far as she would go.

"That is between the late Miss Dearborn and me," Farber said.

"You should read the statutes on withholding evidence, Mr. Farber," Charleen said.

"What evidence?" Farber asked with exaggerated innocence.

"The evidence in Polly Dearborn's computer," Charleen said. Fiona was beginning to feel uncomfortable. No point in opening that Pandora's box.

"You are mistaken, Officer," Farber said smugly. "You are referring to Miss Dearborn's private material, hers to dispose of as she sees fit."

"I think we can go now, Officer Evans," Fiona interjected. The subject was not theirs to debate. But Charleen persisted.

"Have you seen the material in the computer?" Charleen asked. Fiona's heartbeat accelerated suddenly.

"I don't have to answer that question," Farber said. He, too, seemed surprised at the depth of Charleen's probing.

"No, you don't." Fiona said firmly, turning to Charleen. "I think it's time to go."

"Didn't find what you were looking for, girls?" Farber said mockingly. Fiona grabbed Charleen's elbow and led her out of Farber's office.

"You were challenging him to get into that computer," Fiona admonished as they stood in the corridor.

"I was not. I was merely trying to find out if he had tried to get into the computer."

"And if you did find out?" Fiona asked.

The alternatives were dawning on Charleen again. Her answer was a shrug. As always, it was hard to know what she was thinking.

"I have a question for you, Charleen," Fiona said.

Charleen eyes locked into hers.

"Have you read the statutes on withholding evidence?"

At that moment, the receptionist poked her head out of the office door and looked toward them.

"Which one of you is Sergeant FitzGerald?"

Fiona raised her hand and the receptionist ushered her back into the office and pointed to the telephone on an end table in the reception area. Fiona picked it up.

"Find it?" he asked in a hoarse whisper.

"No," Fiona answered.

"That's the bad news," the Eggplant said.

"And the good news?"

It was meant as a facetious question and she hadn't expected a response.

"The good news is that we've got Polly Dearborn's killer."

"Is this a joke?"

"Not to Charleen. There'll be no living with her."

Fiona looked at Charleen, who was studying Fiona's face.

"All right, Captain. I've braced myself."

"Robert Downey," the Eggplant said. "He walked in here a half hour ago and confessed."

19

ROBERT DOWNEY WAS sitting at one end of a long table in one of Homicide's nondescript interrogation rooms. The vomit-green paint was peeling and there were large lightning bolt–shaped cracks in the wall. The windows, despite the fact that they were six floors up, were barred.

He seemed much calmer than when they had seen him the day before, like a man who had made peace with himself.

"You did the right thing," Charleen said. "Sooner or later we would have got you." She had not gloated. To her, Fiona supposed, this was simply the expected course of events, although even she could not have expected this dramatic a denouement.

"Before you sign your statement, I wanted you to talk with those assigned to the case," the Eggplant said to Downey. Apparently, Downey had already made his statement to a police stenographer and was waiting for it to be typed for his signature.

"I understand," Downey said.

"Do you feel any remorse for this act?" Fiona asked.

"None at all," Downey said crisply. "She had it coming."

183

The Eggplant said, "Officer Evans, would you care to do the honors?"

She was entitled to that, Fiona thought. It was, after all, her instinct, her theory.

"Would you tell us exactly how it was done?" Charleen asked.

"Of course," Downey said. He coughed into his fist. "It was easy getting in. I came through the garage, hid behind one of the pillars, waited for a car to come through, then just ducked through the gate as it closed. No problem at all. Then I went up the rear elevator. I carried the rope in a shopping bag." He looked at his watch. "It was just before midnight."

Fiona had a yellow pad in front of her on which she jotted down notes. Charleen simply watched the man as he spoke.

"Getting into her apartment was also no problem. I rang the buzzer. She asked who it was. I told her I was Robert Downey, and she opened the door."

"Just like that?" Charleen asked.

"Oh no," Robert Downey said calmly, smiling. His complexion was ruddy but had not reddened. Nor did he seem agitated in any way. He could be discussing a tennis match. "We talked through the door and I could tell she was looking at me through the door's peephole. I took care not to look threatening. I told her that I simply wanted to come forward to set the record straight and that I had new evidence to impart."

"And then she let you in?" Charleen asked.

"Well, it took a lot more time. She probed me pretty hard. I told her I felt foolish standing out there in the hall." He laughed. He seemed to be enjoying the attention. "I must admit I was pretty persuasive. Finally she opened the door. But she did not stand there waiting for me to enter. She let me in and I closed the door. She was wearing a nightgown and she ran into the bedroom and told me to wait for her in the living room."

"Did you?" Charleen asked.

"Afraid not," he said calmly. "I followed her into the bedroom, taking the rope out of the bag. When I got to the bedroom, she had her back turned to me while she was putting on a dressing gown. I simply threw the noose around her neck and pulled it tight. She went down easy, without a sound."

"And then?" Charleen asked.

Although it was a ghastly, gruesome act, as he described it, it seemed somehow banal, uneventful.

"Don't forget, my objective was to make this look like a suicide by hanging. I had to make sure everything was in its place. I straightened the room out, then dragged her through the apartment to the terrace."

"Did you wear gloves?" Charleen asked.

"Most of the time. I took them off only to work the knot that fastened the rope to the stanchion on the terrace. It was hard to do with gloves on."

They had asked Flannagan to send one of his boys to do another dusting to see if they could pick up any prints that had been missed. That report had not come in yet, but they expected it momentarily.

"Was it you who went to the apartment yesterday posing as her brother?"

He nodded.

"A little ridiculous, wasn't it? But, you see, I had left the shopping bag. It was one of these plastic bags with the name of the hardware store where I had purchased the rope. A store in Baltimore, actually. I was still harboring the hope that I was going to get away with this. Of course, you'd already ruled out suicide, but if you found the bag, you'd surely trace the rope to me."

"Where was the bag?" Charleen asked. She was determined to show the others a healthy skepticism. So far nothing had been said to dispute her theory.

"Actually, I put it behind one of the potted plants. It was out of sight. It was so out of sight that I forgot it."

Fiona did not remember looking behind all of the potted plants.

"Did you find it?" Charleen asked.

"Yes." Downey nodded in emphasis.

"What did you do with it?"

"I burned it," Downey said.

"If it was so simple to enter the building, why did you go to the front desk?" Charleen asked. It was her first stupid question.

Downey chuckled.

"There would have been no one inside to open the door. I needed a key."

Charleen showed the barest flicker of annoyance.

"You realize that we're here to punch holes in your confession," Charleen said. What she really meant was that she wanted to corroborate her theory beyond a shadow of a doubt.

"Punch away."

"Why hanging?" Charleen asked.

Again he smiled.

"There was something... well, appropriate about it. Something public. Like she did to others. Publicly hung them."

No doubt about it, Fiona thought, the man was convincing. He seemed to have all the psychological implications in place. On the matter of the garroting and the dragging of the body across the apartment, that, too, was convincing, but he might have pieced that together from newspaper and television stories. She made brief notes of her doubts as Charleen continued. Of one thing she was dead certain. Charleen was having a ball.

"All right," Charleen said. "You fastened the end of the rope around the stanchion, then..."

"Actually, I spent about a half hour before I put the body over the terrace, simply making sure that the scene would suggest a convincing suicide. As you now know, I made a lot of mistakes. Shows you I'm not much of an expert on these matters. Then I eased the body over the railing. She was either dead or dying at that point. I did not stop to find out. Getting out of the building was no trouble at all. I came out the way I got in." Again he looked at his watch. "By twelve forty-five I was out."

"Then what did you do?"

"I went home and slept like a baby. I felt, well, serene, fulfilled. This woman was garbage and I felt that I had struck a great blow for humanity."

"When did you decide to come forward?" Charleen asked.

"Somewhere around four this morning. I realized how important it would be to show the world to what lengths people will go to clear their names after being assassinated by the media. Pamela Dearborn was a murderer. She murdered my father. Frankly, I felt proud that I had struck back. This woman told lies about me and my Dad. In a way, I'd say I vindicated him."

It was, of course, the convoluted reasoning expected from a remorseless killer. But so far it was only his word that warranted his act. More was needed. Missed prints could buttress his confession. Of course, that might have been the real reason for his returning to the apartment. Fiona's mind raced with rebuttals.

"We'll see what the tech boys come up with," the Eggplant said, revealing his own skepticism.

"He might have put them there when he went back," Fiona interjected. It was an important distinction and she wanted to be sure it was emphasized.

"Well?" Charleen asked Downey.

"Yes, it could have been, although I was quite careful when I went through there that second time. I never took off my gloves. There weren't any knots to tie."

"Problem is," the Eggplant said, "you can never be sure. The tech boys always miss things, although they do the best they can."

"I'm confessing, Captain," Downey said with a touch of indignation. He had been remarkably cool up to then. Now his knobby cheekbones were growing redder. "I killed that woman. I'm proud of it. I'm prepared to accept whatever punishment is meted out. I can assure you I will die a happy man because of what I did."

"You have a lawyer?" the Eggplant asked.

"No. But a public defender will do if any more paperwork is needed. There is no need of a trial. I'm guilty."

No need of evidence, either, Fiona thought with some relief until she remembered the unresolved issue between Barker and Farber. Suddenly, a ray of hope exhilarated her. Now they could destroy the disks and the hard copies. No longer would it be a case of withholding evidence. Simple theft was another matter. All right, it was not a purist notion, but it might satisfy the Eggplant's pangs of conscience.

On the other hand, said the little devil's advocate that lurked in a camouflaged part of her brain, if Barker won in his fight for the possession of the computer, it would ultimately result in the discovery that disks were missing, creating a further mystery. A clever deducer might one day get to the answer. Besides, the whole idea of a three-way conspiracy was anathema to the Eggplant and, for that matter, to Fiona. Charleen, as they had seen, could be an unguided missile. She shook these gloomy thoughts away. First things first, she told herself.

The Eggplant suddenly motioned them to leave the room, which they did. They talked in hushed tones in the corridor.

"What do you think?" the Eggplant asked.

"Open and shut." Charleen said.

They both looked toward Fiona.

"I don't know." she said hesitantly.

"What's troubling you?"

"I'm not sure," she admitted. "I need time to think about it."

The Eggplant turned to Charleen.

"Not a shadow of a doubt?" he asked.

"None."

"I'm inclined to go along," the Eggplant said. "I'm enjoying the prospect of telling that tough bastard Barker that the Witch of Watergate got knocked off because she ruined a couple of lives. That I'm going to enjoy."

"Are we really ready to turn it loose?" Fiona asked. "Convinced beyond all reasonable doubt?"

"I told you. I am," Charleen said.

The Eggplant shrugged.

"If you think he's lying, you'll have to give us more, FitzGerald."

She needed more time to dance around it.

"What about the other?" Fiona asked, meaning the business of the computer.

"I've been thinking about how to handle that one." He looked at Fiona. It seemed a plea for understanding. "You people have taken enough risks. You're out of it. I want the material in my hands by tonight. Then I want you both to forget about it. I understand your motives and I think they're damned fine, but wrongheaded. You don't need that on your heads. You understand?"

Charleen nodded.

"Whatever you say, Captain," Fiona said, somewhat reluctantly. It was upsetting having to worry about that when she still wasn't convinced about Robert Downey. She foresaw long nights of second thoughts, lost sleep and worry.

"Let me have him for an hour, Captain," Fiona said.

Fiona and Charleen locked eyes.

"Do you think that's necessary?" Charleen asked.

"I need to be sure," Fiona said.

"The man confessed," Charleen said. Fiona could sense the anxiety beneath the inscrutable surface. Catching killers was all, the root of her obsession. Her understanding of Charleen was growing by the second.

Fiona turned to the Eggplant and looked him squarely in the eyes.

"I insist on this, Captain. I want to talk to Downey alone."

The Eggplant hesitated, but he did not turn his eyes away. See my determination, Fiona begged him silently.

"What's another hour?" Fiona pressed.

"Because it was my hunch, Sergeant FitzGerald," Charleen said acidly.

The Eggplant turned to face her, studied her, then turned back to Fiona.

"You got it, FitzGerald." He swept his arm in a wide arc and pointed to the room where Robert Downey sat waiting.

"Be my guest."

20

FIONA KNEW SHE could put holes in his story, undermine it with technicalities. His counter would be that in the heat of the moment he might have missed a point or two. He had it close enough and the system might buy it. Guilty or not, the media would send it sailing round the world and back.

"Statement ready to sign?" Downey asked. He sat at the end of the table where they had left him, relaxed and casual. She hadn't noticed how neatly dressed he was: pressed blazer with gold buttons, clean light blue button-down shirt, a red paisley tie on a field of olive. His hands were delicate, the networks of blue veins visible beneath the pinkish freckled skin covered by reddish hair, the nails clean and clipped squarely.

"They're getting it ready," Fiona said, taking her seat on the chair closest to him, at touching distance. For the first time, it seemed, she noticed his eyes set deep behind his knobby cheekbones. They were hazel, the pupils surprisingly large as they watched her with a feral alertness and anxious curiosity.

"It got too much to carry, did it?" Fiona asked pleasantly.

"I feel better with it off my chest," Downey replied.

"You seem almost euphoric," Fiona said.

"I am. I feel that I have rid the world of a disease. I hadn't realized it would make me feel so good to confess it. But you have to admit, it made an appropriate statement. Don't you just love the versimilitude?"

"You feel you've paid her back for what she did to your father?"

"In spades."

"What do you think your father would think about your having done this?"

"He'd understand."

"Did you tell him that you did it?" Fiona asked casually.

His feral eyes snapped into greater alertness.

"Why are you asking me this? I've confessed. That's enough. No, I did not tell my father. And, if you don't mind, I'd like him kept out of this. I did this on my own." He had straightened in his chair and put his hands palms down on the table. She remembered that gesture from their meeting at his father's house. He was, she decided, preparing to guard himself carefully. She recalled how uptight he had gotten when she had crossed the boundary he had set for himself.

"It certainly is a logical question," Fiona said reasonably. "You could have told him, and that information might have triggered his suicide."

"That is a disgusting allegation," Downey said.

"Is it? More than the other?"

"What other?"

"That he killed himself because of the shame of exposing your incestuous affair."

He stood up abruptly.

"Where is my statement? You have no right to discuss that. It was a lie. That beastly woman dredged up a lie."

"A lie that you told in testimony before a court of law," Fiona pressed.

"I was coerced by the cult. I did not know what I was doing."

Again the knobs of his cheekbones reddened. He was standing at the table, his fingers pressed to its surface, bent almost backward.

"You deny it, then?"

"Of course I deny it." His head shook, his lips trembled. "How dare you?"

She knew she had to press forward relentlessly now, give him no time to mount a defense, rattle him, force him into an emotional outburst. Still, she wasn't certain that he had concocted the confession, but she was determined to find out the truth of it.

"Your father blew his brains out because he couldn't take the exposure, am I right?"

"She was bent on destroying him, would stop at nothing. Even this terrible, awful lie..."

"But your father killed himself rather than face it."

"It turned out that he didn't have to," Downey said, fighting for control. He sat down but kept his hands on the table.

"But he couldn't face it. The taboo was too monstrous..."

"He couldn't bear the idea that I would suffer." A sob gurgled in his throat. "He loved me."

"But he left you to face the music."

"No. He did it to spare me."

"But the story never ran."

"He didn't know that."

"But you did and the guilt was too much for you. You needed to punish yourself. You cooked up this phony confession to expiate your sins. The sin of incest, this filthy, dirty secret between you and your father." She sensed the cruelty of her statement, but waved aside all compassion. For her the bottom line was to find out the truth. The greater wrong would be for Polly Dearborn's real killer to get away with it.

"You're going too far," he said, still in charge of himself, still unbroken.

"Not far enough. You're a liar, Downey. You and your father had this illicit relationship since you were a child, just as you testified. It was so strong that you continued it all your lives. Nothing could break it. Nothing could stop it."

"No. No. Absolutely not. That is a lie. I demand you stop this." His voice rose. "I want my statement. I killed Polly Dearborn. You are tormenting me."

Still, he wasn't breaking. She had broken others with this type of staccato interrogation. Perhaps he was telling the truth. Perhaps he had killed her. Perhaps he had not had this incestuous relationship with his father. It was, after all, the ultimate accusation, the ultimate disgrace.

"I don't believe you," she said. But she could tell that the emotional crescendo was lessening, that he was getting himself under control.

Then, in one of those wildly insightful moments, when an idea springs from some unknown subconscious wellspring, she took a three-hundred-and-sixty-degree turn in tactics. She was wearing a blue skirt held up by a thin leather ropelike belt, which her fingers had touched by pure accident. She unfastened the buckle. He could not see her do this, since that part of her was out of his field of vision.

"You say you killed Polly Dearborn. Garroted her from behind, dragged her across the apartment, threw her over the side of the terrace?"

"It's all in my statement," he said. "If you don't mind, I'd like to sign it and get it over with once and for all. Let's end it, why don't we?"

"That's okay with me. But first..." She pulled the rope-like leather belt out of its loops and threw it on the table. "Show me how you made the knot."

He looked at the belt in front of him. But he made no move to reach for it.

"Just replicate the hangman's noose that you used on Polly Dearborn. Do that and it's case-closed."

Fiona watched him. The color had drained from his face, even from the reddened knobs of his cheekbones. He had clasped his hands in front of him but he made no move toward the belt.

"This is ridiculous," he said, trying to override his anxiety by indignation.

"That was your choice of weapon," Fiona pressed. "A little demonstration shouldn't be a problem."

"I refuse," he said, his voice shaking.

"You can't. Not now."

He was silent for a moment, averting his eyes. She watched his hands move toward the belt. He lifted it with trembling fingers.

"You've made me too nervous," he said, his eyes pleading.

"Your lies have made you nervous, Downey."

He picked up the belt and began to create the knot. For a brief moment, Fiona thought he was about to get it. His fingers continued to shake as he made what seemed like the appropriate loops. But when he pulled at it, the plaited leather rope unraveled. He did not look at Fiona. Beads of perspiration began to gather on his upper lip.

"It's all right. We're in no rush," Fiona said soothingly.

He tried again.

"This is not real rope," he muttered, stopping for a moment to brush away the perspiration.

Again he tried making the right loops. Again the belt unraveled. It did not deter him as he continued to try, always without success.

"I'm too ... too nervous." He looked toward her. Perspiration was running down the sides of his chin. Drops were falling on his tie.

"You can't, can you?"

He hesitated, turned away from her, concentrating once again on making the knot. After numerous tries, he seemed to have succeeded, creating what looked like a hangman's knot.

"There," he taunted, throwing the looped end in her direction. She took it, pulled, and it unraveled. An odd strangulated sound issued from his throat. Tears of frustration seemed to fill his eyes.

"You didn't," she rebuked. "You didn't kill Polly Dearborn."

"I ... I ..." He couldn't get any further words out.

"It wouldn't solve it, Robert," Fiona said gently. "It would always be there, wouldn't it?"

He bowed his head, his shoulders shook with sobs. He had clasped his hands, knuckles white, and rested them on the edge of the table, a child's gesture. Fiona reached out and touched them.

"You musn't be too hard on yourself," Fiona said. The man's agony had touched her. He lifted his head and took deep breaths, trying to get himself under control.

"How can people possibly understand?" he whispered. "I loved that man with all my heart and soul and body. And he loved me. As far back as my memory goes, I loved my father."

"Yes," she said gently.

"It was more than twenty years ago. How dare she dredge that up. Everybody had forgotten. Even the FBI check on Dad never found it. We thought we were home free. Pamela Dearborn was a cruel beast, a cruel beast. She killed him and I needed to kill her." He turned his tear-stained face toward Fiona. "You understand that."

"Of course I do," Fiona said. "But, you see, our job is to catch her real killer. Forcing the system to punish you wouldn't help anything, Robert. Leastwise, yourself."

He was gaining control. She took a packet of tissues out of her pocketbook and gave it to him.

"Do you think we can keep this ... well ... you know."

"Quiet?"

He nodded.

"I feel like a fool," he said.

At that moment, Charleen burst through the door, followed by the Eggplant. She threw an envelope on the table.

"They found prints. It's confirmed. They belong to Robert Downey."

Fiona turned to face her, looking up slowly. Charleen's eyes glistened with the pride of victory.

"Do they?" she said.

"Captain Greene has his statement for his signature," she said. Poor Charleen, Fiona thought. No insight. One searching look at Robert Downey should have convinced her. It quickly convinced the Eggplant. He took a folded paper from his pocket and ripped it up, sprinkling the remains on the table.

Even then, Fiona wondered when it would finally dawn on Charleen Evans.

21

FOR THE FIRST time in days Fiona awoke refreshed from a dead, dreamless sleep. Often in her experience, bearing witness to another's catharsis had a sympathetic effect on her own emotions.

Lying in bed, stretching in the delicious warmth, watching bright sunbeams spear through the blinds, she felt an odd sense of peace and satisfaction, as if she had finally said goodbye to yet another brief bout of depression.

It would pass. She knew it would. A realist, she had learned to trust her self-knowledge. It had been a legacy of her father, who had, for most of his life, relied rather heavily on self-delusion and fantasy, never really confronting himself. His epiphany, which changed the course of his life, profoundly altered her own.

The sense of it had burned into her memory, invaded, then embedded itself in her tissue forever. He had assembled his tiny family, consisting of her mother and herself, in the dining room. Perhaps the fact that she continued to live in the house deeply influenced the pristine recall of the moment.

The memory was further reinforced by another event that had occurred to her almost at the same moment in time, perhaps a day or two before. She had had her first period, had become a woman.

For weeks before, her father had seemed catatonic, alarmingly so, since he was the very model of the gregarious Irish politician, a man who had parlayed charismatic charm and a gift for blarney to membership in the most exclusive club in the world, the United States Senate.

It was early morning. She remembered the special quality of the sunlight filtering through the curtains.

"I have reached a decision," he said. Perhaps it was the light, but she noted that the fatigue wrinkles in his facial skin had miraculously smoothed and his eyes sparkled with happiness. "I intend to oppose the Vietnam war," he said. To Fiona it had sounded momentous, although she had absolutely no true understanding of the implications. "It will probably ruin my career and change our lives."

"Is that wise?" her mother had said, ever the cautious conservative. Despite the hardships of being a Senator's wife, she would not have traded her position for anything.

"Remember what Lou Gehrig said when they gave him that tribute at Yankee Stadium?" her father said. It made absolutely no sense to her. Not then. Who was Lou Gehrig?

"What are you talking about?" her mother had said.

"I am the happiest man on the face of the earth," her father had replied.

Only later did she learn who Lou Gehrig was . . . the first baseman for the New York Yankees who had just been diagnosed as having a rare form of infantile paralysis. More importantly, she had finally grasped the full import of what he had meant.

Since then, her life had been through enough peaks and valleys to validate her own self-knowledge. Being true to yourself was always the best remedy for depression. She had traversed yet another valley. It was always difficult to know what caused this. Something to do with loneliness, a protracted famine of loving, both physical and psychic. It would come again. She was sure of it. Optimism returned. Hope was on the horizon. She felt good, joyous, sexy. Life was a kick again. A thousand hosannas.

She met the Eggplant and Charleen at Sherry's for breakfast. The Eggplant had assumed his usual morning sourness. A good sign, she decided. In fact, there were good signs everywhere this morning. There hadn't been a single murder in this city on the previous night.

And Charleen Evans showed signs of humility and remorse.

Sherry's was a police hangout, a ramshackle coffeeshop stuck somewhere in the 1950s. It was furnished with naugahyde-covered booth benches, chipped and faded white plastic tables and countertops. Most of the chrome trim was dented. Sherry grunted her usual indifferent greeting as she poured strong black coffee into their chipped white mugs.

Beside Charleen on the bench was a dispatch case, which, Fiona assumed, contained the computer disks from Polly Dearborn's computer.

They had all read the morning *Post*'s account of the Dearborn investigation. There was no mention of Robert Downey's abortive confession. Most of it was a rehash, since there wasn't much that was new to impart except that, as the story said, "the investigation was continuing."

"I resisted temptation," the Eggplant said, as if he had tuned in on Fiona's thoughts. He did not wait for her questioning response. "I nearly told Barker about the Downey thing." He gestured with his thumb and index figure. "Came this close. Just to show the bastard how the media can curdle people's guts."

"Downey's been through enough hell as it is," Fiona

said, casting a glance at Charleen, who lowered her eyes. Her remorse was palpable.

"I wasn't thinking of Downey. I couldn't give a shit." He paused and sipped his coffee. "I was thinking how sweet it was to deliberately keep something out of that rag."

"I was wondering about that," Fiona said. It was somewhat unusual. Leaks were everywhere in the department.

"We were lucky. The guy walked in when I was there. He would only speak to me alone, and Sally, the stenographer, is a buddy. I would trust her with my life."

He looked at Charleen.

"Gut instinct," he said. Fiona wondered whether Charleen would see the rebuke in it.

"I feel like a fool," Charleen said.

"About time," Fiona chided.

Charleen looked into the steaming coffee in her mug.

"I may not have the right stuff for Homicide," she said. Fiona was surprised at the extent of her contrition.

"Maybe not," the Eggplant muttered. Fiona wondered if his undue toleration was because he feared Charleen's knowledge. Whatever happened, he would have to contend with the fact of their conspiracy. Charleen, despite her newfound humility, was still a cipher to Fiona, although less so than yesterday.

Fiona was on the verge of coming to her defense when the Eggplant said:

"We haven't got time for that shit, Evans. We still have a killer to find."

His rah-rah sense of urgency seemed misplaced. The fact was that they were back to square one. The computer complication had slowed them down considerably and the Downey matter hadn't helped. Being shorthanded was also an obstacle.

"I don't think we're going to be able to move as fast as Harry Barker would like," Fiona said.

"Fuck Harry Barker," the Eggplant snapped.

Brave talk, she thought, remembering their first meeting with Barker, at which the Eggplant had reached new heights of humility and deference. He hadn't been too forthcoming at the second meeting either. There was no point in pushing for an explanation. It would come in its own sweet time.

"We'll just have to develop leads." She looked at Charleen. "Split things up between us." Then, turning to the Eggplant, "Just don't expect miracles."

"I don't," he said. Then he took a deep sip of his coffee. When he had put down the mug he looked at Charleen. "The disks in there?"

Charleen nodded. She picked up the briefcase and handed it to the Eggplant. He opened it and looked inside.

"Hard copies, too," Charleen said.

He nodded, seeming satisfied, then his eyes shifted, studying both their faces.

"Let's go," he said, picking up the dispatch case.

He got up and they followed him out. His car was parked on the street and he opened the door on the driver's side, throwing the briefcase onto the rear seat. Fiona got in beside him and Charleen behind her, next to the briefcase.

He headed the car toward the Capitol, then swung a sharp right and headed toward Independence Avenue. No one spoke. They passed a construction site where land was being cleared for a large office building. Some of the laborers were standing around a fire in a barrel, warming their hands against the early morning chill, their shovels, picks and sledgehammers lying helter-skelter around them.

The Eggplant pulled up adjacent to the site and reached over for the briefcase. Then he got out of the car, carried it to where the men were standing, opened it and fed papers into the fire, much to the astonishment of the men warming their hands. The fire flared up and the men backed away. But the performance wasn't over yet.

The Eggplant removed the disks from the briefcase, picked up one of the sledgehammers lying about, then proceeded to demolish them until there were only bits and pieces left. Then he picked up the remains and dumped them into the fire.

"Won't burn, mister," one of the men said.

"All they need is a good charring," the Eggplant said as he headed back to the car.

"Felt good," he said, as he gunned the motor and headed back to Sherry's, where Fiona had parked the car. "Got the idea this morning when I passed this site."

"I'd say that was a pretty decisive act," Fiona said.

"Just completed the other half of the job is all." He turned to look at Fiona, showing his broad, gummy smile.

Charleen seemed speechless with astonishment.

"Have we missed something?" Fiona said. It was not the first time she had witnessed the Eggplant's passion for histrionics and game-playing.

"You mean I haven't told you?" He chuckled.

"Told us what?"

"Farber destroyed the computer."

"How can you be sure?" Fiona asked.

"He sent Barker a handwritten letter, validating its destruction." The Eggplant laughed. "For some reason Barker faxed it over to me last night."

"What happened with the injunction?" Fiona asked.

"Beats the shit out of me," the Eggplant said. "Guess he just called off the dogs."

"I thought he was so determined to get at it," Fiona said.

"Guess he changed his mind. He wrote a cover note.

Said better to let sleeping dogs lie. That's one thing me and the son-of-a-bitch agree on. Let sleeping dogs lie. Especially these."

Which explained to Fiona his sudden cavalier attitude toward Barker. With the material out of play, nothing would threaten his becoming Police Commissioner.

Not that there weren't still some moral niceties that had to be overlooked. After all, one day the Mayor, if he was still in political life, might have some explaining to do. Without Polly Dearborn's research, that possibility was not imminent. Nor was it incumbent on any of them to provide the media with the weapon to destroy the Mayor. Who were they to be judge and jury?

"But why?" Fiona asked. "Yesterday he seemed so adamant at getting the material."

"I guess he didn't think it was worth the hassle," the Eggplant replied.

"Or he paid Farber's price," Fiona suggested.

"And what would he have gotten for that?" the Eggplant asked. "The computer had no disks."

"He wouldn't know that until he got the computer," Fiona persisted.

"I thought of that. But he seemed perfectly content with the way the situation was. Knowing the bastard, he would have bitched like hell if he thought that Farber had screwed him."

"So we let the sleeping dogs lie," Fiona said.

"May they sleep in peace forever," the Eggplant said.

He dropped them back at Sherry's and sped away in the direction of headquarters, leaving them still somewhat in a state of shock. Sherry brought them coffee. It suddenly occurred to Fiona that Charleen hadn't made a comment on the Eggplant's action.

"What do you make of all this, Charleen?"

Charleen picked up her mug and drank. She looked somewhat vague and uncertain and made no effort to reply.

"Listen, Charleen, we all make mistakes," Fiona pressed.

"This is more than a mistake. It shakes your confidence in me, makes me lose credibility. Everything I say is suspect. I've made a damned fool of myself."

"You just haven't got all the answers, Charleen. No crime in that. None of us has."

"I don't even have the right questions," Charleen said.

"Not always. Neither do I."

"You know your stuff, FitzGerald."

Fiona took a deep drag on her coffee and looked at Charleen.

"Enough of this bullshit, woman, we've got work to do. Problem is I don't exactly know where to start."

They were silent for a long time. Charleen looked into the black coffee of her mug as if she were searching for alien bacteria.

"All right, FitzGerald," Charleen said. "I've got a question."

Fiona looked up in response.

"What caused Harry Barker to change his mind about obtaining the material?"

Fiona thought about it, let the idea sink in, then nodded her head vigorously.

"There's hope for you yet, Charleen. That's one fucking good question."

22

FOR THE NEXT two weeks, murder was not Washington's number-one topic. Not that crime was off the front pages. There was a major coke bust, a sting operation that bagged fifty-three thieves and the arrest of the leaders of a major black gang in Southeast Washington.

The Mayor had created task forces and various committees to come up with ideas to combat crime. Having little choice and backed to the wall by media-fed public opinion, the Mayor cranked up his public-relations machine.

More significantly, the cherry blossoms were popping, signaling the start of the tourist season. The *Post*, perhaps honoring Barker's pledge to the Eggplant, no longer used the sobriquet that Washington was the murder capital of the United States and stopped bashing the Mayor. More cynical minds, like Fiona's, determined that this was more in deference to the paper's advertisers than to any pledge to a mere captain of Homicide.

It seemed a watershed time, a respite. Fiona and Charleen continued their investigation of the Dearborn murder. They made lists of possible suspects, gleaned from those newspaper clippings provided by Sheila Burns.

Because of the manpower shortage, Fiona and Charleen had to work alone, returning each evening to headquarters to compare notes. Even Fiona's friend Chappy was a suspect and worthy of an interview.

Fiona visited him at his Georgetown house.

"Drink?" he asked, inviting her into the sitting room.

"This is official," Fiona said with a wink. "I'm on duty."

"Two olives or one?" Chappy asked.

"I'm tracking a killer," Fiona said, holding up one finger.

"Rocks or straight up?"

"Not a lead in sight. Rocks."

"Gin or vodka?"

"Did you do it, Chappy? Stolly."

He mixed the drinks, popped in the ice and olives and sat opposite her in the little sitting room that overlooked his elegant but small English garden.

"In my mind, a thousand times," Chappy said, lifting his glass in a silent toast. "In reality, I couldn't, and I doubt any of us mowed down by her ferocious pen could do it. Public men, in the final analysis, are cautious realists. The fact is that there is another life beyond the limelight. All right, I'm no longer viable for the perks and ego satisfactions of the diplomatic life, but life is not over." He sipped his drink. "As you can see." He swept his arm to take in the antique-filled room and the garden.

"Chester Downey had another view," Fiona said.

"That is an enigma. His downside, while devastating, need not have been fatal. A public scolding, a resignation and temporary limbo. There had to be more to it."

She studied his face, wondering if he knew more than he was saying.

"There are also the realities of being a public person. You know up front that the media is gunning for you. That is a given. The media barons know that there is nothing more tantalizing to curiosity than watching a star fall and no posture more fearsome than righteous indignation. We are a nation of watchers and the media is the surrogate for all of our frustrations. It is a lethal combination, especially for a public person who has made a tiny misstep. And who hasn't?"

"Should I believe my ears, Chappy?" Fiona said.

"Polly Dearborn was a master of the half-truth. Or should I say the half lie. In my case, she accused me of using my position to gain inside information of a certain transaction for personal profit. Well, it's half true. I made the transaction and I made the profit."

"And the other, the inside information?"

Chappy took another sip and put his drink down on the table beside him. He smiled.

"Hearsay, rumor, an overheard tip. That doesn't qualify as inside information. The fact remains that I was in the position to hear it."

"Are you defending the lady?" Fiona asked.

"Defending? Not at all. I'm commending her for her skillful use of the language, for creating high art out of vagueness, and drawing masterful conclusions from inconclusive information. The fact is that I knew the game and the house rules. I gambled on the play and lost."

"What about her dredging something out of the distant past? A youthful indiscretion."

"If it's on the record, fair game."

"A sexual aberration?"

"Aberration? What's that?"

"Homosexuality?"

"Tame stuff. It's called sexual preference. No mileage in that any more."

"Womanizing?"

"Image-enhancing, unless a scorned woman blasts away. Or the lady is underage."

"Whips and chains, sadism, masochism."

"Almost over the edge."

"Incest, child abuse."

"Beyond the pale. You're hiding that, stay out of public life."

"What about crime?"

"Crime is also fair game. But that, too, has to be beyond the pale. Like murder, dope peddling, burglary. Not drunken driving or car theft for joyriding. The public can forgive that if no one got hurt. Her research in that area was dogged. If there was a record anywhere to be found, she found it."

"Computers. She was hooked into data banks."

"God help us. Still, you can't blame the messenger."

"My, Chappy. All this defense. I thought you rejoiced in her death," Fiona said.

"Not really. I rather liked having an enemy, gave the adrenalin a lift."

"So you don't think she was done away with by her victims?"

"As a victim, I tend to doubt it," Chappy said. He finished his drink. "But hell, I'm no detective."

Her conversation with Chappy seemed a bellwether to their investigation. Other victims of Polly Dearborn seemed to express the same point of view. A public person is the media's target of convenience. They are in the business of gaining attention, attracting notice. Only a familiar star can do that.

They interviewed those with whom Polly Dearborn spent social time. Most were catalysts of the social scene, people who reveled in collecting powerful persons. Polly Dearborn was sought after because of her power, not her social graces. All agreed that she was mostly a loner, secretive and protective of herself. Most felt that she was always in a working mode, a lion in lamb's clothing. Nor was she averse to probing her social contacts, sometimes relentlessly.

It seemed obvious after a number of interviews that Polly Dearborn had been sought after by people of prominence more as a defense mechanism than for her scintillating company. Nobody admitted close friendship with her, only casual acquaintanceship.

Essentially she was a loner, her modus operandi quite transparent, and there were always people available with scores to settle to provide her with information laced with nasty gossip that might form the basis for one of her scalpel-wielding performances. Now that she was dead, there seemed to be no reluctance to tell the real truth about her. Such was the hypocrisy of the Washington social system.

Aside from interviews with those who touched Polly Dearborn's life, Charleen and Fiona contacted hardware stores that sold the brand of rope used to hang her. It proved a common type. Every store carried it and every lead provided led nowhere.

Even the story of Polly Dearborn's murder, after a surge of interest in the national media, seemed to fade away, yet another brief titillation to pique the public's interest and pass into history.

Because of the stringent manpower shortage, Charleen and Fiona's pattern was to go their separate ways during the day and review their findings when they came back to the squad room each evening, It was a painstaking process, mostly discouraging, since they could not develop a single lead.

Charleen's awareness of her own vulnerability and self-doubt was not helped by the failure to produce any results in the Dearborn killing. She grew increasingly morose and depressed, which did little for Fiona's morale.

"Patience, Charleen. It's a tough case."

"I just feel I'm not pulling my weight," she said often.

"We just stay with it, something will develop," Fiona told her, but without much conviction. This one was getting away from them. Nevertheless, the reality was that not every homicide was solved. Who knew this better than Charleen?

Although they were encouraged by the Eggplant to pursue the case diligently, it was beginning to seem more for show than for substance. Their reports to the Captain were getting briefer and subject to cancellation by more pressing matters. A number of gang murders and random killings had been solved, and better police protection of the combat zones seemed to be holding down the killings.

Besides, Fiona knew that the Eggplant was merely marking time for the day when he would take over as Police Commissioner. Rumors were rampant about his impending appointment. Apparently the present Commissioner was waiting for the most propitious moment to announce his resignation, a moment of calm, to allow him to save face and point with pride.

Unfortunately, the calm was not to be. The nightly bloodbath began again, triggering a new round of daily meetings and even more pressure on the Homicide squad. And once again the Washington *Post* began to describe Washington as "the murder capital of the U.S.A." and resumed its bashing of the Mayor.

"The bastard broke his word," the Eggplant ranted as they met with him one morning. The new round of murders had broken the calm in his disposition as well. "His Honor has been chewing carpets all morning. Can't say that I blame him."

"Have you discussed this with Barker?" Fiona asked.

"Left messages at his home and office," the Eggplant said. He took a deep drag on his panatela, then blew a smoke ring toward the ceiling.

"What do you make of it?" Fiona asked.

"Maybe he's saving things up. One day he'll use it to fry us. Do a story on the great unsolved murder of Polly Dearborn. His Honor is giving me the I-told-you-so routine."

"Sounds strange. He seemed so anxious to be kept in the loop," Fiona said.

"Fact is, there's no loop to keep him in. Nothing's happening. Right?"

"I wish there was," Fiona said, exchanging glances with Charleen, who looked away.

"Maybe Barker feels that because we hadn't busted the Dearborn case fast enough, all deals are off."

"We're trying, Captain," Fiona muttered.

They had reported to him at every step of the investigation.

"Considering the circumstances, I know you're giving it your best shot." He shot a glance at Charleen. "Both of you."

"Give us some extra manpower, we might get something going," Fiona said. It was a futile gesture and they both knew it.

The telephone rang, a welcome relief for all of them. He picked it up and turned away, a clear gesture of dismissal.

Charleen and Fiona went back to their desks in the squad room.

"Any ideas?" Fiona asked.

Charleen began to speak, then hesitated, and said nothing. In two weeks she had become reticent, gun-shy.

"Open up, for chrissakes, Charleen. Take a chance."

Charleen shrugged and nodded.

"I think Barker knows something we don't," Charleen said.

Fiona hadn't focused on that point and appreciated the idea. She wanted Charleen to know it, rebuild her confidence.

"Not bad, Charleen. Let it hang out a bit more."

Charleen rubbed her chin.

"Maybe the feds got to him. Maybe there is some aspect of national security to this. Maybe this is all a CIA game, a plot that had as its object the elimination of the Defense Secretary."

"Maybe," Fiona said, half believing the possibility. In the absence of leads, homicide detectives often fantasized. Charleen, intrepid despite her defeats, was having a lulu.

"You think I'm crazy?" Charleen asked.

"You spend enough time in Washington, nothing surprises," Fiona said.

"I . . . I've worked out a theory," Charleen said, encouraged by Fiona's initial response. Charleen paused and cleared her throat. "The CIA could have concocted the whole idea," Charleen continued. "Rather than reveal that the Defense Secretary was a spy, they conspire to knock him off. Kill Dearborn, then orchestrate Downey's suicide. People think it's because of Dearborn's articles. In this way the country is spared a scandal and the world doesn't skip a beat knowing that some other country now has all our secrets."

"And how does Barker figure in this?"

"The President tells him."

"Makes it a cover-up, with Barker participating," Fiona said.

"For national security. For the good of the country."

The stuff of fiction, Fiona decided, unwilling to pour cold water on Charleen's fantasy. She remembered seeing Charleen's extensive library of spy, detective and suspense novels.

"You think it's off-the-wall?" Charleen asked. Coming along, Fiona thought. At least she trusted Fiona enough to ask.

Fiona mulled it over for a long moment. The idea had possibilities, but, as in most of Charleen's theories, despite its imagination, it lacked insight.

"It has a fatal flaw," Fiona said gently.

Charleen frowned.

"Good for the country or not, Barker would never agree to bury a helluva story like that."

"You think not?"

"No way."

Charleen seemed puzzled but did not reply. Fiona felt compelled to explain.

"Whatever the circumstances, Charleen," she said, "would you, as a homicide detective, cover up a government murder of a civilian in our jurisdiction for whatever reason?"

"Absolutely not," Charleen said indignantly.

"Nor would I. Not the Captain, either."

Charleen lowered her eyes, obviously considering the explanation.

"You get my drift," Fiona continued gently. The real talent of a homicide detective was in understanding human behavior. People had parameters, a hard core of pride and identity, even the most amoral. Deduction depended more

214

on insight than bare facts. How could she possibly explain such concepts to someone as literal as Charleen? Indeed, if an explanation was required it defeated the logic. You can't intellectualize instinct. This was something that had to be built into the cells.

"I'm not sure," Charleen admitted.

"Just don't commit to it," Fiona pressed.

"Like Robert Downey?"

"You got it," Fiona said. "Keep an open mind."

The rebuke took its toll. Charleen, tight-lipped and uncertain, began to rifle through papers on her desk.

And yet, Charleen had raised one issue that did linger in her mind, rousing the very instinct she had secretly accused Charleen of not having: "Barker knows something we don't," she had said.

Yes, he does, Fiona agreed.

23

SHE HAD NEVER seen the Eggplant so agitated. A vein palpitated on his forehead, spittle had formed on the edges of his mouth, the whites of his eyes were crisscrossed with red veins and his nostrils seemed unusually wide and distended as if they had expanded to gulp up scarce air.

He was slumped over the wheel of his car. Fiona sat beside him. Charleen was in the back. Their car was parked beside the Eggplant's in a picnic parking spot on a deserted stretch of Rock Creek Park.

It was the Eggplant's idea to meet there, someplace off the beaten track. Not at headquarters. Not at Sherry's. No place that was indoors. The request had all the symptoms of acute paranoia. It was the hour of twilight and only the dark clouds that hovered over the city belied the time. Fiona felt chilled. The mood was ominous.

"I don't know how he got it, but he's got it. No question." The Eggplant shook his head in frustration.

He had just come from the Mayor's office, he had explained. Summoned there out of the blue. What he found was a man on the edge of hysteria and rage.

"The way he tells it," the Eggplant said, "the *Post* had called with allegations about his conduct that were insulting and harassing. Those are the words he used, 'insulting and harassing.' Then he gave me the topper. He said they asked him about something that took place years ago. An indiscretion, he called it."

"Was he specific?" Fiona asked.

"No," the Eggplant said. "He said it was a pack of lies."

"Like Downey," Charleen muttered, as if she were still trying to sell that discredited idea. Fiona and the Eggplant ignored the comment.

"I mean what he said at first," Charleen said, assuming their reaction.

"There is no question but that they've got it," the Eggplant said.

"The computer material?" Fiona asked him.

"I'd bet my life on it."

"They got it and they're going to use it," the Eggplant said. "They're going to have his ass for lunch."

"Maybe you're just jumping to conclusions," Fiona said without conviction.

"Bastard broke his word," the Eggplant said. "Proves you can't do business with those rats. They'd sell their mother for a story."

"That's a given," Fiona said, cutting a sharp glance at Charleen, who thus far had remained silent. "What I want to know is how he got the material. A couple of weeks ago he didn't have it. And you can't accuse him of buying it from Farber, because he didn't have it. And we saw you bust up the hard disks and burn the hard copies."

"Maybe he got it from some other source," the Eggplant speculated.

"Possibly," Fiona said. "Although the chances are that Polly developed it herself."

"Maybe she made copies beforehand," the Eggplant said.

Fiona thought about that for a moment.

"If she was intent on destroying the material on her death," Fiona said, "it would follow that she would not have made any copies. The computer was both her record and her strongbox."

The logic of it seemed to offer little relief for the Eggplant, who must have been seeing his chance at being Police Commissioner slipping away.

"I thought at first," the Eggplant said, clearing his throat, "that maybe they, one of their other reporters, had found some other indiscretion, something that Polly Dearborn had failed to find. You know. Where-there's-smoke-there's-fire kind of thing."

"That's a possibility," Fiona agreed.

"There is another possibility," Charleen said suddenly. They turned to face her. She seemed somewhat tentative.

"We're listening, Evans," the Eggplant snapped.

"The murderer may have dumped the information from Polly's computer to another one," Charleen said.

"Are you suggesting that he came up with his own computer?"

"That or Polly Dearborn might have had another computer in the apartment. Maybe a portable. And when the murderer saw that there weren't any disk slots in Polly's machine, he fished around for a computer to which she could transfer the information."

"And miraculously, there was one handy," Fiona said.

"With connecting cables," Charleen said without skipping a beat. "You can't hook them together without connecting cables."

"Or he could have brought his own computer," Fiona said. She was conscious of the Eggplant's gazing from face to face as if he were watching a Ping-Pong match.

"What about the computer key, the one you found around the woman's neck?" Fiona asked.

"The murderer could have removed it," Charleen said, "used it to open the computer, dumped the information into the other computer, relocked the computer, then replaced it around the woman's neck and thrown her over the terrace."

"How would he have known that the key was around Polly Dearborn's neck?" Fiona asked.

"It would seem like a logical place to keep a key of such significance," Charleen said. She seemed to have given the matter a great deal of thought. As she spoke, she appeared to be getting back her old confidence. A tinge of arrogance was also becoming visible. But Charleen was making every effort to drown the tendency in humility.

"Explain the sequence, then," Fiona pressed, her mind racing. "He garrotes Polly. Does he go for the computer before or after he throws her over the terrace wall?"

Charleen wavered, pausing, biting her lip, not responding. Fiona pressed on.

"He kills her, leaves her strangled on the floor, goes to the computer, sees it's locked. Figures out where the key is. Then he opens the computer, makes his copy and tosses her over the terrace. That it, Charleen?"

"You're going too fast," Charleen muttered.

"Or this. He garrotes her, tosses her over the terrace. Goes to the computer. Discovers that it's locked. Looks for the key. Can't find it anywhere. A light goes on. He pulls the body up, removes the key, does the copy, replaces it."

Fiona felt herself boring in, as if Charleen possessed the guilty secret that held the solution to the Polly Dearborn case. Even as she pressed forward, Fiona knew it was ex-

cessively aggressive. By now Charleen was responding with
confidence and increasing arrogance, enjoying the deduc-
tive clash between them.

"The former scenario fits better," Charleen said. "Neither the body nor the rope indicated that the woman had
been pulled up again. Besides, it would have been too big
a chance for the killer to take. Throwing her over the
terrace would have been his last act."

"I think you got that right, Evans," the Eggplant said.
Actually, although it was difficult to decipher, this was
meant as a compliment, which seemed to please Charleen.

"But why leave the information intact on Dearborn's
computer?" the Eggplant said. "The killer couldn't have
known that one of the detectives on the scene was a computer expert and would take the disks. As far as he knew,
the information was left at the scene and might or might
not be discovered."

"But why make copies?" Fiona asked.

"Or take the disks," the Eggplant said. "Like we did."

Charleen listened, but said nothing, rubbing her chin in
contemplation.

"It was supposed to be a suicide. If he took the disks,
we would have known immediately it was a murder."

"Got an answer for everything, Evans," the Eggplant
said. He was, of course, agreeing with the logic but not
liking it. He shook his head. "Seems to me that someone
is hell-bent on getting the Mayor. Somehow the killer has
learned that there's critical information on Dearborn's
computer. He..." The Eggplant stopped suddenly, then
blew out air in frustration. "That's stupid. What the hell
does he have to kill Dearborn for? She's working to get
the Mayor herself. Why interfere with that?"

It was an endless circle and, at that point, Fiona was
certain that they had all reached the same conclusion.

Whatever happens, the Mayor loses. And if the Mayor loses, Captain Luther Greene loses, and if Captain Greene loses...

"No choice," the Eggplant sighed. "We see Barker, open the can of worms and get ourselves a killer."

He did not seem too happy about it.

24

"THIS IS A rotten time, Captain," Barker said. At first he had refused to see them.

"The paper's going to bed," his secretary had explained. "Can't this wait?"

"No, it can't," the Eggplant said firmly. When he was determined, he could be tremendously intimidating. Finally, Barker had relented.

"Five minutes—no more," Barker grunted.

"It's urgent," the Eggplant told him, slipping into the same chair that he had sat in during their first meeting. Fiona also took the seat that she had sat in that first time. They had sent Charleen back to headquarters. Three cops would be one too many for confronting Barker.

Once again, Fiona was there to bear witness. She knew that. She also knew that they were there to determine the source of the information on the Mayor. After all, the Eggplant had destroyed what they believed was the original material. Although they had not discussed it in depth, she had a good idea what was in his mind. Find the source. Find the killer.

"Hold on until I finish this. The presses won't wait," Barker said.

Warren Adler

They watched him pore over page proofs, then pick up the telephone and bark out orders. He was obviously a man used to command, whose word at the paper was law. Finally, he took off his glasses, laid them still opened beside him on the desk and put his feet up. Again, Fiona noted that his shoe soles were remarkably clean and unscuffed.

"Okay," he said. "What've you got?"

There was an edge of belligerence in his voice.

"Nothing yet," the Eggplant said.

"So what's the urgency?"

Gone was the charm of their first meeting with Barker. He seemed annoyed by their presence.

"It's what you've got that's the problem," the Eggplant said.

Barker seemed taken aback by the Eggplant's attitude, which was unmistakably confrontational.

"You'll have to make yourself clearer, Captain," Barker said. He was calm, confident, offering a thin, menacing smile. As they had learned earlier, Barker had no tolerance for anyone who defied him.

"One of your reporters called the Mayor a few hours ago asking for confirmation..."

"I am aware of that, Captain," Barker interjected.

"We had an agreement," the Eggplant said. Fiona was proud of his firmness, but apprehensive. He was taking on a dragon.

"What agreement?" Barker sneered.

"You were going to stop bashing us, stop referring to our town as the murder capital of the United States, laying off the Mayor..."

"I kept my promise," Barker shot back. "It wasn't open-ended." He removed his feet from the desk and slid forward on his elbows. "Problem is, you didn't deliver your end. Not one fucking clue to Polly Dearborn's murder and

223

they're still butchering each other like mad dogs out there."
He stood up and began to pace his office, working up a
good head of steam. "We have a responsibility to this city.
Our Mayor is a goddamned phony. As a kid he was a drug
pusher himself. We got him on that dead to rights. Also
he killed someone in a hit-and-run. He was in jail. An ex-
con, a murderer and a drug pusher. The public needs to
know that, needs to know that that's the kind of flawed
character that runs this city. He's also an incompetent."
Barker stopped and pointed a finger at the Eggplant's nose.
"Damned straight we're gonna get the bastard. Damned
straight."

The Eggplant looked Barker in the eye.

"Where did you get that information, Mr. Barker? The
material about the drug-pushing and the hit-and-run?"

Barker smiled, stopped pacing and sat down again.

"Do you seriously believe, Captain, that I would answer
that question?"

"How do you know it's the truth?"

"I won't print it if it isn't," Barker said. "That's why
we're checking it out. That's why we called the man."

"You sure as hell didn't have this information the last
time we were here," the Eggplant said, accusatory now.
He was definitely taking chances, baiting his hook. The
problem was that the fish at the other end was too for-
midable. It could never be brought in.

"Well, whaddayaknow. Now he's none other than Sher-
lock Holmes," Barker sneered.

"If you had it you would never have agreed to stop
beating up on the Mayor," the Eggplant said calmly.

"I don't believe this," Barker said, shaking his head,
offering a sarcastic cackling laugh, staring now into the
Eggplant's eyes.

"Am I right or wrong?" the Eggplant asked.

Barker frowned and continued to stare at the Eggplant. It was Barker who finally yielded.

"So what if you're right?" he grumbled.

"You didn't have it then," the Eggplant pressed.

"We have it now," Barker sneered.

"And apparently you have faith in the source. Otherwise you wouldn't have had your people call the Mayor to confirm it. Am I right?"

"Are you telling me how to run my business, Captain?"

"Problem is," the Eggplant said slowly, "the source of your source is my business."

Barker looked puzzled.

"What the hell are you talking about?"

"You got the information from Polly Dearborn's computer," the Eggplant said.

"I don't think it's any of your goddamned business where I got it," Barker said.

"It's evidence in a homicide," the Eggplant shot back.

Frown lines etched Barker's forehead.

"You're kidding me, right?"

"I'm dead serious," the Eggplant said.

Barker shook his head.

"What is this, some kind of a ploy? Are you telling me I can't use this information about the Mayor because it's evidence in a homicide? My nostrils are beginning to twitch. Do you realize the position you're putting yourself in? The Mayor's not worth it, Captain." He turned to Fiona. "And they've enlisted you, FitzGerald. Sounds to me like an act of desperation by the Mayor. Sending two sacrificial lambs to the slaughter. Are you trying to cover this up, protect that jackass in City Hall? Do you realize that I have every right to tell our readers about this ploy? Have you lost your mind, Captain?"

"Polly Dearborn got killed for that information," the

225

Eggplant snapped. He was doing a good job of holding in his anger.

This is more than you can handle, Captain, Fiona thought, frightened for him. He was pushing too hard.

"You're not making any sense at all, Captain," Barker said calmly, obviously confused. "If, as you contend, the information was on Polly's computer, the chances are that it would have found its way to our readers one way or another. Are you saying that Polly was killed to repress the information? That would make the Mayor and his allies suspect. Are you accusing the Mayor of masterminding Polly's murder?"

"You're twisting it," the Eggplant said.

"Or is there a more sinister agenda here?" Barker said. In this mode, Fiona thought, he was fearsome. "You think I bought it from Farber?"

"No, I don't," the Eggplant said.

"He sure as hell didn't give it to me," Barker said. "He destroyed it, just as he said he would. He gave me a dead-line. I told you that."

"You also said you'd be sending out your lawyers to get an injunction. You didn't." The Eggplant was calm, his eyes steady. He did not look at Fiona, who watched the duel between the two men with growing apprehension for her boss. Barker, if he chose, could ruin him with barely a flick of his figurative wrist.

"Oh, that," Barker said, his evasiveness patently transparent. "We decided against that. Too much of a hassle."

"For who? You said it yourself. You have lawyers on the payroll and had a good chance of getting Dearborn's material. Why didn't you?"

Barker's eyes narrowed as he studied the black man who sat across his desk. He seemed to be reassessing his tactics, exploring the implications of the Eggplant's questioning. He might have guessed correctly that Captain Luther Greene was a stubborn and tenacious man.

"I don't understand any of this, Captain. What's your game? Do you seriously believe that the *Post* will stop its investigation of your Mayor? Are you looking for brownie points in this confrontation? What the hell is going on?"

"I made it perfectly clear at the beginning of this interview. Did the material come from Polly Dearborn's computer?"

"Surely, Captain, you must know that a newspaperman would rather die than reveal his sources." The Eggplant did not answer, nor did he draw away his gaze from Barker's.

Fiona could sense the approach of the critical moment. In order to make his case persuasive he had to tell Barker the truth about the computer information, in effect to put his professional life in the hands of a man with no real stake in the secret, a man to whom revelation was everything.

"Even if it would help to catch a killer?" Fiona interjected.

The Eggplant looked at her, obviously unhappy with her intervention.

Barker grew contemplative. He studied them both.

"What I don't understand," Barker said, "is why you believe that this information about the Mayor came from Polly's computer."

The Eggplant and Fiona exchanged glances. Moment-of-truth time, Fiona knew. The Eggplant was about to say something, but Barker was not finished.

"Was it because it was Sheila Burns who called the Mayor?"

There it was. For some reason the Eggplant hadn't told

her. Or the Mayor had not told the Eggplant. But Barker's revelation was the push that started the dominoes falling. Of course. Sheila Burns.

"You promoted her, did you?" Fiona asked.

"Now you're going to tell me who I can promote?" Barker said, somewhat defensively.

"Put her in Polly's place?" Fiona pressed.

"She was the logical choice," Barker said.

"Because she knew what was on Polly's computer," Fiona snapped.

"Not specifically. Only in general terms," Barker said.

"Sheila Burns lied to us, then," Fiona said.

"Lied? That's a strong accusation, Sergeant FitzGerald."

Not strong enough, Fiona thought, looking toward the Eggplant. His features expressed approval. Carry the relay stick, his eyes told her.

"She told us that Polly Dearborn was paranoid about secrecy."

"Where is the lie in that?" Barker asked smugly.

"Then how would she have obtained the information?" Fiona asked.

"I told you. She was Polly's assistant. She knew what Polly was working on in general terms. She also knew about data banks, about the way Polly bird-dogged a story through her computer. Hell, the Mayor's stuff is public domain. It's all out there. You. Me. Everybody. Polly was a ferret. Sheila is a clone. She developed the information on the Mayor herself." He stood up and looked at his watch.

"I've got a paper to put out," he said, standing up, dismissing them. In that attitude he exuded power. They were mere flies ineffectually buzzing around him. He could scatter them with a brush of his hand. "Maybe you've got a point. Maybe the killer of Polly Dearborn was looking

228

for that stuff in her computer. If you're implying that Sheila Burns killed Polly, you're way off base. The only person who could benefit from destroying the material on Polly's machine was the Mayor himself."

Fiona looked toward the Eggplant. He had come within a hairsbreadth of confessing what they had done with the disks and she had deliberately deflected it. Yet the fact remained that without the computer evidence, any case against Sheila Burns would collapse under the weight of hearsay.

"We don't intend to drop this, Mr. Barker," the Eggplant said.

"Neither do we, Captain. Neither do we," Barker said.

"You've got a paper to get out, Mr. Barker," Fiona said. "And we've got a killer to catch."

Barker's eyes narrowed. The ends of his lips rose in the beginning of a smile. Then they stopped.

"You can tell your damned Mayor it won't work," Barker said. "And get the fuck out of here."

25

IT HAD STARTED to rain during the night, one of those interminable and relentless showers that would last for days. Sheets of driven rain spattered the windows at Sherry's, where Fiona and the Eggplant nursed chipped mugs of Sherry's muddy black coffee.

During a lull in the rain gusts, Fiona saw Charleen intrepidly holding her umbrella against the wind as she moved toward Sherry's. Her posture was ramrod straight, unbowed against the elements as she walked toward the coffee shop.

The *Post* had gleefully reported three more murders the night before. An indignant editorial called for more efficient police protection and less bureaucracy in municipal government, a veiled indictment of the Mayor.

They were setting the stage, conditioning the turf. Within the next few days, the other shoe would drop. They would run the story about the Mayor's early indiscretions and the sinking process would begin with a vengeance.

The Eggplant, although fatigued and gloomy, was far from comatose. Fiona had often seen him show remarkable resourcefulness during a crisis. Consistently, when his

230

choice was fight or flee, the Eggplant fought.

He was fighting now and he had inspired her to join in what seemed a hopeless struggle. The Mayor was as good as politically dead. The powerful *Post* would call for a new broom, especially in law enforcement. The likelihood would be that a "neutral" Police Commissioner would be chosen, someone from outside of the District jurisdiction.

"I've written it off," the Eggplant had confessed earlier. She had expected that. He seemed calmer for it. "Doesn't mean we're going to lay down and die, FitzGerald."

There were some encouraging signs. During the last twelve hours, despite the continuing onslaught of homicides, they had brought in three dozen suspects for the various gang killings. That action had taken some of the edge off his pessimism.

But the problem at hand was not the spate of gang murders. There seemed far more at stake in the Polly Dearborn case. As homicide detectives, they had committed the ultimate faux pas. They had become personally involved. They had compromised police ethics, disobeyed police procedures and destroyed evidence.

They had come through a round robin of "ifs." If only they had brought the evidence into headquarters as procedures demanded. If only the Eggplant hadn't destroyed the disks. They had behaved like a bunch of Keystone cops. And a killer remained loose, unwittingly under the protection of one of the most powerful people in Washington.

After they had left Barker's office, they had gone down to Sheila Burns' office. She was busy working on her computer.

"I can't," she said, when she saw them. "I'm on deadline."

It was a different Sheila Burns than they had seen a few

days ago. Then she had been open and relaxed, with an uncertain future. Now she was a busy, intent Sheila Burns, a new and more powerful Sheila Burns.

"This is Captain Greene, the head of MPD Homicide," Fiona said, ignoring her irritation. Sheila continued to pound the keyboard, paying no attention to their presence.

"Come back later for chrissakes," Sheila muttered.

"You told me you didn't know who Polly was going to write about next," Fiona said as they moved toward where Sheila was sitting. As they came closer, Sheila shut down the computer and swiveled in her chair, facing them.

"I lied," Sheila sneered. "Now will you please leave."

"You told us you didn't know much about computers," Fiona pressed.

"I don't."

"You told us that Polly was paranoid about anyone getting into her computer. Even you."

"She was." Sheila's eyes had narrowed as they rotated from Fiona to the Eggplant's face.

"All right then, Sheila, how did you get into Polly Dearborn's computer?" the Eggplant asked.

A frown crossed Sheila's forehead and her eyelids fluttered as she looked up at them. Fiona recognized the hardened expression of a stonewaller.

"I don't know what you're talking about," Sheila said.

"The material about the Mayor," Fiona said cautiously, with a glance at the Eggplant. "It was on Polly Dearborn's computer."

"How could you possibly know that?" Sheila asked, as if she were the soul of innocence.

"Do you deny it?" the Eggplant asked.

"Of course I deny it. This is material I developed myself." She paused and glared at them. "Frankly, I don't know why you're here. I've told you all I know."

She swiveled in her chair and picked up the phone.

"Mr. Barker, please," she said sweetly, looking at them over her shoulder with an air of contempt. "Mr. Barker, Sheila Burns. I have these two detectives here."

Fiona could hear a rising crescendo of sound emanate from the phone.

"I will." Sheila said finally, hanging up. Then she swiveled back to face them.

"I don't have to tell either of you anything. You have no right to interfere with the story I'm doing." She paused for a moment. "Please leave," she said, her voice rising.

"You're lying to us," Fiona said. "That material on the Mayor is from Polly Dearborn's computer." She felt the ineffectiveness of her statement. All she could do was to offer the accusation and provide no proof. If they were going to break Sheila Burns, this was not the way.

"Oh," Sheila said calmly, as if reading her mind. "Have you proof of this? I understand that Polly's computer was destroyed by her lawyer according to her wishes."

"You won't get away with this," the Eggplant said. He was obviously suffering from the same degree of exasperation, made worse by the knowledge that he had destroyed the only evidence to support their accusation.

"I don't know what you're talking about, sir," Sheila said. Her rejoinder was laced with ridicule. "So why don't you get out of here and start looking in earnest for Polly Dearborn's murderer."

"Maybe we're looking at her," Fiona said, shooting a knowing look at the Eggplant, who remained uncharacteristically silent and noncommital.

Sheila's reaction was a broadening smile.

"I'll forget that I heard that," she said sweetly.

"I wouldn't if I were you," Fiona said as they went out the door. On her part it was pure bravado.

The memory of the humiliation rankled her, adding to their frustration. So far neither she nor the Eggplant had come up with any substantial idea on how to make a case against Sheila Burns, who was now their prime suspect. They might take various actions in the hope of breaking her into a confession, but that would be dangerous, especially since Sheila could hide comfortably behind the First Amendment and count on the resources of the most powerful editor in the country to protect her.

They had better, they both had agreed, resist further tangling with Harry Barker until they had something, something concrete and persuasive.

They watched as Charleen Evans came in, shook out her umbrella and raincoat and slid in the booth beside them. Fiona had briefed her the night before about their conversation with Barker and Sheila Burns, then sent her home to think about it.

"I've thought about it," she said, watching Sherry fill her coffee mug.

"No harm in listening," Fiona responded. The Eggplant shrugged his consent.

Charleen took a sip of her coffee.

"We may be jumping to conclusions," she said, putting her mug back on the cracked plastic surface of the table. She did not wait for a response. "Maybe she didn't take the material out of Polly Dearborn's computer."

"I'll say this for the lady," the Eggplant said. "She does listen to a different drummer."

"It's only an assumption on your part," Charleen said.

"You think we're wrong?" Fiona asked.

"I think we should keep an open mind until we're certain," Charleen argued.

"And just how do we know for sure?" the Eggplant asked.

"We find out," Charleen said. "Chances are that the material is in a computer in Sheila's house, where it's been all along. We get a search warrant."

"Which opens up a whole new can of worms," the Eggplant said. "Barker won't stand for that. He now thinks of that material, if it is there, as the property of the paper. He'll accuse us of using gestapo tactics, interfering with the function of a free press, attempting to implicate one of his reporters to counterattack for their exposure of the Mayor. Also don't be so sure that the judge will issue a warrant. We haven't got the remotest hard evidence that connects Sheila Burns with the Dearborn murder. And if the material is not there, Barker will fry me, maybe you two as well, along with the Mayor."

"If we don't check to see whether Sheila Burns has the Dearborn material, we can't go anywhere in this case," Charleen sighed.

"And suppose she does have the material," Fiona said. "How do we prove it came from Polly's machine? What's to prevent her from saying that she had the material all along?"

"She may have," Charleen said cryptically.

"Which means that we're wrong about her being our prime suspect," the Eggplant said. Beads of perspiration had broken out on his lower lip.

"Afraid so." Charleen said.

"You don't think so?" Fiona asked.

"As I said, I'm keeping an open mind."

"I'm not authorizing we go for a search warrant. We're in enough hot water as it is," the Eggplant said.

"I figured you might say that," Charleen said. She was into her tenacious mode, unstoppable, the tentativeness of the last few days gone. "Fact is, we can't get anywhere unless we're certain."

"I don't think we can get anywhere even if we are certain," the Eggplant said. Discouragement was creeping into his mood.

There was a long pause. In the silence the radio that sat on the table between them crackled. It was a call for the Eggplant. He was wanted at headquarters.

"First things first," he said, getting up. "In terms of human life we've devoted more than her due to the murder of Polly Dearborn."

"You're writing it off?" Fiona asked.

The Eggplant shrugged, his face a map of dejection.

"I need that search warrant, Captain." Charleen said, her lips tight with determination.

"No way," the Eggplant said. "We find nothing, we'll be crucified for harassing the press."

"Better that," Charleen said after a long pause. Their eyes had locked. Fiona saw this as primal, the quintessential moment. Charleen was telescoping her threat to him with her gaze. "...than destroying evidence."

"All right," he muttered. But the conviction was gone. Fiona watched his bulky receding back as he walked to the door, carrying his dead dreams with him.

"I feel awful about that. I had to." Charleen said.

"Not your fault," Fiona mumbled. She looked at Charleen, who seemed genuinely disturbed. But it was a more open-faced Charleen than she had ever seen before.

"Yes it is," she insisted. "It's the way I deal with people. I've been thinking about it."

"Jesus, Charleen. It's no time for introspection."

"It is for me," she snapped. "You've accused me of having no insight. You're right. I don't. I've shut myself off from people for too long. You can't be a good homicide detective without insight." She focused on Fiona. "You've got insight...Fiona."

"Taking a chance on intimacy are you, Charleen?"

"You're right to make fun of me."

Fiona felt suddenly ashamed.

"That was dumb," Fiona muttered.

"Not really. I've exasperated you. I'm beginning to exasperate myself." She turned her eyes away, concentrating instead on the oily surface of the coffee in the chipped mug.

"Now you're going overboard, Charleen," Fiona said, trying to pull away. The woman was on the verge of self-revelation, confession. "It's too early in the morning."

"I've been identifying with Polly Dearborn," Charleen said, her voice barely above a whisper.

"Sometimes that can be a plus in a murder investigation."

"People obsessed with computers are often lonely, frustrated people."

"You're being too hard on yourself, Charleen."

"I've always been too hard on myself," Charleen sighed. "Never letting go. Spending a lifetime looking for Momma and Daddy's murderer. How can I be an objective homicide detective if I'm carrying around baggage like that?"

"I'm not a shrink, Charleen," Fiona said. There she was, Fiona thought, being tenacious.

"It's important that I say these things. Important to me. All you have to do is listen."

"I'm listening."

"It's also important that I make this up to you." She motioned with her head. "And him. I owe both of you."

"Stage two. Blame yourself," Fiona said. "If you didn't get into Polly Dearborn's computer...hell, what's the difference? Besides, you didn't destroy the material, the Captain did. And so what if you were wrong about Downey. Big deal. We've all made mistakes."

"I'm going to get into Sheila Burns' computer," Charleen said suddenly.

"Only if he gets that search warrant," Fiona said.

"You know he will." She paused, "He also hate me forever."

"Only if you're wrong about what's in the computer."

"I know," Charleen said with resignation.

"Don't expect any help from me," Fiona said.

"I don't want any.

"Yes you do," Fiona said. She felt her anger rising.

Charleen shook her head and sighed.

"Typical of me. I'm a damned fool."

"I'll buy that."

Charleen lifted her mug, sipped, then spat the coffee back into the mug. The action somehow deflected Fiona's anger and she laughed.

"It's not necessary, Charleen. You're really going too far. So what if we don't crack the Dearborn case. There'll be others. We've had cases before where we had a pretty good idea who the murderer was, but we still couldn't get enough to make our case. If I were you..."

"You're not me, Fiona. Thank your lucky stars."

Charleen had opened her emotional dikes and her guts were spilling out.

"All that self-effacement is making me nauseous."

"Better this way, than the other," Charleen said.

"I'm not so sure."

Fiona's thoughts lingered on what Charleen was going to do. She had given the Eggplant little choice. If they failed to find any incriminating evidence, Barker would hang the three of them in the pages of his newspaper.

"Above all, Charleen, what you're contemplating is not smart," Fiona said. In fact, Fiona thought, nothing that they had done in the past few weeks qualified as smart.

"Maybe," Charleen said. Then she grew silent. They sat through a long pause. The rain battered the windows and the coffee shop began to empty. Sherry came over and poured more coffee.

"There's something else," Charleen said suddenly.

"I was afraid of that," Fiona replied, taking a deep sip of the strong coffee. Charleen looked at her. Fiona noted tiny flecks of yellow in her brown eyes.

"Polly Dearborn and I had another thing in common."

Fiona did not reply, waiting.

"I'm also a virgin," Charleen said.

26

Sheila Burns lived in what was once a large home just off Massachusetts Avenue near Dupont Circle. It had been converted to eight apartments and Sheila's was on the second floor. The Eggplant had gotten their search warrant, probably at great risk, perhaps calling in a favor. They knew, too, that the method of entry would be suspect.

Utilizing Charleen's knowledge of locks from her Burglary squad days, they had entered the front hallway, then Sheila's apartment with comparative ease. Charleen carried a laptop computer.

"Like falling off a log," Charleen said as they opened the door to Sheila Burns' apartment. Fiona had checked to make sure that Sheila was still at the paper. She was. It was two in the afternoon. The wind had slackened and the rain had settled into a steady drizzle.

Before they had entered the building, Charleen had asked for the tenth time since their meeting at Sherry's, "Are you sure about this?"

"No, I'm not," Fiona had answered with scrupulous honesty. "But I'm coming anyway."

"Why?"

"Because you need somebody to protect you," Fiona

said. The point was, Fiona had decided, that they were in it together anyway. "In for a penny, in for a pound," she muttered. It was foolhardy and dangerous. But fascinating and compelling, Fiona had reasoned, if reason was the right term, which it wasn't.

Now she was here with Charleen in Sheila Burns' apartment, a party to it, in up to her ears.

Charleen found the computer, a portable on a desk in an alcove extension of the living room. It was connected to a dot matrix printer. The apartment was modest, but neat. There was a small library of computer books on a bookshelf in the alcove.

"So she didn't know much about computers, did she?" Fiona remarked.

"Basic stuff," Charleen said. "She is apparently just learning."

There were more pictures of Sheila on the walls, particularly ones showing her in her mountain-climbing gear. Fiona discovered a number of books on mountain climbing on the bookshelves. She took one out, opened it. It looked highly technical, not at all rudimentary. This was not just a hobby with Sheila Burns. It was a passion. There were also a number of books on journalism.

Fiona watched as Charleen sat down at the computer and fired it up.

"Good. She hasn't set it up like Polly's. No key needed."

While Charleen pounded the keyboard, Fiona looked about the apartment. She looked in closets and the medicine chest. Sheila obviously lived alone. Fiona sensed an atmosphere not unlike that encountered in Polly Dearborn's apartment. On a dresser in the bedroom stood another picture of Sheila Burns. She was actually climbing the face of a mountain swaddled in rope.

Rope!

Bells went off in Fiona's mind. She returned to the living room and studied the mountain climbing books on the shelves. Taking some out, she thumbed through them. Rope was an essential ingredient of mountain climbing. There were many illustrations on the use of rope, on knots.

It was, of course, a frustrating discovery. More circumstantial evidence. Aside from the other ramifications, Barker would ridicule her assumptions.

"Got it!" Charleen cried as she sat back in the chair and folded her arms.

"Got what?"

Charleen motioned with her hand for Fiona to come closer to the screen. She pointed with her finger to a line on the screen.

"This," Charleen said.

Fiona looked to where Charleen was pointing.

"Absolutely brilliant," Fiona said.

"I wasn't dead certain," Charleen said. "I am now. Sheila Burns is our killer."

Charleen proceeded to connect a cable from her machine to Sheila's machine and copy the information.

"It won't solve it, though," Fiona said as the clacking and purring noises indicated that the transfer was in progress. "Considering the way it was obtained." Then Fiona explained about the rope.

"Sly little bitch," Charleen said.

"Body probably ripples with muscles," Fiona said.

"No sweat strangling the lady, moving her body, getting it over the side of the terrace."

"We've done our job," Charleen said. For the first time since Fiona had met her, her face lit up in a broad smile. "We got us a killer."

"That was the easy part," Fiona said. "How the hell do we put her away?"

On the way back to headquarters, Fiona pondered the problem. The rain had quickened, pounding the windshield, making it difficult to drive. The realities of the case quickly dispelled her elation. Charleen, however, continued to be upbeat. She had, after all, solved the case, fingered the killer. That was no small accomplishment considering her earlier failures.

But the major problem remained. Then there was the fact that Polly Dearborn's original material had been destroyed, making it impossible to prove that the material on Sheila Burns' computer was an actual copy of Dearborn's material.

The Eggplant's credibility could be easily destroyed by Barker's contention that the accusation against one of his reporters was an act of vengeance for the *Post*'s campaign against the Mayor. A can of worms, Fiona sighed.

Unless!

There was only one possible course of action. Fiona quickly contemplated the downside, then pushed the ominous thought from her mind.

They had reached Connecticut and K Streets. The *Post* was around the corner. Fiona made a sharp left and brought the car to a halt in front of the *Post* building.

"Your turn to make a choice, Charleen," Fiona said. She explained what she had in mind.

Charleen's eyes narrowed in thought. She was silent for a long moment. Then she shrugged.

"In for a penny, in for a pound."

27

HARRY BARKER WAS throwing a tantrum.

"You people," he said with contempt.

They had barreled past his secretary, brought in the portable computer and placed it on his desk. Charleen went calmly about the business of putting the plug into an outlet, opening up the computer and firing it up.

Fiona could see the bustle of the city room. It was getting near deadline time. Barker watched the process of setting up the computer with distaste.

"Better be good, beyond good." he said. He had not questioned why their superior was absent, although the answer was a simple one. They had not told the Eggplant what they were up to.

Fiona had not sat down. She loomed over the desk, looking at the seated recalcitrant editor watching her with, despite his negativity, curious anticipation. Fiona looked toward Charleen, who was seated in front of the computer. She hit the keyboard.

"You don't have to worry, Mr. Barker," Fiona began. She felt calm and focussed, unafraid. Being right, she had learned, had a way of boosting one's courage. "Your fear that Polly Dearborn was killed by one of her..." She wanted to say victims, but demurred. Why antagonize the bastard? "...Her subjects. She wasn't killed by any of them."

"I didn't think so," Barker said with manufactured bravado. *Oh yes you did*, Fiona told herself silently. "And it's about time you came up with something."

"It's a scoop for you, Mr. Barker."

"Maybe so. But it won't get your Mayor off the hook." He smiled maliciously, holding up a galley proof. "Running tomorrow, kiddies. The whole shebang. And a sorry bucket of shit it is."

"One of your own did the deed, Mr. Barker. A cynical grab for power is all it was."

His eyes opened wide.

"This had better knock my socks off," he snapped.

"The killer of your star reporter, Mr. Barker, is none other than your new protege, Sheila Burns."

"Bullshit."

She watched his face, the deepening frown, the pull at the edges of his mouth, the sudden vague expression in his eyes. From his point of view it had to be a far worse catastrophe than Dearborn's killer being one of her "targets." This accusation struck at the heart of the vaunted morality of his reporters. Worse, Fiona had left the implication that Sheila Burns' motive was blind ambition, which merely underlined the idea, promoted by Barker himself, that *Post* reporters were encouraged to compete without mercy.

"You had better have absolute proof," he said angrily. A nerve had begun to palpitate in his jaw.

"You be the judge. Bring her into this office," Fiona said, adding, "If you have the guts."

He seemed on the verge of one of his tantrums, and she watched him repress it. His face flushed. He pointed a finger at her.

"I'll bury your Mayor and the police with it, if this is a ploy—"

"We've had quite enough threats from you, Mr. Barker," Fiona said, very aware of her position and its dangers. "We're homicide detectives doing our job and I'd suggest that you not try to interfere with it."

"You're in trouble," Barker said, pointing his finger again. He picked up the phone. "Barker here, Sheila. Will you please come into my office?"

They sat in silence for five minutes. Barker had instructed his secretary to take no calls. He spent the time glaring at both of them. Neither Fiona nor Charleen faltered, forcing him to turn his eyes away. *Show no weakness*, Fiona urged herself. We need his penchant for intimidation.

Sheila Burns came into Barker's office. Although she was small with delicate features, Fiona saw her in a new light. Under those clothes was an athlete's body, the strength to climb mountains and move deadweight. She maintained the pose of arrogance that they had seen earlier. Barker motioned Sheila to take a chair.

"These people have not let up. They've made some very serious charges against you, Sheila. I want you to know I don't believe them. I never have. I think they've trumped something up to keep us from running our Mayor's story." Sheila's color left her face, but her expression remained arrogant. "Frankly, I am reluctant to put you through this."

"It's all right," Sheila said, clearing her throat.

"If they had anything, they would read you your rights and arrest you," Barker said. "The fact is I want them to hang themselves. Could add some bite to your Mayor's series. It's crazy, I know, to allow this. But bear with me."

"Of course," Sheila said.

Fiona debated how to approach her, head-on or obliquely. She decided on the former.

"We have reason to believe that you are responsible for the murder of Polly Dearborn."

The pupils seemed to dance in Sheila's eyes. Not a muscle moved in her face, although her complexion grew more ashen. Fiona waited for a reaction. Sheila's arms shot out, wrists together.

"Well, then, arrest me," she said, looking toward Harry Barker.

"You are treading on extremely thin ice, Officer FitzGerald," he said, barely opening his mouth.

"An accusation is not an arrest," Fiona said. "I have a right to interrogate her."

"It's all right, Mr. Barker," Sheila said. She had recovered her arrogance. "I think we should get this behind us as quickly as possible."

"Might make good grist for our Mayor's story," Barker said threateningly. He pulled a tape recorder out of his desk drawer and pressed a button. "Fire away, Officer."

The tape recorder made Fiona uncomfortable, but she did not challenge its use. To mask her discomfort, she turned toward the window.

"Changes the tune a bit, hey, lady?" Barker said.

"The tune maybe," Fiona said. "But not the facts."

"Which are?" Barker said.

It was a dangerous game, Fiona knew, especially with the recorder going. No theory was ever airtight. She studied Sheila Burns' face, calmer now, less ashen, her expression controlled. Charleen wore her most efficient neutral look. Harry Barker, she knew, would show no mercy, would use his media power ruthlessly. The Mayor, the Eggplant, Fiona, even Charleen, would be grist for the media mill, a quartet of scapegoats.

"All right, then," Fiona said, anger rising, committing herself fully, feeling the adrenaline surge. She turned to Barker, who sat watching and waiting and wearing a thin smile. Okay, Mr. Judge and Jury, here goes.

"Sheila knew the layout and Polly's routine. She knew that the security system had flaws, especially using the garage for access. She got in, went up the garage elevator to Polly's apartment. She rang the buzzer. Polly looked through the peephole, recognized Sheila, opened the door. Sheila carried a briefcase in which she had stored the rope, a portable computer and connecting cable. She worked fast. As soon as Polly had turned her back, she was garroted and strangled. Sheila took the custom-made computer key that Polly wore around her neck, quickly unlocked Polly's computer and copied the material onto the portable computer. Then she dragged Polly's body to the terrace, anchored one end of the rope to the terrace and threw Polly over the side. Then she left, went out the garage and home."

Finishing, Fiona turned toward Sheila, who shook her head.

"That is utter, complete nonsense," Sheila said. Considering the accusation, she was surprisingly calm.

"That's a mighty heavy chore for such a small woman as this," Barker said. He did not seem to be taking Fiona seriously. Sheila nodded, fluttering her eyes in approval.

"Hardly your feminine, helpless-flower type," Fiona said. "This little woman climbs mountains." Fiona paused, turning to face Barker squarely. "Uses rope. Knows knots."

"That it?" Barker asked, but not before he had hesitated briefly, just enough to show the first evidence of concern.

He turned toward Sheila, who also might have noticed his hesitation.

"Typical of the accusations made to Polly," she said, still controlled, although her tone was changing, revealing the beginnings of a hysterical edge. "They were always coming up with tactics like this. Polly and I used to laugh about it. The object was to scare off Polly from doing the story. Now they're trying to do it with me."

Barker rubbed his chin. Then he looked toward Charleen and the portable computer opened before her and frowned.

"And that?" he asked, pointing. "What the hell is that?"

Charleen looked at him and said nothing. Then she turned to Fiona.

"That is what we found in Sheila Burns' computer," Fiona said. She was, of course, completely aware of the risk. She nodded and Charleen turned on the computer.

"And what does that prove?" Barker asked.

"It proves that Sheila Burns copied the information on Polly Dearborn's computer to her own," Fiona said, anticipating what was to follow.

"That is not my computer," Sheila said, hysteria rising.

"No, it's not," Fiona countered. "We copied it from the one in your apartment."

"You broke into my apartment?" Sheila shouted.

"With a search warrant, I presume," Barker asked.

"Yes," Fiona said firmly, remembering the running tape recorder.

"Show him the screen, Charleen," Fiona said.

Charleen turned the computer so that the screen was visible to Barker. Fiona ducked behind the desk and pointed.

"You see that?" she asked.

Barker, despite his continued smugness, put on his glasses and looked at the screen.

"There," Fiona said, pointing with her finger.

"So what," Barker said.

"That is the exact time and date that Sheila took the information off Polly's computer."

Barker read the date and time, then looked at his calendar.

"May sixth, two A.M." he read.

"Exactly in the time frame of Polly Dearborn's murder."

"She doesn't really know that much about computers," Charleen said, now that they were getting into her territory. "She made a subdirectory first, then dumped Polly's stuff into it. It automatically stamps date and time."

"Don't listen to them, Mr. Barker. They're trying to frame me. It's wrong. A lie."

"Then explain it," Fiona said.

She was trying her best to hold herself together. Barker looked toward her, taking off his glasses.

"It was not Polly's material," Sheila said. "It was my own. I developed it." She paused, then smiled. "How can you say that that material was on Polly's computer? The material on that has been destroyed."

Barker turned toward Fiona.

"She's right there," Barker said with considerably less heat, but still showing an attitude of skepticism.

"You break into my apartment, steal my computer material, then accuse me of murder. It is beyond the pale." She turned toward Barker. "I demand that the police be called and these people be charged."

"With what?" Fiona asked.

"Interfering with my first Amendment rights," Sheila Burns said.

But Barker seemed to be engaged, calmer, curious.

"To convince me," Barker said, "you'd have to prove that"—he pointed to the computer screen—"that that material had come out of Polly Dearborn's computer."

Without a word, Charleen stood up and walked to Barker's side of the desk. Bending over, she worked the keyboard. Again Barker put on his glasses and watched the screen. The material on the Mayor flashed onto the screen. Charleen scrolled it slowly so that it could be read.

"All right, that's material about the Mayor. But it still doesn't prove that it came from Polly's computer."

"Which has been destroyed," Sheila said calmly. "Meaning that this may have serious repercussions for both of you and your superiors. Believe me, I do not intend to let it pass." She looked toward Barker, who averted his eyes, again took off his glasses and turned in his chair to look out of the window. Judge and jury, Fiona thought again. He was weighing their fate. Finally he swiveled in his chair and looked directly at Fiona.

"The fact is that you haven't got any evidence," Barker said. "All this, as the lawyers say, is circumstantial and . . ." He paused and shook his head. "It won't stand up in court."

"This woman is a murderer," Fiona said.

"Then arrest me," Sheila taunted. "Show me your evidence."

Suddenly Charleen opened her bag and threw a number of soft computer disks on the desk.

"But we have evidence," she said with conviction. Fiona's heart jumped into her throat. What evidence? "Direct from Polly Dearborn's computer, transferred the morning we found the body. I also have a portable computer, Sheila. And I qualify as an expert. I came back to Polly's apartment with my own portable, dumped the material into it, then made copies on those disks. I deliberately made a subdirectory. You'll note the date and time stamped to indicate my subdirectory. It is undoubtedly a mirror image of the material on your computer, Sheila."

"They're lying," Sheila cried. Hearing the word seemed like an explosion in Fiona's ears.

"Sit down, Sheila," Barker commanded.

She stared at him for a moment. Her lips began to tremble, her nostrils quivered. She started to back away, then held on to the back of one chair, angled herself around and flopped heavily into it.

"They make a convincing argument, Sheila," Barker said firmly.

"They're lying to protect that damned Mayor. Polly had him dead to rights—"

"Polly?" Barker snapped "I thought you said you developed the material yourself."

"We worked on it together," Sheila mumbled, but without conviction.

"That, I know, is not true, Sheila," Barker said. "That was Polly's material, wasn't it, Sheila?"

"No, Mr. Barker. I...she had assigned it to me. I told her I wanted to write it. So she gave me the material, promised me a by-line..."

"Polly Dearborn, the Witch of Watergate," Barker said. "She would kill rather than share."

"She promised..." Sheila said. Clearly, she was beginning to unravel.

"Promised what?" Barker pressed.

"That I would get some recognition, that she would give me greater authority, that she would talk to you about it..."

"She never did, Sheila," Barker said, shaking his head.

"Never did anything for anybody, that bitch," Sheila shouted. "She deserved what she got, hanging out there for the whole world to see. Oh, that was beautiful, beautiful. I have no regrets...none at all."

Fiona had seen it before, the unburdening, letting out the pressure, like air out of a punctured tire. She looked toward Barker, whose face reflected utter disgust.

"Read her her rights, Charleen," Fiona said as she reached for her handcuffs.

28

"HE HAD NO choice," the Eggplant said.

The morning *Post*'s front page was spread before them on one of Sherry's cracked plastic chrome-legged booth tables.

"He wouldn't pass up a story even if it dealt with him, Barker himself, raping his mother."

"Not that tough son-of-a-bitch," the Eggplant agreed.

There on the front page was the story of the arrest of Sheila Burns for the murder of Polly Dearborn.

They had given it big play on the left side above the fold. There were pictures of both Sheila Burns and Polly Dearborn, and a quote before the jump to the inside page of Harry Barker expressing "shock and dismay" on behalf of all the employees of the *Post*.

Sheila had signed a confession and her lawyer was in the process of plea-bargaining a sentence with the District Attorney. The Eggplant considered it a closed case, although his elation was somewhat dampened by three more drug-related gang murders during the night.

The puzzle, of course, was why Barker had not run the story on the Mayor.

"Maybe he was impressed with the way we broke the case," Charleen said.

"Meaning he was impressed with your dramatic moment," Fiona said. "Showing those disks."

"It did the job," Charleen said. Her confidence had returned fully, although her arrogance was tempered now. Fiona could tell she felt secure, qualified for Homicide.

It was a strange meeting. The Eggplant was amazingly calm, almost too calm. Fiona knew that to be a bad sign.

"We had agreed to make no copies the Eggplant muttered." Under other circumstances, he would be raging.

Charleen, for the first time since Fiona had met her, suddenly broke into a broad toothy smile. Then she giggled, actually giggled like a mischievous kid.

"I never made copies. I promised I wouldn't. They were empty disks. I keep my promises." She looked pointedly at the Eggplant. The giggle turned into a laugh and tears rolled down her cheeks.

The Eggplant shook his head.

"Evans, why are you always telling me things I do not wish to hear?"

Charleen's shoulders continued to shake with laughter. It became infectious. Then Fiona started, and the Eggplant. Sherry looked at them and frowned.

"You telling filthy jokes again, Luther?" she asked.

"This one's a lulu, Sherry," the Eggplant said when he had calmed. Then he turned to Charleen. "You really think you're a smart-ass, woman?"

They watched Charleen's face.

"Yeah," she said.

"Think you found a home in Homicide?" the Eggplant said ominously.

"Yes." Charleen said with dead certainty, her chin raised pugnaciously.

"Cocky bitch, aren't you?" the Eggplant said. It was hard to tell whether he was serious or mocking. But the remark induced a long silence. "No. For once. Realistic."

"Question is," Fiona said, quickly changing the subject, "Is a person's past a barometer of a person's future?"

"People don't change," the Eggplant muttered, deflected from his confrontation with Charleen.

"The Mayor, too?" Fiona asked. It was, she knew, a loaded question. He was, as everyone knew, an imperfect Mayor. Certainly not the best. But then, in politics, one could never depend on getting the best. Also, they were privy to the Mayor's earlier indiscretions, the ones on the verge of exposure by the *Post*, which would destroy his political career. They all knew that Barker would run the story and, therefore, destroy any chance that the Eggplant would be Police Commissioner.

"Him, too," the Eggplant said.

His frankness did not surprise her. Conspiracy had bonded them, an odd triumvirate.

"There is something," Charleen volunteered. She waited until Sherry had refilled their mugs. They looked at her, waiting. "Back home in Indiana, he served six months for assault and battery."

"Who?" Fiona asked.

"Harry Barker."

Fiona and the Eggplant exchanged glances.

"I have this data bank..." Charleen began.

"Don't say it," the Eggplant said. "Please."

Charleen didn't. Instead she sipped her coffee.